THE WEIGHT OF WORDS

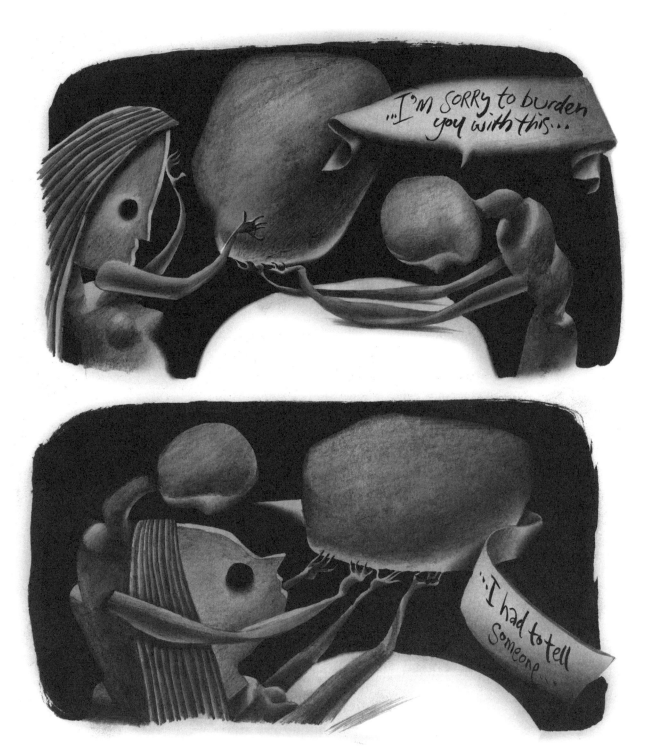

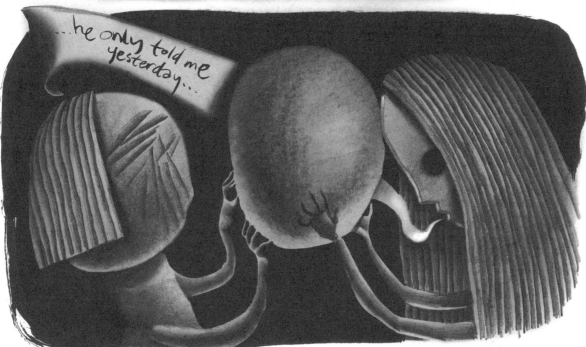

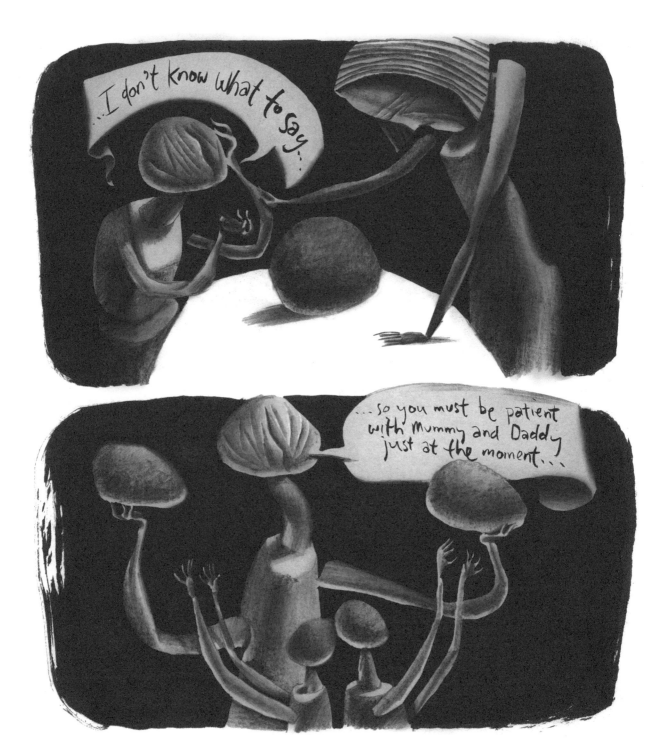

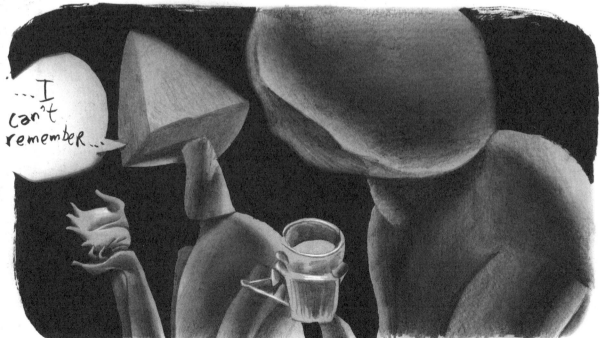

The WEIGHT of WORDS

Edited by Dave McKean and William Schafer

Subterranean Press 2017

Table of Contents

The Weight of Words by Dave McKean — 1

Belladonna Nights by Alastair Reynolds — 15

The Orange Tree by Maria Dahvana Headley — 35

Monkey and the Lady by Neil Gaiman — 67

No One Dies in Nowhere by Catherynne M. Valente — 75

Objects in the Mirror by Caitlín R. Kiernan — 107

Yummie by M. John Harrison — 133

Robo Rapid by Joe R. Lansdale — 145

All I Care About is You by Joe Hill — 183

The Language of Birds by Dave McKean — 215

Broken Face by Iain Sinclair — 227

The Train of Death by Neil Gaiman — 243

Belladonna Nights

Alastair Reynolds

I had been thinking about Campion long before I caught him leaving the flowers at my door.

It was the custom of Mimosa Line to admit witnesses to our reunions. Across the thousand nights of our celebration a few dozen guests would mingle with us, sharing in the uploading of our consensus memories, the individual experiences gathered during our two-hundred thousand year circuits of the galaxy.

They had arrived from deepest space, their ships sharing the same crowded orbits as our own nine hundred and ninety nine vessels. Some were members of other Lines—there were Jurtinas, Marcellins and Torquatas—while others were representatives of some of the more established planetary and stellar cultures. There were ambassadors of the Centaurs, Redeemers and the Canopus Sodality. There were also Machine People in attendance, ours being one of the few Lines that maintained cordial ties with the robots of the Monoceros Ring.

And there was Campion, sole representative of Gentian Line, one of the oldest in the Commonality. Gentian Line went all the way back to the Golden Hour, back to the first thousand years of the human spacefaring era. Campion was a popular guest, always on someone or other's arm. It helped that he was naturally at ease among strangers, with a ready smile and an easy, affable manner—full of his own stories, but equally willing to lean back and listen to ours, nodding and laughing in all the right places. He had adopted a slight, unassuming anatomy, with an open, friendly face and a head of tight curls that lent him a guileless, boyish appearance. His clothes and tastes were never ostentatious, and he mingled as effortlessly with the other guests as he did with the members of our Line. He seemed infinitely approachable, ready to talk to anyone.

Except me.

It had been nothing to dwell over in the early days of the reunion. There had been far too many distractions for that. To begin with there was the matter of the locale. Phecda, who had won the prize for best strand at the Thousandth Night of our last reunion, had been tasked with preparing this world for our arrival. There had been some grumbles initially, but everyone now agreed that Phecda had done a splendid job of it.

She had arrived early, about a century in advance of any of the rest of us. Tierce, the world we had selected for our reunion, had a solitary central landmass surrounded by a single vast ocean. Three skull-faced moons stirred lazy tides in this great green primordial sea. Disdaining land, Phecda had constructed the locale far from shore, using scaper technology to raise a formation of enormous finger-like towers from the seabed.

These rocky columns soared kilometres into the sky, with their upper reaches hollowed out into numerous chambers and galleries, providing ample space for our accommodation and celebrations. Bridges linked some of the towers, while from their upper levels we whisked between more distant towers or our orbiting ships. Beyond that, Phecda had sculpted some of the towers according to her own idiosyncracies. Music had played a part in her winning strand, so one of the towers was surmounted by a ship-sized violin, which we called the Fiddlehead tower. Another had the face of an owl, a third was a melted candle, while the grandest of them all terminated in a clocktower, whose stern black hands marked the progression of the thousand nights.

Phecda had done well. It was our twenty second reunion, and few of us could remember a more fitting locale in which to celebrate the achievements of our collective circuits. Whoever won this time was going to have quite an act to follow.

It wouldn't be me. I had done well enough in my circuit, but there were others who had already threaded better strands than I could ever stitch together from my experiences. Still, I was content with that. If we maintained our numbers, then one day it might end up being my turn. Until that distant event, though, I was happy enough just to be part of our larger enterprise.

Fifty or more nights must have passed before I started being quietly bothered by the business of Campion. My misgivings had been innocuous to start with. Everyone wanted a piece of our Gentian guest, and it was hardly surprising that some of us had to wait our turn. But gradually I had the sense that Campion was going out of his way to shun me, moving away from a gathering just when I arrived, taking his leave from the morning tables when I dared to sit within earshot.

I told myself that it was silly to think that he was singling me out for this cold-shoulder treatment, when I was just one of hundreds of Mimosa shatterlings who had yet to speak to him personally. But the feeling dogged me. And when I sensed that Campion was sometimes looking at me, directing a glance when he thought I might not notice, my confusion only deepened. I had done nothing to offend him or any member of his Line—had I?

The business with the flowers did not start immediately. It was around the hundredth night when they first appeared, left in a simple white vase just outside my room in the Owlhead tower. I examined them with only mild interest. They were bulb-headed flowers of a lavish dark purple colour, shading almost to black unless I took them out onto the balcony.

I asked around as to who might have left the flowers, and what their meaning might have been. No one else had received a similar puzzle. But when no one admitted to placing the flowers, and the days passed, I forced myself to put them from mind. It was not uncommon for shatterlings to exchange teasing messages and gifts, or for the locale itself to play the odd game with its guests.

Fifty or sixty nights later, they reappeared. The others had withered by this time, but now I took the opportunity to whisk up to my ship and run the flowers through *Sarabande*'s analyser, just in case there was something I was missing.

The flowers were Deadly Nightshade, or Belladonna. Poisonous, according to the ship, but only in a historic sense. None of us were immortal, but if we were going to die it would take a lot more than a biochemical toxin to do it. A weapon, a stasis malfunction, a violent accident involving the unforgiving physics of matter and energy. But not something cobbled together by hamfisted nature.

Still I had no idea what they meant.

Somewhere around the two hundredth night the flowers were back, and this time I swore I was nearly in time to see a figure disappearing around the curve in the corridor. It couldn't have been Campion, I told myself. But I had seen someone of about the right build, dressed as Campion dressed, with the same head of short curls.

After that, I stationed an eye near my door. It was a mild violation of Line rules—we were not supposed to monitor or record any goings-on in the public spaces—but in view of the mystery I felt that I was entitled to take the odd liberty.

For a long time the flowers never returned. I wondered if I had discouraged my silent visitor with that near-glimpse. But then, around the three hundredth and twentieth night, the flowers were there again. And this time my eye had caught Campion in the act of placing them.

I caught his eye a few times after. He knew, and I knew, that there was something going on. But I decided not to press him on the mystery. Not just yet. Because on the three hundred and seventieth night, he would not be able to ignore me. That was the night of my threading, and for one night only I would be the unavoidable focus of attention.

Like it or not, Campion would have to endure my presence.

"I suppose you think us timid," I said.

He smiled at me. It was the first time we had looked at each other for more than an awkward moment, before snatching our glances away.

"I don't know. Why should I?"

"Gentian Line has suffered attrition. There aren't nine hundred and ninety nine of you now, and there'll be fewer of you each circuit. How many is it, exactly?"

He made a show of not quite remembering, although I found it hard to believe that the number wasn't etched into his brain. "Oh, around nine hundred and seven, I think. Nine hundred and six if we assume Betony's not coming back, and no one's heard anything from *him* in half a million years."

"That's a tenth of your Line. Nearly a hundred of your fellow shatterlings lost."

"It's a dangerous business, sightseeing. It's Shaula, isn't it?"

"You know my name perfectly well."

He grinned. "If you say so."

He was giving me flip, off-the-cuff answers as if there was a layer of seriousness I was not meant to reach. Smiling and twinkling his eyes at me, yet there was something false about it at all, a stiffness he could not quite mask. It was the morning before the night of my threading, and while the day wasn't entirely mine—Nunki, who had threaded last night, was also being congratulated and feted—as the hours wore on the anticipation would start to shift to my threading, and already I was feeling more at the centre of things than I had since arriving. Tonight my memories would seep into the heads of the rest of us, and when we rose tomorrow it would be my experiences that were being dissected, critiqued and celebrated. For these two days, at least, Campion would be obliged to listen to me—and to answer my questions.

We stood at a high balcony in the Candlehead tower, warm blue tiles under our feet, sea air sharp in our noses.

"How does it work, Campion, when there are so many of you dead? Do your reunions last less than our own?"

"No, it's still a thousand nights. But there are obviously gaps where new memories can't be threaded. On those nights we honour the memories of the dead. The threading apparatus replays their earlier strands, or makes new permutations from old memories. Sometimes, we bring back the dead as physical imagos, letting them walk and talk among us, just as if they were still alive. It's considered distasteful by some, but I don't see the harm in it, if it helps us celebrate good lives well lived."

"We don't have that problem," I said.

"No," he answered carefully, as if wary of giving offence. "You don't."

"Some would say, to have come this far, without losing a single one of us, speaks of an innate lack of adventure."

He shrugged. "Or maybe you just choose the right adventures. There's no shame in caution, Shaula. You were shattered from a single individual so that you could go out and experience the universe, not so that you could find new ways of dying."

"Then you don't find us contemptible?"

"I wouldn't be here—I wouldn't keep coming here—if I felt that way. Would I?"

His answer satisfied me on that one point, because it seemed so sincerely offered. It was only later, as I was mulling over our conversation, that I wondered why he had spoken as if he had been our guest on more than one occasion.

He was wrong, though. This was our twenty second reunion, and Campion had never joined us before. So why had he spoken as if he had?

I felt foolish. We had communicated, and it had been too easy, too normal, as if there had never been any strange distance between us. And that was strange and troubling in and of itself.

The day was not yet done, nor the evening, so I knew that there would be more chances to speak. But I had to have all my questions ready, and not be put off by that easy-going front of his. If he wanted something of me, I was damned well going to find out what it was.

The flowers meant something, I was sure, and at the back of my mind was the niggling trace of half an answer. It was something about Belladonna, some barely-remembered fact or association.

Nothing came to mind, though, and as the morning eased into afternoon I was mostly preoccupied with making last minute alterations to my strand. I'd had hundreds of days to edit down my memories, of course, but for some reason it was always a rush to distil them into an acceptable form. I could perform some of the memory editing in my room in the Owlhead tower, but there were larger chunks of unconsolidated memory still aboard my ship, and I realised it would be quicker and simpler to make some of the alterations from orbit.

I climbed the spiral stairs to the roof of the Owlhead and whisked up my ship. For all the charms of Phecda's locale, it was good to be back on my own turf. I walked to the bridge of *Sarabande* and settled into my throne, calling up displays and instrument banks. My eyes swept the glowing readouts. All was well with the ship, I was reassured to note. In six hundred and thirty days we would all be leaving Tierce, and I would call on *Sarabande*'s parametric engine to push her to within a sliver of the speed of light. Already I could feel my thoughts slipping ahead to my next circuit, and the countless systems and worlds I would visit.

Beyond *Sarabande*, visible through the broad sweep of her bridge window, there were at least a hundred other ships close enough to see. I took in their varied shapes and sizes, marvelling at the range of designs adopted by my fellow shatterlings. The only thing the ships needed to have in common was speed and reliability. There were also a handful of vehicles belonging to our guests, including Campion's own modest *Dalliance*, dwarfed by almost every other craft orbiting Tierce.

I worked through my memory segments. It didn't take long, but when I was done something compelled me to remain on the bridge.

"Ship," I said aloud. "Give me referents for Belladonna."

"There are numerous referents," *Sarabande* informed me. "Given your current neural processing bottleneck, you would need eighteen thousand years to view them all. Do you wish to apply a search filter?"

"I suppose I'd better. Narrow the search to referents with a direct connection to the Lines or the Commonality." It was a hunch, but something was nagging at me.

"Very well. There are still more than eleven hundred referents. But the most strongly indicated record relates to Gentian Line."

I leaned forward in my throne. "Go on."

"The Belladonna Protocol is an emergency response measure devised by Gentian Line to ensure Line prolongation in the event of extreme attrition, by means of accident or hostile action."

"Clarify."

"The Belladonna Protocol, or simply Belladonna, is an agreed set of actions for abandoning one reunion locale and converging on another. No pre-arranged target is necessary. Belladonna functions as a decision-branch algorithm which will identify a unique fallback destination, given the application of simple search and rejection criteria."

A shiver of disquiet passed through me. "Has Gentian Line initiated Belladonna?"

"No, Shaula. It has never been necessary. But the Belladonna Protocol has been adopted by a number of other Lines, including Mimosa Line."

"And have we…" But I cut off my own words before they made me foolish. "No, of course not. I'd know if we'd ever initiated Belladonna. And we certainly haven't suffered extreme attrition. We haven't suffered any attrition at all."

We're too timid for that, I thought to myself. Much too timid.

Weren't we?

I whisked back to Tierce. Campion was lounging in the afternoon sunlight on the upper gallery of the Candlehead, all charm and modesty as he fielded questions about the capabilities of his ship. "Yes, I've picked up a weapon or two over the years—who hasn't? But no, nothing like that, and certainly no Homunculus weapons. Space battles? One or two. As a guiding rule I try to steer clear of them, but now and again you can't avoid running into trouble. There was the time I shattered the moon of

Arghul, in the Terzet Salient, but that was only to give myself a covering screen. There wasn't anyone living on Arghul when I did it. At least, I don't *think* there was. Oh, and the time I ran into a fleet of the Eleventh Intercessionary, out near the Carnelian Bight…"

"Campion," I said, his audience tolerating my interruption, as well they had to on my threading day. "Could we talk? Somewhere quieter, if possible?"

"By all means, Shaula. Just as long as you don't drop any spoilers about your coming strand."

"It isn't about my strand."

He rose from his chair, brushing bread crumbs from his clothes, waved absent-mindedly to his admirers, and joined me as we walked to a shadowed area of the gallery.

"What's troubling you, Shaula—last minute nerves?"

"You know exactly what's troubling me." I kept my voice low, unthreatening, even though nothing would have pleased me more than to wrap my hands around his scrawny throat and squeeze the truth out of him. "This game you've playing with me…playing *on* me, I should say."

"Game?" he answered, in a quiet but guarded tone.

"The flowers. I had a suspicion it was you before I left the eye, and then there wasn't any doubt. But you still wouldn't look me in the face. And this morning, pretending that you weren't even sure of my name. All easy answers and dismissive smiles, as if there's nothing strange about what you've been doing. But I've had enough. I want a clear head before I commit my strand to the threading apparatus, and you're going to give it to me. Starting with some answers."

"Answers," he repeated.

"There was never any doubt about my name, was there?"

He glanced aside for an instant. Something had changed in his face when he looked back at me, though. There was a resignation in it—a kind of welcome surrender. "No, there wasn't any doubt. Of all of you, yours was the one name I wasn't very likely to forget."

"You're talking as if we've already met."

"We have."

I shook my head. "I'd remember if I'd ever crossed circuits with a Gentian."

"It didn't happen during one of our circuits. We met here, on Tierce."

This time the shake of my head was more emphatic. "No, that's even less likely. You ignored me from the moment I arrived. I couldn't get near you, and if I did, you always had some excuse to be going somewhere else. Which makes the business with the flowers all the more irritating, because if you wanted to talk to me…"

"I did," he said. "All the time. And we did meet before, and it was on Tierce. I know what you're going to say. It's impossible, because Mimosa Line never came to Tierce before, and these towers aren't more than a century old. But it's true. We've been here before, both of us."

"I don't understand."

"This isn't the first time," Campion answered. Then he looked down at the patterned tiles of the floor, all cold indigo shades in the shadowed light. "This day always comes. It's just a little earlier this time. Either I'm getting less subtle with the flowers, or you're retaining some memory of it between cycles."

"What do you mean, cycles?" I reached out and touched his forearm, not firmly, but enough to know I was ready to stop being mocked with half-truths and riddles. "I asked my ship about the flowers, you know. *Sarabande* told me about the Belladonna Protocol. It was there at the back of my mind somewhere, I know—but who'd bother caring about such a thing, when we haven't even lost a single shatterling? And why do you leave the flowers, instead of just coming out with whatever it is you need to share?"

"Because you made me promise it," Campion said. "The flowers were your idea. A test for yourself, so to speak. Nothing too obvious, but nothing too cryptic, either. If you made the connection, so be it. If you didn't, you got to see out these thousand nights in blissful ignorance."

"They weren't my idea. And blissful ignorance of what?"

I sensed it was almost more than he could bear to tell me. "What became of Mimosa Line."

He took me to the highest lookout of the Clockhead tower. We were under a domed ceiling, painted pastel blue with gold stars, with open, stone-fretted windows around us. It surprised me to have the place to ourselves. We could look down at the other shatterlings on the galleries and promenades of the other towers, but at this late afternoon hour the Clockhead was unusually silent. So were we, for long moments. Campion held the upper hand but for now he seemed unsure what to do with it.

"Phecda did well, don't you think," I said, to fill the emptiness.

"You said you returned to your ship."

"I did." I nodded to the painted ceiling, to the actual sky beyond it. "It's a fine sight to see them all from Tierce, but you don't really get a proper sense of them until you're in orbit. I go back now and then wherever I need to or not. *Sarabande*'s been my companion for dozens of circuits, and I feel cut off her from her if I'm on a world for too long."

"I understand that. I feel similarly about *Dalliance*. Purslane says she's a joke, but that ship's been pretty good to me."

"Purslane?"

Something tightened in his face. "Do you mind if I show you something, Shaula? The locale is applying fairly heavy perceptual filters, but I can remove them simply enough, provided you give me consent."

I frowned. "Phecda never said anything about filters."

"She wouldn't have." Campion closed his eyes for an instant, sending some command somewhere. "Let me take away this ceiling. It's real enough—these towers really were grown out of the seabed—but it gets in the way of the point I need to make." He swept up a hand and the painted ceiling and its gold stars dissolved into the hard blue sky beyond it. "Now let me bring in the ships, as if it were night and you could see them in orbit. I'll swell them a bit, if you don't mind."

"Do whatever you need."

The ships burst into that blueness like a hundred opening flowers, in all the colours and geometries of their hulls and fields. They were arcing overhead in a raggedy chain, sliding slowly from one horizon to the other, daggers and wedges and spheres, blocks and cylinders and delicate lattices, some more sea-dragon than machine, and for the hundred that I presently saw there had to be nine hundred and more still to tick into view. It was such a simple, lovely perceptual tweak that I wondered why I had never thought to apply it for myself.

Then Campion said: "Most of them aren't real."

"I'm sorry?"

"The bulk of those ships don't exist. They're phantoms, conjured into existence by the locale. The truth is that there are only a handful of actual ships orbiting Tierce."

One by one the coloured ships faded from the sky, opening up holes in the chain. The process continued. One in ten gone, then two in ten, three in ten…

I looked at him, trying to judge his mood. His face was set in stone, as impassive as a surgeon administering some terrible, lacerating cure, sensing the patient's discomfort but knowing he must continue.

Now only one in ten of the ships remained. Then one in twenty, one in thirty…

"Mine is real," he said eventually. "And three vehicles of Mimosa Line. None of the others were present, including all the ships you thought belonged to your guests."

"Then how did they get here?"

"They didn't. There are no guests, except me. The other Line members, the Centaurs, the Machine People…none of them came. They were another illusion of the locale." He touched a hand to his breast. "I'm your only guest. I came here because no one else could stand to. I've been coming here longer than you realise." And he raised his hand, opened his fist, and made one of the ships swell until it was larger than any of Tierce's moons.

It was a wreck. It had been a ship once, I could tell, but that must have been countless aeons ago. Now the hull was a gutted shell, open to space, pocked by holes that went all the way through from one side to the other. It was as eyeless and forbidding as a skull stripped clean of meat, and it drifted along its orbit at an ungainly angle. Yet for all that I still recognised its shape.

Sarabande.

My ship.

"You all died," Campion said softly. "You were wrong about being timid, Shaula. It was the exact opposite. You were too bold, too brave, too adventuresome. Mimosa Line took the risks that the rest of us were too cowardly to face. You saw and did wondrous things. But you paid a dire price for that courage. Attrition hit you harder than it had any Line before you, and your numbers thinned out very rapidly. Late in the day, when your surviving members realised the severity of your predicament, you initiated Belladonna." He swallowed and licked his tongue across his lips. "But it was too late. A few ships limped their way to Tierce, your Belladonna fallback. But by then all of you were dead, the ships simply following automatic control. Half of those ships have burned up in the atmosphere since then."

"No," I stated. "Not all of us, obviously…"

But his nod was wise and sad and sympathetic. "All of you. All that's left is this. Your ships created a locale, and set about staging the thousand nights. But there were none of you left to dream it. You asked about Gentian Line, and how we commemorated our dead? I told you we used imagos, allowing our fallen to walk again. With you, there are only imagos. Nine hundred and ninety nine of them, conjured out of the patterns stored in your threading apparatus, from the memories and recordings of the original Mimosa shatterlings. Including Shaula, who was always one of the best and brightest of you."

I forced out an empty, disbelieving laugh.

"You're saying I'm dead?"

"I'm saying all of you are dead. You've been dead for much longer than a circuit. All that's left is the locale. It sustains itself, waits patiently, across two hundred thousand years, and then for a thousand nights it haunts itself with your ghosts."

I wanted to dismiss his story, to chide him for such an outlandish and distasteful lie, but now that he had voiced it I found it chimed with some deep, sad suspicion I had long harboured within myself.

"How long?"

The breeze flicked at the short tight curls of his hair. "Do you really want to know?"

"I wouldn't have asked if I didn't." But that was a lie of my own, and we both knew it for the untruth it was. Still, his reluctance was almost sufficient answer in its own right

"You've been on Tierce for one million, two hundred and five thousand years. This is your seventh reunion in this locale, the seventh time that you've walked these towers, but all that happens each time is that you dream the same dead dreams."

"And you've been coming along to watch us."

"Just the last five, including this one. I was at the wrong end of the Scutum-Crux arm when you had your first, after you initiated the Belladonna Protocol, and by the time I learned about your second—where there was no one present but your own residuals—it was too late to alter my plans. But I made sure I was present at the next." His face was in profile, edged in golden tones by the lowering sun, and I sensed that he had difficulty looking me straight in the eyes. "No one wanted to come, Shaula. Not because they hated Mimosa Line, or were envious of any of your achievements, but because you rattled their deepest fears. What had happened to you, your adventures and achievements, had already passed into the safekeeping of the Commonality. None could ignore it. And no Line wants to think too deeply about attrition, and especially not the way it must *always* end, given enough time."

"But the dice haven't fallen yet—for you."

"The day will come." At last he turned to face me again, his face both young and old, as full of humour as it was sadness. "I know it, Shaula. But it doesn't stop me enjoying the ride, while I'm able. It's still a wonderful universe. Still a blessed thing to be alive, to be a thing with a mind and a memory and the five human senses to drink it all in. The stories I've yet to share with you. I took a slingshot around the Whipping Star…" But he settled his mouth into an accepting smile and shook his head. "Next time, I suppose. You'll still be here, and so will this world. The locale will regenerate itself, and along the way wipe away any trace of there ever being a prior reunion."

"Including my memories of ever having met you."

"That's how it has to be. A trace of a memory persists, I suppose, but mostly you'll remember none of it."

"But I'll ask you to pass a message forward, won't I. Ask you to leave flowers at my door. And you'll agree and you'll be kind and dutiful and you'll come back to us, and on some other evening, two hundred thousand years from now, give or take a few centuries, we'll be in this same lookout having much the same conversation and I won't have aged a second, and you'll be older and sadder and I won't know why, to begin with. And then you'll show me the phantom ships and I'll remember, just a bit, just like I've always remembered, and then I'll start asking you about the next reunion, another two hundred thousand years in the future. It's happened, hasn't it?"

Campion gave a nod. "Do you think it would have been better if I'd never come?"

"At least you had the nerve to face us. At least you weren't afraid to be reminded of death. And we lived again, in you. The other Lines won't forget us, will they? And tell me you passed on some of our stories to the other Gentians, during your own Thousand Nights?"

"I did," he said, some wry remembrance crinkling the corners of his eyes. "And they believed about half of them. But that was your fault for having the audacity to live a little. We could learn a lot."

"Just don't take our lessons too deeply too heart."

"We wouldn't have the nerve."

The sun had almost set now, and there was a chill in the air. It would soon be time to descend from the Clockhead tower, in readiness for the empty revelry of the evening. Ghosts dancing with ghosts, driven like clockwork marionettes.

Ghosts dreaming the hollow dreams of other ghosts, and thinking themselves alive, for the span of a night. The imago of a shatterling who once called herself Shaula, daring to hold a conscious thought, daring to believe she was still alive.

"Why me, Campion? Out of all the others, why is it me you feel the need to do this to?"

"Because you half know it already," he answered, after a hesitation. "I've seen it in your eyes, Shaula. Whatever fools the others, it doesn't escape you. And you're wrong, you know. You do change. You might not age a second between one reunion and the next, but I've seen that sadness in you build and build. You feel it in every breath, and you pick up on the flowers a little sooner each time. And if there was one thing I could do about it…"

"There is," I said sharply, while I had the courage.

His expression was grave but understanding. "I'll bring you flowers again."

"No. Not flowers. Not next time." And I swallowed before speaking, because I knew the words would be difficult to get out once I had started. "You'll end this, Campion. You have the means, I know. There are only wrecks left in orbit, and they wouldn't stand a chance against your own weapons. You'll shatter those wrecks like you shattered the moon of Arghul, and when you're done you'll turn the same weapons onto these towers. Melt them to lava. Flush them back into the sea, leaving no trace. And turn the machines to ash, so that they can't ever rebuild the towers or us. And then leave Tierce and never return to this place."

He stared at me for a long moment, his face so frozen and masklike it was as if he had been struck across the cheeks.

"You'd be asking me to murder a Line."

"No," I said patiently. "The Line is gone, and you've already honoured us. All I'm asking for is one last kindness, Campion. This wasn't ever the way it was meant to be." I reached for him then, settling my hand on his wrist, and then sliding my fingers down until I held his in my own. "You think you lack the courage to commit grand acts. I don't believe a word of it. And even if you did, here's your chance to do something about it. To be courageous and wise and selfless. We're dead. We've *been* dead for a million years. Now let us sleep."

"Shaula…" he began.

"You'll consider it," I said. "You'll evaluate the options, weigh the risks and the capacity for failure. And you'll reach a conclusion, and set yourself on one course or another. But we'll speak no more of it. If you mean to end us, you'll wait until the end of the Thousandth Night, but you'll give me no word of a clue."

"I'm not very good at keeping secrets."

"You won't need to. This is my threading, Campion. My night of nights. It means I have special dispensation to adjust and suppress my own memories, so that my strand has the optimum artistic impact. And I still have the chance to undo some memories, including this entire conversation. I won't remember the phantoms, or the Belladonna protocol, or what I've just asked of you."

"My Line frowned on that kind of thing."

"But you got away with it, all the same. It's a small deletion, hardly worth worrying about. No one will ever notice."

"But I'd know we'd had this conversation. And I'd still be thinking of what you'd asked of me."

"That's true. And unless I've judged you very wrongly, you'll keep that knowledge to yourself. We'll have many more conversations between now and Thousandth Night, I'm sure. But no matter how much I press you—and I will, because there'll be something in *your* eyes as well—you'll keep to your word. If I ask you about the flowers, or the other guests, or any part of this, you'll look at me blankly and that will be an end to it. Sooner or later I'll convince myself you really are as shallow as you pretend."

Campion's expression tightened. "I'll do my best. Are you sure there's no other way?"

"There isn't. And you know it as well. I think you'll honour my wish, when you've thought it over." Then I made to turn from him. "I'm going back to the Owlhead tower to undo this memory. Give me a little while, then call me back to the Clockhead. We'll speak, and I'll be a little foggy, and I'll probably ask you odd questions. But you'll deflect them gently, and after a while you'll tell me it's time to go to the threading. And we'll walk down the stairs as if nothing had changed."

"But everything will have," Campion said.

"You'll know it. I won't. All you'll have to do is play the dashing consort. Smile and dance and say sweet things and congratulate me on the brilliance of my circuit. I think you can rise to the challenge, can't you?"

"I suppose."

"I don't doubt it."

I left him and returned to my parlour.

―――――

Later we danced on the Fiddlehead rock. I had the sense that some unpleasantness had happened earlier between us, some passing cloudy thing that I could not bring to mind, but it could not have been too serious because Campion was the perfect companion, attentive and courteous and generous with wit and praise and warmth. It thrilled me that I had finally broken the silence between us; thrilled me still further that the Thousand Nights had so far to run—the iron hands of the Clockhead tower still to complete their sweep of their face.

I thought of all the evenings stretching ahead of us, all the bright strands we had still to dream, all the marvels and adventures yet to play out, and I thought of how wonderful it was to be alive, to be a thing with a mind and a memory and the five human senses to drink it all in.

The Orange Tree

Maria Dahvana Headley

Shelter me in your shadow
Be with my mouth and my word
Watch over my ways
So I will not sin again with my tongue.
—Solomon ibn Gabirol, 11ᵗʰ century

1.

Since the beginning of the world, there've been a thousand ways invented to be lonely. In a market stall, surrounded by speechless wooden wares, or banished to a black rock in the center of the sea. In a tower, feet forced into standing, floor too small for kneeling down, the only view a high window, the world below made of fire. On a road, parched, nothing but horizon. In the dark, visited by spirits jealous with their leavings.

At the tops of certain mountains there are places for those the world refuses, and at the bottoms of other mountains there are prisons for those the world regrets. There have been boulders installed for leapers once the never is too much.

The quiet is never quiet, not to the lonely. The quiet is full of newborn babies crying and lovers murmuring. The quiet is full of wineglasses and whippoorwills. Screaming quiet is the way the world lets a man know he's alone forever, with no remedy but death or sorcery.

2.

Málaga isn't a city where loneliness should overtake a man. Sweet milk, grapes and almonds, figs, lemons, bitter oranges, pomegranate, a view across the ocean from Spain to the coast of Africa. It's beautiful everywhere, everywhere but where Solomon is. Wherever he steps, there is sorrow and pain.

Solomon's come South from Saragossa to the city of his birth in a last attempt to heal himself. He's saltfish. Something's climbed beneath his skin, creating scabrous ridges on the sides of his ears and lips, and a cough, sometimes bloody. It isn't leprosy, but it looks enough like it that the neighbors shun him. No medical man can help him, and no woman will have him.

Alone in his house, Solomon names a cloud of dust, picturing an Avra with delicate fingers and a quick smile. Then he sweeps her into the street and watches her blow away. God doesn't permit men to knead dust into something with a heart. There is a short history of forbidden creations, a litany of longing. To defend a city, one might permissibly make a warrior of clay. One is not allowed to do that in order to fulfill selfish desires. There will be no blank-faced brides made of mud in Solomon's house. There's no hope of love now, not the way he looks. He's spent twenty years describing the thousand ways, and no time on any softer arts.

The four-hundred-thirty-fourth way to be lonely is the loneliness of the sleepless, awake while the world is not, moon risen, bats with it. Small owls, and teeth in the walls. A coverlet made of sand, a bed made of blisters.

When Solomon wakes each morning his mind is filled with words chewing at each other's tails, tangling toes and tongues. Unspoken poems run through his house, little long-legged darknesses. When he's on his pallet at night, words stand on their hind feet and stare at him. He can't sleep, nor can he organize words into sentences. When he lights a candle, he sees books he'll never finish. Words hide in the shadows and in the cracks in the walls, refusing to be written.

All he has are words, and none of them serve him. None of them even care for him.

Solomon sits alone at supper, taking figs from a dish painted with a lustered ship. He touches the ship's outlines, the oars, the rigging.

Had he a ship, he might sail to some far off country where women had never seen men, and thus wouldn't recognize him as a ruined specimen. He has no ship.

He idly makes a heap of fine sawdust and positions it across from him. *Tziporah*, he thinks, and then, realizing what he's doing, brushes her abruptly from the table. That dust isn't a wife.

Solomon spends an hour staring bitterly at the sky, mapping more of the ways of loneliness. The spheres above him, the sky filled with planets, and all of them are in love. He's a solitary star in the process of dying, the last of a galaxy, the only point of light in a bad piece of darkness.

As a young man, he walked the roads of Andalusia, and mapped brightness instead of the night. Black lace on golden skin, copper glances, the gentle mouth of a serving maid as she circled the table with a jug of wine. He was invited to meals in fine houses, and published as a philosopher, but he made more enemies in such houses than friends. There was something wicked in his soul as well as in his skin. Perhaps the almighty means him to live in solitary misery, a scalded man, but he finds himself in rebellion.

There are options. Witchcraft or suicide. Death or sorcery. The choices are clear.

Solomon has two new texts, bought during his last travel North. He has, for years, called himself a translator, bartering and wheedling, when in truth he wanted these volumes for something else. He's translated words, but he wants to translate other things. At last—this is his seventh night sleepless—he takes the books down and unwraps them from the linens that keep them safe from dust. The Banū Mūsā's treatise on the construction of ingenious devices, and the *Sefer Yetzirah*. There are instructions in both, recipes for things more complicated than joy. Nothing in it is obvious, but he's a poet. What he lacks in logic, he adds in lyric. He combines the instructions, and draws a diagram.

The five-hundred-ninety-third variety of loneliness is the loneliness of first light, a dawn unwitnessed by anyone else, sun rising over the sea, a cracking seam in the world.

When he was sixteen and ignorant of his future miseries, Solomon boasted *"I am the Song and the Song is my slave."* Even if that was true then, it's no longer enough.

The two-hundred-fifth way to be lonely is to hear an echo and think it is the voice of a friend.

At twilight, Solomon dresses himself in a wide-brimmed hat, long gloves, a scarf about his throat and shoulders, a thin saffron-dyed robe, and a veil over his face. He goes into the Jewish quarter.

The nine-hundred-sixty-eighth variety of loneliness is the loneliness of planning magic and keeping it to oneself.

The moon rises as Solomon walks. It's spring and the trees are in bloom, but Solomon prefers the stars: they're brighter in winter. Lightning laughs in the distance. Nighttime is, at least, less lonely. He's free of the house. No one draws back from him in horror, because his garb covers everything.

He passes a garden and smells salt, clove and cinnamon. The sky blooms with the roses of Venus, constellations of pale pink nard, falling stars of jasmine. He stops to inhale, and imagines sharing what he's seen. He could bring a wife a bouquet of all the flowers of this city, both poetic and actual. He could tell her every secret he's stored in his skull, every desire for murder, every yearning for love. He could pile them all at her feet and wait for her to look up and smile at the precious things he'd given her. He'd tell her about the assassination of his mentor, the way he wandered adrift after it. He'd tell her about the hundreds of elegies he's written, and about the grammars, the dictionaries. He'd recite them all from memory, until she knelt before him to tell him that it was time to sleep. He would go. He would not be an unreasonable husband.

At last he arrives at the orange grove.

"I need a tree," says Solomon. "Not too small a tree." He shows the grove man the size he means, stretching his arms.

"The entire tree?" the owner asks, looking at Solomon. "What will you do with a tree? How will you carry a tree?"

"The roots as well," says the poet.

The treeseller sighs. "It won't grow back, once it's cut. The roots should stay here in the earth, to feed the ground."

"The roots," says Solomon again.

The seller takes Solomon's coins, shrugging, and brings out his shovel. The five-hundred-sixth form of loneliness is the loneliness of drought, trees dropping their leaves and fruit, humbled by heat, a treeseller amongst them, praying in vain for the clouds to burst.

The treeseller shovels.

Solomon has a cart's worth of orange tree in the end, and he hires a donkey to haul it.

The seven-hundred-thirteenth variety of loneliness is the loneliness of driving a cart back to town in the dark, a donkey breathing loudly, smelling blossoms. The oranges from these trees are too bitter to eat, but their blooms are perfumed with the smell of sweat and sex.

At the carpenter's house, Solomon gives the carpenter the tree with its heady blossoms and wilting leaves, the roots a tangle of black soil and beetles. With the tree, he passes over a green glass cup from his own kitchen, and the lusterware dish painted with the ship. At last, he gives the carpenter his diagrams. He pays him in maravedís from the publication of *The Fountain of Life*, the only thing he's written that seems likely to pay. Planets devoted to God, each one with its own section. He's out of fashion now, he fears. No one pays for poetry.

"Hinged," Solomon says, pointing at various places on the diagram. The carpenter usually makes doors. Solomon wonders if he's literate.

He has no certainty, only longing. He'll do the most difficult part of the magic himself, but for this part, the handwork, he has no skills. He goes home and waits, alone, alone, alone.

3.

"The poet's commissioned a cabinet," the carpenter tells his father. "But it's a strange one. He insists I use the entire tree to build it, the shavings and the dust, the roots and the leaves, the flowers. It'll take days of planing and shaping, and even then, I'll have to bend the wood in too many places. He wants it hinged at every compartment, and he wants a musical instrument built into it. I don't know what to tell him."

The carpenter's father shakes his head, and so the carpenter goes to his mother. She's not from Spain at all, but from a city across the sea. She has different skills than those his father possesses.

"He pays us well for this?" she asks.

The carpenter shows the coins, looking uneasily at the branches he's meant to shape.

"Well enough," she says, counting them. She examines the diagram with interest, annotating it, drawing the outlines of an instrument from her homeland. At last she scratches in another small alteration, a tiny compartment to be placed deep within the creation, and sealed.

"I should not make this," the carpenter says. "It will offend."

The carpenter's mother glances sharply at him. "The commission is a kind of cabinet, whatever it looks like. Deny what you've made if anyone asks who made it. But we'll take his payment."

She hides the poet's coins away in her apron, then brings her son sheets of metal, pounded thin, a curved knife, and a tiny hammer. She consults the diagram again, goes to the market, and returns with a stillborn goat, bought for its tender hide, and the tanned skin of a doe. She brings tools for carving and stitching: awls, a vial of a particular oil, sand for polishing.

What the poet has commissioned is no sin to her people. The desert has wandering fountains, and the holy have help.

The thirty-ninth form of loneliness is the loneliness of a woman who can see her home from across a sea, but cannot return to it. The loneliness of childbirth in a foreign land, none of the rituals, none of the other women. The loneliness of a marriage made across a table, cooking food, the sound of men talking the language of this country, not of the one you came from.

The carpenter's wife comes from a family whose men made objects for kings. Her son and husband are not what she'd have chosen for herself, had she been doing the choosing. If she were a man, she'd have spent her life working metal and dark wood, inlaying it with gemstones and camel bones.

Instead, she lives on the southern coast, looking over the water at the weather of the continent she's lost.

So the carpenter and his mother work the wood of the orange tree, sanding and polishing, putting in hinges. They work at night when the other work is done, and in the dark, the workshop fills with the scent of sap, fruit and pitch. There are the sounds of strings being plucked and then bowed, the sounds of taut leather being tapped. The carpenter's mother adds an instrument from her home, and while she builds the instrument she sings the songs it should play.

The carpenter's mother sits on her heels, looking at the blistered hearth where the fire caught out of control one afternoon beneath a spitted goat. The goat, with its twisted horns and yellow eyes, is long gone, but she remembers its voice, the song it sang, beheaded. She takes a handful of the ash, presses it hard into her palm, shapes it.

Her son crouches beside her. "People want strange things," he says. "Nothing I'd wish for."

"Most people don't," she says, working the ash, adding a tiny piece of parchment with something scrawled upon it, a word in her own language, and then more ash. "Most people want things to remain the same forever, but the world changes, and we change with it."

She pets the wood, finds a long splinter and tests its sharpness. She soaks it carefully in the oil until it shines. Perhaps things like this cabinet are made all over the world, and always have been, but she only knows them from her home city, and then only small ones, playthings for the wealthy. This one is different.

She kneels, and opens doors, until she arrives at the secret door hidden deep within the commission. She places her handful of ash there, a gift to it.

The carpenter's mother closes that door again and seals it with beeswax. She closes the next door and the next, until all the doors are tightly shut.

4.

The golem isn't alive, and then she is.

The first loneliness is the loneliness of birth. The golem opens her eyelid hinges, delicate doe leather. Her eyes are cold and dry, but she can see the man she's been created to serve, standing over her.

"You," he says. "You."

The golem has pale yellow-brown skin, smoothly sanded. Her hair is made of creamy white flowers with canary streaks, and there are shining green leaves throughout it. She smells of biting honey. She's small and slender, her waist narrow. No taller than he is. Her arms show the tracks of the tools that made her. There's a gouge between her breasts where there was a knot in the orange tree's trunk.

The poet has hammered one of the secret names of God into her palate, and this is what has brought her to life. She tries to speak but she has no tongue. There is a pain, a stabbing where the silver tablet is. She can't tell what it is, only that it hurts.

It stretches inside of her body, a tentacled name. There is a loneliness in this too, the two-hundred-sixty-seventh, the loneliness of the only name one can speak being unspeakable.

"My name is Solomon ibn Gabirol," the man says, and blinks nervously. "You are my wife and servant. You'll help me write. I've need of someone to keep my words contained."

She examines the man before her. His hair is turning white, and his skin is red, black and yellow. His cracked flesh bleeds. Salt water runs from his eyes.

Solomon, she mouths. There is no sound.

"Yes," he says. "You're a thing made for me."

The man feeds her a piece of paper, on which is written a line of a poem, and then he feeds her another. They taste like termite, wasp, worm. A hinge creaks in her jaw.

She's never seen a man before, not from this angle. She wants to take his tears and use them for some purpose. *A ship,* she thinks, catching a bewildering taste of his old thoughts. *On a salt sea. An island where they have never seen a woman.*

She tries to make a noise, but only a rattle comes out. There's a lock on her lips, a bent metal hook through a bent metal eye, and he has latched it. He takes her through his house, showing her its rooms.

"You'll clean for me," he says. "You'll rid my house of dust."

She understands. She begins to shovel with her hands. She buries her fingers in the mess, and thinks of rooting there, falls to her side and stretches, planting herself, but he pulls her up, telling her he wishes her to sweep the dirt, not roll in it like a sow.

She learns quickly. She's made to learn.

5.

When he ordered her, Solomon gave only the measures of the golem's body, writing figures in the margins of his diagram. The carpenter was no sculptor. The golem is full in the hips and breasts, but one breast is bigger than the other, and her hips are tilted.

She has no heart, and no soul. She is therefore no sin.

This is what Solomon thinks to himself when he is trying to sleep in a house in which he is no longer alone.

Solomon's diagrams included no more than suggestions for her face. She therefore has crude features, a mosaic of lustered ceramic for a mouth, and green glass eyes neither the same size nor the same shape. One is oval, and the other is wide and round. The lids, at least, are neat half-moons. Her nose is an angled slope with a bump at the bridge where the grain of the orange tree arcs. She has only an approximation of a woman's looks, but her hinges are perfect. All over her body, there are metal hinges, and wooden ones, leather hinges, and string ones.

She's held together to come apart.

Sometimes, after the first days when she has to be kept from dropping in the garden and pressing her long fingers into the soil, or from standing too many hours outside with her face upturned, waiting for bees to land on her skin, the poet opens a door in her abdomen to remove a word and use it in a sentence. He talks more and more, all day, all night. He paces the room, telling her of injustices, years of woe, jealous companions and patrons murdered. He tells her of his childhood and his disease. He reports every injury done to him, and then writes more lines and feeds them to her.

"*My throat is parched with pleading,*" he scribbles. "*I am buried in the coffin of my home. I combine my blood with my tears, and stir my tears into my wine. I am treated as a stranger, despised—as though I were living with ostriches, caught between thieves and fools, who think their hearts have grown wise.*"

Solomon wonders why he still feels lonely. What kind of loneliness is this? One that hasn't been given a number. It makes him itch, all over, everything from his fingertips to his brain.

6.

The golem is busy. She sweeps the house's dust into the street. She washes the clothes. She clatters on the stones of his floor, her feet too loud in the night, and sometimes she sits, looking out the window, waiting for him to wake, breathing in the new dust that falls from the old walls of the city. She doesn't sleep or eat. She has no need for it.

He writes a list of his enemies and puts them into her mouth. He wants them dead or forgotten, himself remembered. He burns his name onto her wooden skin, a thin line of characters, black and smudged, a circle around her wrist. She looks at the words, curious. They're nothing magical. He is, for all his labor and verse, an ordinary man.

I am your thing, she thinks. *Thing.* She has no name. It is his job to give her one, and he has not.

The poet writes poems, and the golem walks in circles. She lifts his pallet with one hand, to dust around and beneath it. She beats a rug with her fist.

There is a thumping and pleasurable loneliness in this, the loneliness of a drummer in the desert, pounding a sound into leather, untethered by any city. She pounds the rug and feels a song inside herself, the song of falling oranges in a storm, the noise of their ripe roundness rolling away. The rug is silk, and she ravels a strand of scarlet loose and wraps it around her fingers, weaving it through her hinges. There is pleasure in this too, the feeling of an orange tree surrounded by dancers, the feeling of a gourd strung across by strings. She pulls the silk through her hands, stretching it, thinking of spiderwebs. She was once companioned by hundreds of spiders, each one using her branches as an anchor for an instrument of its own, fishing at night. She unravels the whole rug and makes a delicate web in a doorway.

"What is that?"

She has no answer, of course. She's standing beside her web, moving silk over silk, patterning the web to mimic the ones she's seen in her own twigs. With dawn there would be dew on each thread, and the spider in the center, waiting quietly for whatever might be drawn to something with so much gleam.

"This is nothing you'll do again," he says to her, taking the threads in his fist, tugging at them until they detach. He takes the tangled silk and throws it over the cliff. She watches it unspool, red loops caught in the wind, spun strings. Scarlet words in the air for a moment and then gone.

The loneliness of a bird trapped in a web, its wings twisting backward as it swings, struggling, and trapped. The spider's venom, the twisting of thread to cover the beak, the glittering eyes, the feet and flight. The loneliness of being too much body to eat, and killed anyway. A mummified silence, a veiled singer dangling from a chain of silver threads.

Solomon leaves her mouth unlocked one night, and she tests it, stretching the hinges, coughing up half a poem. She feels dirty, and so she goes out into the rain and opens nearly every door in her body.

She thinks of sap. There are roots inside her, her stomach and her intestines made of them, and she places a hand on the ground and takes water from the soil. The sun is part of her skin, and so are the wind and the salt from the sea. She's three hundred years old, and grew from an orange seed dropped by a gull. She's birthed thousands of oranges, and they've fallen from her boughs, taken into the ocean, and into compote dishes. A few of them grew into trees.

Now she's a golem, but she's still what she used to be.

In the morning the poet finds her with her head still upturned, and screams at her, fearful of rust stiffening her smallest hinges.

She looks toward the blaze on the horizon, her jaws wide for the rain until he closes them again, muttering that his hidden words will get wet. He locks her mouth. She grinds her tiny wooden teeth, tasting dust, which she swallows, but she isn't built for anger at her maker.

She's seen the stars now, and she longs to see them again. They're familiar, the green haloes around them, the way the bird-hunting bats swoop and hang from her fingers, the way darkness turns to dawn, bleeding at the edge of the sky.

7.

The poet brings her inside the house, and locks the front door, just as he locked her lips.

"You must be as a wife," Solomon says, his hands shaking. "That is what you were created to do."

The house is very clean. He arranges her on the bed, and she opens for him. She is built to do this. Her diagrams were clear. The secret hinges he requested are small and soft, made of the leather of the stillborn goat. They unfold, door after door, until the second to last door unhinges. He shoves himself inside it.

There's still the final sealed compartment. He doesn't know it exists. Nothing of him gets in.

The golem wonders suddenly if the house is like her, if she's inside the mouth of a larger golem. The loneliness of the motherless daughter, the loneliness of the daughter eaten by the mother, the loneliness of a roomful of wooden teeth. She looks at the chairs and table. She looks up over the poet's shoulder to see if the name of god is hammered to the ceiling. The loneliness of the result of magic.

When he's finished with her, the golem's doors shut themselves, one by one. She stands up and sands herself; there's a spot of blood on her breast from a wound on his. Sawdust flies until she's clean again. He coughs blood, and curses. She sweeps the dust away.

He give her a chestnut to crack between her teeth. She hands him the meat and keeps the shell for herself to suck. It's like a nub of tongue. The golem makes a tiny sound, balancing it in her mouth, a rattle. She wedges it there with her fingers, pressed against the metal name.

She feels liquid drip down her wooden thigh. Startled, she closes the doors tighter.

"I thought I'd be happy with you." Solomon says from the pallet. "But you're not a real woman. You're a thing I made."

You didn't make me, she thinks. *I grew.*

With the shell in her mouth, she makes a tiny noise, a moaning sound not a word, but not the sound of nothing. She chirrs a note. Everything that ever sang through her branches, every gust of wind, every bat, every bee, every bird. They all spoke to her and she spoke back to them when she was a tree. Now she is a hinged woman, muted by magic, and she moves the shell in her mouth, looking for a voice she's not been made to have.

8.

Solomon gets up, dresses in his loosest garments and writes. His skin is boils and snakes. His bones feel breakable, and even his thoughts feel diseased. Talking doesn't help his loneliness. He wants to have her again, because she is all he'll ever have.

She isn't what he wants. He had a different woman in mind. Copper glances, black lace, a living woman willing to wrap him in bandages, a woman willing to carry him to a warm tub, a woman to cure his agonies.

This one is cold and has no heart. This one is ugly and has no mind. She's only an orange tree.

He writes of the loneliness of the poet, years of shunning, the way his life has bent itself into a hoop of suffering. He writes of the eight-hundred-sixty-first form of loneliness, the loneliness of the scratching quill plucked from some dead swan. He writes of the forty-eighth form of loneliness, the loneliness of the moment of orgasm, when all the sky rushes from the blue and into the sea, leaving nothing in its place.

He goes to the golem and stares at her, considering the conditions of the magic. He asks for one thing he hasn't had yet.

"Play me a song," he says. "It's too quiet."

9.

The golem is surprised to discover that she's made of music. She has no tongue, but she has noise. The golem's body is a chamber. There are strings made of silk, and a curved bow inside one of the cabinets of her thigh. When she threads three strings through tiny holes drilled in her sternum, and another set just below her stomach, she can play the rabāb. This was part of her diagram, any instrument, and the carpenter's mother chose this one from her own home. There is a thin membrane of doeskin, tanned and stretched taut over the cavity of the cabinet, and this skin vibrates.

She plays the tunes given her by the carpenter's mother, songs of the desert, songs of another religion. There are S-shaped openings in her stomach from which the song pours.

She draws the bow across the strings, filling with greater and greater pleasure, until the poet waves his hand, goes to his bed, and waits for her to stop the noise and come to him.

10.

There's a hard storm that night, and all the pomegranates fall. The golem goes into the street at dawn and kneels to collect them, each one as large as a baby's head.

"Who are you?" a woman says, and the golem looks up, startled, her fingers pushing through the pomegranate's skin and deep into the seeds, groping for something.

The woman is standing over her, looking horrified, and when the golem raises her face, the woman screams, and backs away, gasping.

The golem feels the seeds slick and fat between her fingers. She crushes some, and juice runs out into the dirt. There are tiny ants all over the fruit, and she feels their bodies crushing too, their certainty that they might carry something so tremendous. She feels sorry for that.

"What are you?" the woman says, and makes a gesture of protection. "Demon," she whispers, and runs, dropping her basket.

The golem goes back into the house.

She curls into the cold fireplace, a heap of sticks, and stays there through the day and until the next morning, though Solomon shouts for her when she brings no evening meal. Her blossoms are falling off. The petals are dropping, and she feels as though she will soon be naked.

When the petals are gone, though, there are oranges, tiny green ones. Her skull is beaded with them.

The loneliness of the bee seeking nectar, the journey between trees, a wavering flight, a humming and thrum. The loneliness of the pale flower, a channel of gold at its center, dew and dawn and a white room.

In the morning, she raises Solomon's bed with him on it, and sweeps the dust from beneath it. She swabs water over the new wounds on his skin. He is weak and fevered. She wonders if he will die.

"You serve me," he croaks. She feels her doors opening. She has no say in it.

11.

Solomon presses into her, looking down at her still face, pushing against her hard flesh. He is too sick to leave the house at all. Too sick to enjoy anything. His skin feels like a board being planed, shaven, the scraps tread on by goats. He needs a diet of milk and honey, a balm of olive oil. She can't fetch any of it for him. He is a monster and she is a cabinet. Neither of them can go into the street.

He considers the precious word that brought her to life. He means to pry it loose. She'll be firewood at least. This has been a failure.

"You're not what I wanted," he says when he is finished.

He puts his fingers to the corner of her mouth, intending to open the hinges and remove god from her.

12.

As Solomon approaches her, the golem feels a startling jolt deep inside her body. Something sealed begins to unseal; something forbidden begins to reveal itself. She holds the innermost cabinet door shut, feeling the hinges stretching, the thing behind it trying to be loose. If the poet notices her alarm, he says nothing.

There is shouting from the street. Solomon withdraws from her. The golem smoothes her dress. The poet rearranges his robes. The oranges are ripening. The room is heavy with their smell, sweat and sweetness.

The door inside the golem's body, the last and smallest door, the last and smallest hinge, shakes and swells. She keeps it closed. She refuses. Whatever is in there, it can stay locked behind the door. Liquid on her thigh. She closes all the doors with ferocious resolution.

Men shout to enter. Solomon ties a patterned cloth about her head, over the lumpy oranges.

"Qasmūna," he says. "Your name is Qasmūna. You're a housemaid."

Her fists open and close convulsively as the door pounds.

She wonders if she'll kill his enemies. That is what she was made to do.

13.

The men surge into the house, bearded and cloaked. There are five of them, and they're all elderly, years beyond Solomon. He knows them. The elders are the ones who kept him in this house, unable to walk amongst humans. When he arrived in the city, he was shunned. It was only their permission and their memories of his parents, long dead, that allowed him to live here at all, to stop walking the roads. Otherwise, he'd be dead somewhere, parched and dried to leather.

It might be better than this.

He thinks for a moment that he can take them all, pulverize them. He might crush them into a cupboard and barricade them there. He might make them into the contents of a cabinet, dishes asking to be broken. Then he remembers that they're living men, not his creation. He's lost his understanding of the nature of the world. He is a sickly poet, and they are the men in charge of the city.

The men circle the room, staring at the golem, who stands in the center, waiting, trembling. She's a tree full of birds, and they're foxes.

"What have you done?" they shout at Solomon, and he lies to them, though it's futile. They're holy men with long beards and hundreds of years between them. They know his books and they know the history of his books. They know every corner of the law. Solomon feels himself surrounded by poems he will never write. He'll be taken to executioners. It troubles him for a moment, and then it doesn't. He'll stab out their eyes as he goes. He'll scream his own elegy from his last moments. It's already written and stored inside his cabinet.

"This creature is no woman, Solomon ibn Gabirol," says one. "Do you take us for fools?"

"She's nothing more than a housemaid," Solomon says calmly. "Her name is Qasmūna, and she came from Saragossa. I brought her here to tidy my house and care for me. You know that I've been ill."

The loneliness of capture, the loneliness of guilt, a single intruder caught and tied, burned at the stake. The loneliness of fire touching feet, the loneliness of stones flying toward a target. All he wanted was a wife.

This is no sin, he thinks. This is not a sin. She's a housemaid, and Solomon has a house that needs cleaning. He has a heart that needs polishing. He has a body that needs a companion. He cannot see the problem. There is a map inside his mind of all the sins, and he doesn't believe in most of them. This one? To build a woman out of wood? How could it be wrong? To use her as a wife? She has no heart and she has no soul. She's an instrument and he has played her properly. That's what he'll say. That's how he'll argue.

One of the men nearly touches the golem, and then stops, his fingers inches from her hand. He leans forward and shakes his head.

"This is not a maid," he insists, then lifts a metal cup, and raps it against her wrist. It makes the sound of an axe meeting a tree. "No. We know what this is."

The golem opens her mouth hinge, slightly, to show her teeth. In her mouth, the nub of tongue rattles, and she makes a tiny noise, a cry. A string within her body vibrates and makes a sighing tone.

"We do *not* know fully," another man protests. He looks at the golem, skeptical. "Solomon ibn Gabirol isn't holy enough to make a golem. He's not held in grace. Perhaps she's simply ugly. Open your mouth wider, girl, show us what you have," he says.

She shows her teeth a little more, and her sound grows louder, a humming rattle, a clicking. Her eyelid hinges blink, quickly, a leathery brush against the green glass.

One of the men leans forward and taps her eye with a spoon. She flinches. It rings like a bell calling for prayers.

"She's a living woman," says Solomon, fearful of punishment, but angry too. His fingers curl around the tabletop.

"She is not," one of the men says, and looks at Solomon with something approaching kindness. "Shelomo ben Yehuda ibn Gabirol, you are too lonely. You are fortunate we've come to help. No one knows you've done this, not yet, and we will save you from this sin for the sake of your father."

14.

The golem trembles, bound to protect Solomon. She feels his rage like a windstorm bending her trunk. She is a newborn woman and she is a rabāb full of the songs of an entire country of travelers. She is a tree with hundreds of years of history.

She removes the bow from the cabinet in her thigh and starts to play the strings in her abdomen. The song is not a hymn. The song is a wild high flight from some other shore, the song of a woman shouting in a ship across the sea. The song of the strings bends and weeps, and she plays, her head bowed, while the bow in her hand moves quickly. Tongueless, she is telling them what will happen, but they don't listen.

"Speak," says one of the men.

"She can't," says Solomon. "She doesn't speak our language."

I am speaking, Qasmūna plays. *I am warning you. You should leave.*

"This is a sin. More than a sin. To fornicate with *this*. Speak in Spanish, you serving maid. Speak in Arabic. Speak in Hebrew. Speak any language at all."

Qasmūna plays harder, her wooden fingernails stopping the strings, the bow calling forth the sound of women seizing a ship's crew and tearing them apart. The loneliness of the shore with no one landing on it in a year. The loneliness of hunger. She is an orange tree clinging to a cliffside, oranges falling into the sea. She is a forgotten wife clinging to a village full of forgotten children. She is called to war while the men are at another war. She and her sisters march over the Atlas Mountains. She and her sisters sing warcries, play their instruments, light signal fires.

"SPEAK!" a man shouts. "Or we will know what you are."

I am speaking, the golem plays. *Hear me. Leave before you can't leave.*

Qasmūna can see veins bulging in Solomon's neck. Her hinges flutter. The secret door inside her shakes loudly enough that the men can hear it. It is unsealing. It is opening. She can't help it.

"This is not a sin," argues another holy man. "She doesn't need to be cleansed after menstruation, for she doesn't menstruate. She can't procreate. She can't speak, nor has she any intelligence. She's less than an animal. It can't be fornication if she isn't a woman."

"Her lack of speech reflects the flaw in her creator," the first man says. "He's not holy enough."

The golem listens to them argue over whether she is holy or only wooden. She plays. They look at her in annoyance. She is an instrument and she plays the music she is filled with. She bends and draws the bow over the strings, playing an attack on a tent, playing a moon rising over bloodied sand. They don't understand her. She attempts to give them a final warning, but they are too busy with their debate.

15.

Solomon rages, but doesn't dare do it with his voice. The golem is playing some tilting tune, and he can't get her to stop. Her music is nothing he'd have chosen. Why did he not kill her last night? She could be in the fireplace, heating the house. She could be rising through the chimney, her smoke a small cloud in the sky.

This was a mistake, but now that they are trying to take her from him, he wants her back. Who are they to deny him a wife?

"You must destroy this golem, Solomon ibn Gabirol," concludes the man most in charge. "For though it may not be a sin in the eyes of the law, you're a poet, not a holy man, and you have made a monstrosity for yourself, not for any city. This is forbidden."

"She's not a monstrosity," pleads Solomon. "She's my housemaid. She cleans the dust." His wounds are bleeding. He coughs, wet and red.

The loneliness of seeing one's own blood on a white cloth. The loneliness of a disease impervious to magic, to knowledge, to weather. He is dying, and there is no one to take care of him. He is dying, and soon he will be like an infant, helpless and howling. Soon he will be a body in a bed, bones like kindling.

The thousandth form of loneliness is the loneliness of the dead, rotting just beneath the ground. There will be worms and insects, there will be birds pecking at the earth, but there will be nothing to love any man underneath the world. The thousandth loneliness is a grave with fresh shovel marks, the noise of the dirt being packed down above. He will be, he realizes, down where the orange tree roots snake in the dark, white wooden bones hard as stones.

"You'll remove the name of our lord from her mouth. You'll destroy her, and you'll burn her materials." The men nod. "You'll do it now, for these witnesses, or you yourself will be put to death. Take her apart now. We will watch."

Solomon sways. He's still living, he thinks. His prick pulses. He must retaliate. He must fight.

There's a creak in the room, and a muffled pounding.

"Defender," Solomon whispers to his golem. "Defend."

The golem is already standing, staring at the old man before her. She raises a hand, and looks at it. Slowly she brings her fist down on the man's skull, a neat rapping. He cries out and falls. The holy men scream.

Solomon watches her push her fingers into one of the men's mouths, her fist pressing deeper, deeper until she finds the root of his tongue. She tears out the meat of his voice and crushes it, a splattering gore beneath her foot. Solomon makes a sound, whether of vengeance or of protest, he can't say. He looks at the holy tongue for a moment, watching it bleed, then doubles over, vomiting.

The sound of something breaking open. He turns to see the golem and the last of the holy men, his skull vised in her two hands. She looks at Solomon, her face blank, and there is a grievous crack, sending blood spraying. Her mouth rattles and she breaks the man's neck for good measure, as though he is a hen.

16.

The loneliness of being the last man alive in a room filled with the dead is the nine-hundred-ninety-ninth loneliness.

They're all murdered in his house, the holy men of Málaga. Solomon won't die of illness as he'd imagined. He'll be executed. He has to flee the city, but he can't flee with her. He gathers himself. She has saved him and damned him at once. It can't be his fault. No one would think it was. He would never order his golem to kill for him.

"Open your mouth," Solomon orders his golem. "Give me the name. Take it out, and give it to me."

Slowly, the golem's jaw hinges open, showing the poet the name of god. One of her hands reaches up to remove it.

There is the sound of a sealed door opening. Something changes in the room.

Solomon looks down at the golem's chair. There's a creature in it, small and black, made of ash. It stands, its arms outstretched, a tiny thing, and it shakes the room with a high, wild song, a song like the rabāb and like a singer too, a song of loneliness beyond number. It sings a horde of women in open space, raging across a landscape, swords raised.

Solomon clenches all over. Can he smash it? With a dish, perhaps, or a text. It's small enough. It's no animal or insect he's seen. A rough black creature, the size of a closed fist. The song is something… Solomon tilts his head. His ears feel penetrated.

"What's that?" Solomon manages. "Where did it come from?"

Qasmūna picks the creature up and cradles it. The ash looks at Solomon, its eyes glittering. In its fist, it holds a splinter of orange wood.

A splinter held by a tiny thing. That's nothing. No sword, no matter the feelings roused in him by its song. Whatever those feelings were, they are falsehoods, defenses without teeth. Women running over sand, bloodied swords. This is only a small aberration. He'll consider it later, when this is all done.

What it is, Solomon doesn't know, but it doesn't matter. He'll dismantle the golem and it'll die with her. There will be a heap of wood, leather, metal and string. There'll be some metal hinges, some green oranges. He'll toss it all over the cliff edge. He feels a little stronger suddenly, purposeful. He'll dress and put his books in a sack. He'll hire a cart.

The loneliness of the fleeing poet. The road before him, the dust, the cart rattling, the bones pained. The loneliness he is well accustomed to, traveling by himself, wandering book stalls at night, reading texts he procures from the darkest, dustiest stacks. He will write two hundred verses in mourning for the golem, he decides. He'll write of her smooth skin and fragrant hair, her green eyes and sharp teeth.

He hears the golem moving, and turns to find her quite close to him. She hasn't listened to his request. Why has she not given him the name? Is the magic flawed?

Solomon clasps his golem's wrist, groping for her jaw hinge, but the golem's golem is there, standing on his arm. It stabs the splinter into the poet's hand, deep into the vein at the top.

"You are my thing!" Solomon shouts at her. "My wife!"

She says nothing. There's only that high song from the ash, and the golem, moving the bow across the strings in her stomach. Red threads. A web, Solomon thinks. A spider.

Solomon runs for the door, but almost instantly he's too ill to run, too ill to walk. He falls, shaking and vomiting, feeling his body dismantling itself from the inside out. He's made of hinges and all of them are bending, all the doors inside his body too far open, his heart dropping through staircases, his kidneys swollen, his eyes watering and blasting agony. His skin is shedding and he is a snake. His hinges are rusting and he's alone on a rainy road, floodwater rising. The loneliness of the poet muted. His hands are claws. His mouth feels thick and his throat is closing.

17.

Qasmūna goes to him. She is built to serve, to defend, to protect, and her protections include the cessation of misery. She gives Solomon the juice of bitter oranges in a green glass cup, gently, a drop at a time from her finger. This is all there is left to do. She knows that much.

His heart thunders but after a time, he's quiet.

She picks him up from the floor and carries him, not gently. Now he's only a body, not a master. She ferries him from the house, and with her hands she digs a grave in the garden beneath the roots of a fig tree.

This not loneliness in this garden. The company of trees, the conversation of birds, the discussions between wasps and fruit. The pollen of flowers and the high pallor of clouds. She looks up and breathes in. She spits out the inadequate nutshell, and takes a twig from the tree. She works the twig into the space in her mouth, behind the name of God.

The tiny golem watches her, prepared to defend her city, prepared to do what it is golems do. As she pushes her new tongue into place, a door opens in her chest.

The golem's golem places itself inside the compartment there, a compartment that has previously been perfectly empty, and the hinges close.

Qasmūna's heart beats. The strings of her instrument vibrate.

She speaks a word.

18.

A season passes, and the walled garden grows wild.

The fig tree bears fruit, and the carpenter's mother crosses over the wall and onto the poet's land to pick before the birds and bats can eat them. She can see slender yellow bones bending up from the soil beneath the tree, fingers, and a jaw, long since picked clean by animals. The earth is especially dark here, a bright russet soil, and the bones are beautiful, like jewelry lost after a night's dancing. The carpenter's mother steps barefoot on the dirt and packs it down, leaving it smooth.

She reaches up and plucks figs, dropping them into her smock. The figs are heavy and green, their centers scarlet. The carpenter's mother eats one as she stands in the garden, looking out toward the country that was hers before this one.

She hums a song about marching through sand, a song about homecoming after war. The song can only be played on the rabāb, and the tune runs counter to the music, a twisting blade sung at night while the washing's being wrung. When she was a girl, all the women sang this song at once, and when the men returned from wherever men went, they were nervous at the patterns the women's feet had made in the dust, the way they'd danced together beneath the moon.

Months have passed. The carpenter's mother knows nothing of where Solomon ibn Gabirol has gone. He walked in one day, and surely he walked away the same. His kitchen was full of coins for a time after he disappeared. Then the coins went into the carpenter's mother's apron as payment for a cabinet.

She knows nothing of where the holy men have gone, either. She saw nothing late in the night all those months ago, beneath a moon like a blossom. She heard no music playing, no mournful joyful strings, no echoing resonance and thrum. Those songs were unfamiliar to her. They sounded nothing like wandering fountains in the desert, nothing like shining things made of metal and silk.

The carpenter's mother never saw a woman walking out from the house of Solomon ibn Gabirol, her feet clattering across the stones of the street. A stranger to Málaga! She didn't see that woman lifting five men, and throwing them tenderly, one by one, from the cliffs, nor did she see her digging here, beneath the fig tree.

She didn't see the woman step off the rock path, and walk down to the harbor. Nor did she see her open a door in her abdomen, and remove a thousand pages of words, sections from poems, scribbled lines and wishes. She didn't see her tear these until each word was left lonely, and then begin to rearrange them.

She didn't see this, the carpenter's wife would swear, if anyone asked her. No one will ask her. She's an old woman, and must know little of the world. She's been here too long to read and too long to write. Too long to know anything of the world of magic.

But how quickly that wooden woman went, arranging poem after poem, the words of the poet who called her from the trees taken and changed. She took all the poet's words and made new things with them, a line on the sand.

When she was finished, she looked up at the old woman standing on the cliff.

The old woman, of course, saw nothing.

She didn't watch the wooden woman place herself in a boat, take the oars in her strong hands, and begin to row.

Surely, no mother of Málaga would let a murderess of so many men, all the intellectuals of this part of the coast, all of the holy, and a philosopher poet too, surely no carpenter's wife would let a murderess go free.

19.

On the night the golem left Spain, after it was fully dark, the carpenter's mother climbed down the rocks to the shore. This much was true. She would say it, if she were asked.

The poem on the sand was written in a language she could read, and she thought for a moment about the market stalls in her homeland, the words scrolling over her fingertips, the things made by her father and brothers, brought to life by her own blood and spit.

In dreams, she inlaid a mother of pearl woman with coral, camel bones, ebony eyes. In dreams, she breathed into the woman's lips and sent her to kill those who would sell a talented daughter to wed a lowly carpenter on the southern coast of Spain. Her life is no horror, but it is no glory, either, and who would imagine that a carpenter's wife would be full of poetry, full of spells, a maker of women? She could cause a fountain to spring from the desert, and here she is, sold, sold and spelled, daughter to a magician long dead. She'll never go home again, because the water will refuse her.

She read the poems Qasmūna left for her. Some had already caught the wind and blown out into the salt by the time she'd made it down the cliff, but two remained.

O gazelle, tasting leaves,
here in the green of my garden.
Look at my eyes. Dark and lonely,
just as yours are.
How distant we are from our beloveds, and how forgotten

Standing in the night,
Waiting for fate to find us.

The carpenter's mother looked up, listening to the song coming over the water. She ate a fig and tasted the wasp that had pollinated it, the bones of the poet that had fed it. The second poem was shorter.

The garden is filled with fruit on the vines, but the gardener
refuses to brush a finger over the skin of even one piece.
How sad it is! The season of splendor passes,
and the fruit that ripens only in darkness
Remains lonely.

The gulls followed the wooden woman into a new life, out from Spain and over the sea, but that is nothing the carpenter's mother will admit to knowing. She's merely an old woman sitting in the dark, listening to the sounds of a creature made of ash, and one made of wood, singing their way away.

She sits there a long time beneath the stars, before she writes the poems onto a piece of cloth, before she walks barefoot down the road to another town with them, before she puts them into the hands of a songseller.

"Where did these come from?" the seller asks.

"A woman," she tells him. "Qasmūna."

"Who is her father?" he asked. "Who is her husband?"

"She has neither," the carpenter's wife said, knotting the scrolls with red silk thread. "Will you buy them?"

Coins are never lonely. They clacked and rang out, and the carpenter's wife held them in her palm, though soon they'd disappear like the kind of shining moths which land for only a moment to drink, before lighting again into the night.

Historical Note

The legend of the wooden golem created by the Andalusian Hebrew poet Solomon ibn Gabirol (1021–c.1058) is much less known than that of Rabbi Loew and the Golem of Prague, perhaps because ibn Gabirol's golem was a (rare) female golem brought to life not as a defender, but as a housemaid and likely bedmate. The historic ibn Gabirol was a complicated and brilliantly prolific intellectual figure, a reclusive misanthrope who suffered from a skin disease, possibly cutaneous tuberculosis. His poetry is filled with feelings of ostracisation and rage relating to same—he complains about jealous enemies, among other things—though he also wrote rapturous and religiously ecstatic poems regarding the planets, the gardens of the sky, and laughing lightning. In the accounts, ibn Gabirol was forced to destroy his hinged golem after being accused of fornicating with her. The legend typically comes up in discussions of personhood in Jewish law—and the debate in *Hinge* is typical of that discussion. The *Sefer Yetzirah,* in which mystical information related to golem creation is traditionally thought to be found, was a significant influence on ibn Gabirol's work, and he translated sections of it. The Banū Mūsā's *Book of Ingenious Devices* was written in the 9th century, and contains instructions for creating a variety of automata. The legend of ibn Gabirol's murder and burial beneath a fig tree is historical, though used to new ends here.

The rabāb is a stringed instrument still played all over the world, an ancestor of the violin (which wasn't invented until after the period in which this story is set). It came from North Africa via trade routes to Spain in the 11ᵗʰ century, and there's a very nice drawing of a more pear-shaped variant included in the Catalan Psalter, c. 1050. There's also a version of a rabāb in a fresco in the crypt of Sant'Urbano alla Caffarella, near Rome (c. 1011), and that version looks almost exactly like a modern violin, including S-shaped soundholes. The tones of the rabāb are said, even in early accounts, to mimic those of a woman's voice.

Bitter oranges, a primary crop in Málaga, have recently been discovered to have effects similar to those of the banned diet-aid ephedra—their extract, often marketed as a stimulant, can cause strokes and heart attacks. The pale yellow wood of the bitter orange tree is so hard that it is made into baseball bats in Cuba. The golem's golem, composed of ash and a name written on parchment, is a far more traditional golem than the wood and hinges creation said to have been made by ibn Gabirol (the only golem of that composition in the history, so far as I can tell), but that one is my invention.

Qasmūna (or Kasmunah) bat Isma'il was an 11ᵗʰ or 12ᵗʰ century Andalusian Jewish poet. Her name is likely derived from the Arabic diminutive of the Hebrew root *qsm*, meaning charming and seductive. Charming, in this case in the literal sense—magical. It may also be derived from the Arabic male name Qasmun—someone with a beautiful face. Her two extant poems (my loose translations from the original Arabic) are in the text. She is one of only two documented Spanish Jewish female poets in the period, the other being the Wife of Dunash. Qasmūna bat Isma'il's biography is unknown, though there has been plenty of speculation—the daughter of a scholar, the daughter of a well known poet, or, in this case, something else entirely. Regardless, her poems are erotic, and steeped in the natural world.

Monkey and the Lady

Neil Gaiman

Monkey was in the plum tree. He had only made the universe that morning, and he had been admiring it, particularly the moon, which was visible in the day-time sky, from the top of the tree. He had made the winds and the stars, the ocean waves and the towering cliffs. He had made fruit to eat, and he had been enthusiastically picking and eating fruit all day, and trees to climb and from which he could observe the world he had made. Now he was covered in sticky red juice. He laughed with delight, because it was a good world, and the plums were sweet and tart and sunwarmed, and it was good to be Monkey.

Something was walking, beneath the tree, something he did not remember having created. It was walking in a stately fashion, looking at the flowers and the plants.

Monkey dropped a half-eaten plum onto it, to see what it would do. It picked the plum from its shoulder and flicked the fruit uneaten into the bushes.

Monkey dropped to the ground. "Hello," said Monkey.

"You must be Monkey," said the person. She wore a high-collared blouse, and her grey skirts were full, and went almost to the ground. She even wore a hat, with a rose of a dusty-orange colour tucked into the hatband.

"Yes," said Monkey, and he scratched himself with his left foot. "I made all this."

"I am the Lady," said the woman. "I believe we are going to have to learn to live together."

"I don't remember making you," said Monkey, puzzled. "I made fruit and trees and ponds and sticks and—"

"You certainly didn't make me," said the woman.

Monkey scratched himself thoughtfully, this time with his right foot. Then he picked up a plum from the ground, and devoured it with relish, throwing the plum-stone down when he was done. He picked at the mushy remains of plum from the fur on the back of his arm, and sucked at the fruit he retrieved.

"Is that," asked the Lady, "really acceptable behaviour?"

"I'm Monkey," said Monkey. "I do whatever I want to."

"I am sure you do," said the Lady. "But not if you wish to be with me."

Monkey pondered.

"Do I wish to be with you?" he asked.

The Lady looked at Monkey gravely, then she smiled. It was the smile that did it. Somewhere between the beginning of the smile and the end of it, Monkey decided that spending time in this person's company would be a fine thing.

Monkey nodded.

"In which case," she said, "you will need clothes. And you will need manners. And you will need not to do that."

"What?"

"The thing you are doing with your hands."

Monkey looked at his hands, guiltily. He was not quite certain what they had been doing. Monkey's hands were part of him, he knew, but when he was not actually thinking about them they did whatever hands did when you were not watching them. They scratched and they investigated and they poked and they touched. They picked insects from crevices and pulled nuts from bushes.

Behave yourselves, Monkey thought at his hands. In reply one of the hands began to pick at the fingernails of the other.

This would not be easy, he decided. Not even a little. Making stars and trees and volcanoes and thunderclouds was easier. But it would be worth it.

He was almost certain it would be worth it.

Monkey had created everything, so he intuited immediately what clothes were: cloth coverings that people would wear. In order for clothes to exist, he needed to make people to wear them, to exchange them and to sell them.

He created a nearby village, in which there would be clothes, and he filled it with people. He created a little street market, and people who would sell things in the market. He created food stalls, where people made food that sizzled and smelled enticing, and stalls that sold strings of shells and beads.

Monkey saw some clothes on a market stall. They were colourful and strange, and Monkey liked the look of them immediately. He waited until the stallholder's back was turned, then he swung down and seized the clothes, and ran through the market while people shouted at him in anger or in amusement.

He put the clothes on, just as the humans wore them, and then, awkwardly, he went and found the Lady. She was in a small cafe, near the market.

"It's me," said Monkey.

The Lady examined him without approaching. Then she sighed. "It is you," she said. "And you are wearing clothes. They are very gaudy. But they are clothes."

"Shall we live together now?" asked Monkey.

In response, the Lady passed Monkey a plate with a cucumber sandwich on it. Monkey took a bite of the sandwich, broke the plate experimentally on a rock, cut himself on a section of broken plate, then peeled apart the sandwich, picked the cucumber from it with bloody fingers and threw the remaining bread onto the cafe floor.

"You will need to do a better impersonation of a person than that," said the Lady, and she walked away in her grey-leather shoes with buttons up the side.

I created all the people, thought Monkey. I created them as grey dull land-bound things, to make Monkey seem wiser and funnier and freer and more alive. Why should I now pretend to be one?

But he said nothing. He spent the next day, and the day after that, watching people and following them on the earth, almost never climbing walls or trees or flinging himself upwards or across spaces only to catch himself before he fell.

He pretended that he was not Monkey. He decided not to answer to "Monkey" any more, when anything spoke to him. From now on, he told them, he was "Man."

He moved awkwardly on the earth. He only managed to conquer the urge to climb everything once he stole shoes and forced them onto his feet, which were not made for shoes. He hid his tail inside his trousers, and now he could only touch the world and move it or change it with his hands or his teeth. Monkey's hands were better behaved too—more responsible, now that his tail and his feet were hidden, less likely to poke or pry, to rip or to rub.

The Lady was drinking tea in a small cafe near the market, and he sat beside her.

"Sit on the chair," said the Lady. "Not the table."

Monkey was not sure he would always be able to tell the difference, but he did as she requested.

"Well?" said Monkey.

"You're getting there," said the Lady. "Now you just need a job."

Monkey frowned and chittered. "A job?" He knew what a job was, of course, because Monkey had created jobs when he had created everything else, rainbows and nebulae and plums and all the things in the oceans, but he had barely paid attention to them even as he created them. They were a joke, something for Monkey and his friends to laugh at.

"A job," repeated Monkey. "You want me to stop eating whatever I wish, and living where I wish, and sleeping where I wish, and instead to go to work in the mornings and come home tired in the evening, earning money enough to buy food to eat, and a place to live and to sleep…?"

"A job," said the Lady. "Now you are getting the idea."

Monkey went into the village he had made, but there were no jobs there to be had, and the people laughed at him when he asked them to employ him.

He went into a town nearby, and found himself a job, sitting at a desk and writing lists of names into a huge ledger, bigger than he was. He did not enjoy sitting at the desk, and writing names made his hands hurt, and whenever he sucked absentmindedly on his pen and thought of the forests the blue ink tasted foul and it left inkstains on his face and his fingers.

On the last day of the week, Monkey took his pay and walked from the town back to the village where he had last seen the Lady. His shoes were dusty and they hurt his feet.

He put one foot in front of the other on the path.

Monkey went to the cafe, but it was empty. He asked if anyone there had seen the Lady. The owner shrugged her shoulders, but said that, on reflection, she thought she had seen the Lady in the rose gardens on the edge of the village the previous day, and perhaps Monkey should look there…

"Man," corrected Monkey. "Not Monkey." But his heart was not in it.

Monkey went to the Rose Gardens, but he did not see the Lady.

He was slouching along the path that would have taken him back to the cafe when he noticed something on the dry earth. It was a grey hat with a dusty orange rose in the hatband.

Monkey walked towards the hat, and picked it up, and examined it to see if, perhaps, the Lady was underneath it. She was not. But Monkey noticed something else, a minute's walk away. He hurried over to it. It was a grey shoe, with buttons up the side.

He walked on in the same direction and there, on the ground, was a second shoe, almost the twin of the first.

Monkey kept going, now. Soon, crumpled on the side of the road, he found a woman's jacket, and then he found a blouse. He found a skirt, abandoned on the edge of the village.

Outside the village he found more grey clothes, thin and unlikely, like the shed skins of some scanty reptile, hanging now from branches. The sun would soon be setting, and the moon was already high in the eastern sky.

Something about the branches the clothes were hanging on felt familiar. He walked further into the grove of trees.

Something hit Monkey on the shoulder: it was a half-eaten plum. Monkey looked up.

She was far above him, naked and hairy-arsed, her face and her breasts stained and sticky with red juice, sitting and laughing in the plum tree.

"Come and look at the moon," she said, with delight. "Come and look at the moon with me."

No One Dies in Nowhere

Catherynne M. Valente

First Terrace: The Late Repentant

There is a clicking sound before she appears, like a gas stove before it lights. One moment there is nothing, the next there is Pietta, though this is the last gasp of before/after causality in her pure, pale mind. Now that she is here, she will always have been here. Charcoal-blue rags twist and braid and drape around her body more artfully than any gown. A leather falcon's hood closes up her head but does not blind her; the eyecups are a fine bronze mesh that lets in light. Long jessies hang from her thin wrists. This room which she has never seen belongs to her as utterly as her eyes: a monk's cell, modest but perfect and graceful. Candles thick as calf-bones. Water in a black basin. A copper rain barrel, empty. She runs her hand along the smooth, wine-dark stone of her walls; her fingertips leave phosphor-prints. She lays down on her bed, a shelf for holding Piettas carved out of the rock, mattressed in straw and withered, thorny wildflowers that smell of the village where she was born. From the straw, she can look out of three slim glassless windows shaped like chess bishops. A grey, damp sky steals in, a burgling fog climbing up toward her, a hundred million kinds of grey swirling together, and the stars behind, waiting. Pietta remembers the feeling of the first day of school. She goes to the window and looks out, looks down. Her long hair hangs over the ledge like two thick vines. Black, seedless earth below, dizzyingly far.

As close as spying neighbors across a shared alley, a sheer, knife-cragged mountain stretches up into the dimming clouds and disappears into oncoming night. The mountain crawls with people. Each carries a black lantern half as tall as they. A man with a short, lovely beard chokes on the smoke puking forth from his light, but even as he chokes, he holds it closer to his mouth, desperate to get more. Their eyes meet. Pietta holds up her hand in greeting. He opens his jaw far wider than any bone allows and takes long, sultry bites out of the smoke.

When she turns away, a bindle lies on her bed of stone and straw. A plain handkerchief knotted around a long, burled black branch. She looses the cloth. Inside she finds a wine bottle, a pair of scissors, a stone figure of a straight-backed child in a chair, a brass key, a cracked, worn belt with two holes torn through, and a hundred shattered shards of colored glass. Pietta picks up one of the blades of glass and holds it to her breast until it slices through her skin. The glass is violet. The blood never comes.

Second Terrace: The Proud

On an endless plain where nothing grows lie a mountain as crowded as a city and a city as vast as a mountain. They face one another like bride and bridegroom. The city was enclosed at the commencement of linear time, a great ancient abbey bristling with domes, towers, spires, and stoas, chiseled out of rock the color of wine spilled on the surface of Mars, doorless, but not windowless, never windowless, candlelight twinkling from millions upon millions of arched and tapered clefts in the stone. From every one of these, you can see the mountain clearly, the people moving upon it, their lamps swinging back and forth, their hurryings and their stillnesses. The whispered talk of the people on the mountain can always be heard in the cloisters of the city, as though there is not a mile of churning black mud between the woman emptying her rain barrel after a storm and the ragged man murmuring on the windy crags. A road connects the mountain and the city, lit by blue gas lamps, cobbled by giants. No one has ever seen a person walk that road, though they must, or else what could be its purpose?

The clouded, pregnant sky swallows the peak of the mountain but declines the heights of the city. When there are stars, they are not our stars. They are not even white, but red as watch-fires.

In the city, which is called Nowhere, a man with the head of a heron sat comfortably in the topmost room of the policemen's tower, working on his novel.

It was slow going.

He supposed had everything he needed—a hurricane lamp full of oil, a stone cup full of dry red wine, a belly full of hot buttered toast, a typewriter confiscated from a poor soul he'd caught sledgehammering *Fuck This Place* onto the north stairwell of the Callabrius Quarter, a ream of fresh, bright paper filched from the records office. It was a quiet night in Nowhere. The criminal element, such as it was, seemed content to sleep the cold stars away until morning, leaving Detective Belacqua in peace.

He tried typing: *It was a quiet night in Nowhere,* then, disgusted with himself, abandoned his desk with a flamboyant despair no one could see to appreciate, and stared gloomily out the long, slender stone window onto the mud plain far below. A moonless spring blackness slept on the fields outside the walled city. It was always spring in Nowhere. But there were no cherry blossoms, no daffodils or new hens, only the cold dark mud of snow just melted, the trees stripped naked, bare arms flung up pleading for the sun, the smell of green but not the green itself. Every day was the day before the first crocus breaks the skull of earth, the held breath before beginning can begin. Always March, never May.

Detective Belacqua had several strikes against him as a budding author. For one thing, he had very little conception of time, an essential element in organizing narrative. He was, after all, mostly infinite. He barely remembered his childhood, if he could be said to have had one at all, but he remembered the incandescent naphtha-splatter of the birth of the universe pretty well. What order things happened in and why wasn't his business. He didn't pry. And this was another problem, for Detective Belacqua had not, in all his long tenure in the walled city, felt the urge to question any aspect of his existence. Such restlessness was not marked out on the map of a strigil's heart the way it was scribbled on every inch of the maps of men. Belacqua enjoyed his slow progress through each day and night. He enjoyed hot buttered toast and dry red wine. He enjoyed his job, felt himself to be necessary in a way as profound as food to a body. Someone had to keep order in this orderless place. Someone had to give Nowhere its shape and its self. His world was a simple equation: if crime, then punishment. It didn't matter at all why or how a criminal did his work, only that he had done it. And because he never bothered with the rest, Detective Belacqua was a hopeless novelist, for he had no clear idea of what drove anyone to do much of anything except be a policeman and bear lightly the granite weight of an unmovable cosmos. The actions of others were baffling and mostly unpleasant. He had never moved in the moral coil of clanging and conflicting wills. All he had ever known was Nowhere, and by the time Nowhere happened to a person, they had already made all the choices that mattered.

Yet Detective Belacqua longed to write with every part of his unmeasurable psyche. He had been a happy man before he discovered books. Very occasionally, people brought them to Nowhere in their sad little bindles. The first time Belacqua saw one, during a quickly opened, quickly shut case of petty theft in the Castitas District, he had confiscated it and crouched for hours in a vestibule, transfixed, as he read the crumbling paperback, the very hows and whys Belacqua had never understood. But it was not enough to read. Belacqua wanted more. There were no strigils in any of the books men brought to Nowhere. No one like him. The men had men-heads and men-desires and the women had women-heads and women-ambitions and nowhere could his heron-soul find a sympathetic mirror. And so he tried and tried and at best he plonked out *It was a quiet night in Nowhere* on the back of a blank incident report. He felt deeply ashamed of his desires and told no one. None of his comrades could hope to understand.

But it was, indeed, a quiet night in Nowhere. But a night was not a book.

"Make something happen, you blistered fool," Detective Belacqua grumbled to himself.

A knock comes upon the door.

Rubbish.

Detective Belacqua pushed back from his desk, his belly perhaps slightly less righteously muscled than it had been when the primordium was new. He wrapped a long scarf the color of cigarette ash around his feathered throat, snatched his black duster from the hook near the door, and abandoned his post—only for a moment—in search of something more fortifying than buttered toast to fuel his furtive ambitions.

He had hardly left the tower when the alarm lamps began to burn.

Third Terrace: The Envious

Sixty-six days later, Pietta steps out of her room for the first time. No one has come for her. She has heard no footsteps in the long hall beyond her door. But a kind of rootless fear like thin pale mold forked slowly through her limbs and she could not bring herself to move.

She measures out the time in bears and glass. Each morning, Pietta places a shard of colored glass on her windowsill. They split the candlelight into harlequin grapeshot, firing volleys of scarlet, cobalt, emerald toward the mountain outside. She has developed a kind of semaphore with the smoke-eaters on those icy slopes; at least, when she moves her arms, they move theirs. But perhaps Pietta is the only one who imagines an alphabet.

Each evening, she watches the bears come in across the mud plain and snuggle against the city for warmth. She does not know where they come in from, only that they do, hundreds of them, and that they are not very like the bears she remembers, though the act of remembering now is like reading a Greek manuscript—slow, laborious, full of transcription errors, clarity coming late and seldom. It is possible bears have always looked like the beasts who rub their enormous flanks against the pockmarked burgundy stone of the city walls as the red stars hiss up in the dusk. But Pietta does not think bears ever had such long stone-silver fur, or that they wore that fur in braids, or that they had a circlet of so many eyes round their heads, or that they had tusks quite so inlaid with gold.

So passes sixty-six days. Glass. Arms. Smoke. Bears.

She gathers together her only belongings and secrets them in the slits and knots of her clothes. Beyond the door of the room belonging to Pietta she finds a hall that splits like a vein into a snarl of staircases. Will she be able to find her way back? The fearful mold begins to grow again, but she stifles it. Burns it out. Descends a black iron spiral stair down, down, to another hall, under an arch into which some skilled hand has carved PENURIA, under which some rather less skilled hand has painted *FOR A GOOD TIME FIND BEATRICE*. Pietta looks back in the direction she has come. The other side of the stone arch reads TAEDIUM. She will try to remember that she lives in Taedium. Pietta passes beneath Contemptus Mundi and Beatrice's come-hither into a courtyard under the open sky.

The courtyard thrums with people and forbidding candles standing as tall and thick as fir trees, barked in the globs and drips and wind-spatters of their yellow wax. There is a stone bowl near the yawning edge of the terrace, filled with burnt knobs of ancient wood and volcanic rock. People like her move between the tallow monoliths and the stone bowl, wrapped tight in complex charcoal-blue rags and falcon-hoods, but not like her, for they chatter together as though they belong here, as though the hereness of here is no surprise to them. They huddle around beaten copper rain barrels, looking up anxiously at the spinning scarlet stars. They pass objects furtively from one hand to the next. They stare out at the constant vastness of the mountain pricked with lantern light before plunging their hands into the bowl and devouring the charred and ashen joints of wood.

Pietta is noticed. A middle-aged man with an unusual nose and arthritic hands pulls her urgently behind one of the cathedral-column candles. She can see blue eyes beneath the mesh of his blinders.

"What did you bring?" he whispers.

Pietta remembers the feeling of a husband she did not want. She answers: "I don't know what you're talking about." Because she doesn't. She has nothing.

The man sighs and tries again, more kindly, holding her less tightly. "In your bindle. What did you carry with you to Nowhere? Don't be afraid. It's important, my dear, that's all. It is everything."

Fourth Terrace: The Gluttonous

Detective Belacqua navigated the night-crowded halls of the Temeritatis Precinct with ease. The locals parted into ragged blue waves to let him pass. Some held their hands to their mouths, some fell to their knees—but Belacqua knew the difference between awe and reflex. They genuflected because they thought they should. They thought it might help.

The crowd around the automat is thin. Humans didn't eat at the finer establishments. They had no currency. The wonderful glass wall of cool plates and steaming bowls was for the comfort of the strigils, a small luxury in this rather undistinguished outpost. Behind the bank of windows set into two feet of dark abbey stone, Belacqua saw a woman with the head of an osprey move with mindful grace, clearing the old dishes, bringing in the new. Her black and white feathers shone in the kitchen lights.

"What have you got in the way of savory, tonight, Giacama? I'm in the mood for salt."

Giacama pushed aside the little window on an empty compartment of the automat. Her mild seabird eyes floated in the glass as though they were the night special.

"Good evening, Detective. I've got a lovely [rind of cheese from the gluttons' farms]. It's all yours."

"Detective Inspector soon," Belacqua said with a flush of pride. He took his crescent of cheese from the window. Only then did he see the young girl staring up at him through the blinders of her falcon-hood, rubbing anxiously at the backs of her hands.

"Are you a demon?" she whispered. "Are you an angel?"

"Naw," Belacqua answered around a mouthful of white cheese. "I work for a living."

The child might have said more, but a commotion disturbed the evening throngs. A strapping man with a raven's grand face strode toward Detective Belacqua, out of breath, trembling in his black finery.

Sergeant Tomek—but in all the aeons of known existence Belacqua had only known his sergeant to be a calm and rather cold sort.

Sergeant Tomek clasped his hand roughly, his raven's face handsome and dark and puffed with excitement or terror. His black ruff bristled.

"Sir, I hate to trouble you at this hour and I know you hate to be interrupted when you're…working…but something terrible's happened. Something dreadful. You must come."

Detective Belacqua tightened his long grey scarf and smoothe back his own rumpled feathers.

"Calm down, Tomek. You'll spook the poor creatures. Just present the facts of the case and we'll see to it with a quickness. What can possibly have you in such a state?"

Sergeant Tomek stared at the wine-dark flagstone floor. He swallowed several times before whispering wretchedly:

"A body, Sir."

"Well, that's hardly cause for all this upset, Sergeant. We're nothing but bodies round here. Bodies, bodies everywhere, and hardly one can think. Go home and get some sleep, man, we'll see to it in the morning."

The raven-headed Sergeant sighed and tried again, more miserably and more quietly than before.

"A *dead* body, Sir. A corpse."

Detective Belacqua blinked. "Don't be stupid, Tomek."

"Sir. I know how it sounds," Tomek glanced around at the passing folk, but most gave the policemen a wide berth. "But there is a dead woman lying face down with her throat cut and there's blood everywhere and *things* on her back and she is very, *very* dead."

Detective Belacqua grimaced with embarrassment. "Sergeant Tomek," he hissed, "they can't *die*. It's not possible. They steal, they cheat, they vandalize, they fornicate, they lie, they curse God, but they do not kill and they do not die. That's not how it *works*. That's the whole *point*."

But the raven would only say: "Come see."

Detective Belacqua thought of his novel and his dry red wine waiting safe and warm for him in the watchtower. They called to him. But he knew what duty was, even if he did not know how to begin his opus. "Where is she?"

Sergeant Tomek trilled unhappily. He ran his hand along the black blade of his beak.

"Outside."

Fifth Terrace: The Covetous

Pietta follows the man with the unusual nose. They have exchanged names. His is Savonarola. He spits the syllables of himself as though he hates their taste. He leads her through a door marked CONTEMPTUS MUNDI.

"My home," he sighs, "such as it is."

"I live in Taedium," Pietta answers, and it is such a relief that she has remembered it, that the information was there when she reached for it, solid, heavy, cold to the touch. She almost stumbles with the sweetness of it. Savonarola grunts in sympathy.

"Too bad for you. You'll find no fraternity among your neighbors, then. They keep to themselves in Taedium. They do not come to cloister, they do not trade, they do not attend the rainstorms. They don't even take Christmas with the rest of us. But perhaps that's to your taste. Taedium, Taedium, so close to Te Deum, you know. What passes for cleverness around here."

Pietta remembers the feeling of longing for something lost before she ever had it. "I have made friends with a man on the mountain. He moves his arms. I move mine. We are up to the letter G. But there is no G in my name, so he cannot know me. I am...I am lonely. I thought someone would come for me."

"No one on the mountain is your friend, girl," snaps Savonarola, and they emerge into a wide piazza full of long tables with thick legs and glass lanterns the size of parish churches shining out into the mist of the night. Wind pulls at them like a beggar pleading. The tables are full of handkerchiefs unknotted,

their contents laid out lovingly, more men and women in charcoal-blue rags closely guarding each little clutch of junk.

Savonarola introduces her to a small, dark woman with a beautiful, delicate mouth. The woman is called Awo. She has an extraneous thumb on her left hand, small and withered and purpled. Pietta touches the objects on Awo's handkerchief, running her hands over them gently. They awake feelings in her that do not belong to her: a drinking cup, a set of sewing needles, a red brick, a pot of white paint, several ballpoint pens, and a length of faded paisley fabric. When Pietta touches the sewing needles, she remembers the feeling of embroidering her daughter's wedding dress. But Pietta had only sons, and they are babies yet.

"You have lovely things," Pietta whispers.

"Oh, they aren't mine," Awo says. The wind off of the mountain dampens all their voices. "I long ago traded away the objects I brought with me into this place. And traded what I got in return, and traded that again, and so on and so forth and again and again. Everything in the world, it turns out, is escapable except economy. Those objects which were once so dear to me I can no longer even name. Did I come with a cup? A belt? A signet ring? I cannot say. Now, what will you give me for my fabric? Savonarola says you have scissors."

Pietta touches her ribs, where she hid the shears. She looks away, into the crystal doors of a massive lantern and the flames within. "But what are these things? What is this place? Why do I have this pair of scissors in this city at this moment?"

Savonarola and Awo glance at one another.

"They are your last belongings," Savonarola says. "The things you lingered over on your last day."

Rain comes to the city. It falls from every dark cloud and splashes against the lanterns, the tables, the buyers and the sellers. Everyone runs for their rain barrels, dragging them into the piazza, the copper bottoms scraping the stone. The rain that falls is not water but wine, red and strong.

Pietta remembers the feeling of dying alone.

The Sixth Terrace: The Wrathful

Detective Belacqua stood over the woman's body. He let a long, low whistle out of his beak and reached into his pocket for a cigarette. Sergeant Tomek opened his black jaws; a ball of blue flame floated on his tongue. Belacqua lit his wrinkled, broken stump of tobacco and breathed deep.

"Isn't there someone else we can hand this off to? Someone higher up. Someone…better?"

Tomek stared down at the corpse as it lies face down on the slick blue-black cobblestones of the road that connects the city and the mountain. The blue of the gas lamps makes her congealing blood look like cold ink.

"You had the watch, Detective Inspector," he said, emphasizing his soon-to-come promotion. But they both knew this woman, the very fact of her, makes all ranks and systems irrelevant.

Belacqua scratched the longer feathers at the nape of his neck. The clouds boiled and swam above them, raveling, unraveling, spooling grey into grey. He could not remember the last time he'd set foot outside the city. Probably sometime around the invention of music. The air smelled of crackling pre-lightning ozone and, bizarrely, nutmeg fruits, when they are wet and new and look like nothing so much as black, bleeding hearts.

"Is she going to…rot, do you think?" Sergeant Tomek mused.

"Well, I don't bloody well know, do I?" the man with the heron's head snapped back. Detective Belacqua had closed thousands of cases in his infinite career. The Nowhere locals got up to all manner of nonsense and he didn't blame them in the least. On the contrary, he felt deeply for the poor blasted things, and when it fell to him to hand out punishments, he was as lenient as the rules allowed. He was a creature of rules, was Belacqua. But the vast majority of his experience lay in vandalism, petty theft, minor assault, and public drunkenness. Every so often something spicier came his way: attempted desertion, adultery, assaults upon the person of a strigil. But never *this*. Of course never *this*. *This* was against the rules. The first rule. The foundational rule. So foundational that until tonight he had not even thought to call it a rule at all.

Detective Belacqua knelt to examine the body. He suspected that was the sort of thing to do. Just pretend it was a bit of burglary. Nothing out of the ordinary. Scene of the crime and all that. Good. First step. Go on, then.

"Right. Erm. The deceased? Should we say deceased? Are you writing this down, Tomek? For God's sake. The, em, *re*-deceased is female, approximately twenty-odd-something years of age. Is that right? It's so hard to tell with people. I don't mean to be insensitive, of course—"

"Oh, certainly not, sir."

"It's just that they all look a *little* alike, don't they, Sergeant?"

Tomek looked distinctly uncomfortable. His dark ruff bristled. "About forty, I should say, Detective Inspector."

"Ah, yes, thank you. Forty years of age, brunette, olive complected, quite tall, nearly six foot as I reckon it. Her hood seems to have gone missing and her clothes are…well, there's not much left of them, is there? Just write 'in disarray.' Spare her some dignity." Now that he'd begun, Belacqua found he could hardly stop. It came so naturally, like a song. "Cause of death appears to be a lateral cut across the throat and exsanguination, though where she got all that blood I can't begin to think. Bruises, well, everywhere, really. But particularly bad on her belly and the backs of her thighs. And there's the…markings. Do you think that happened before or, well, I mean to say, *after*, Tomek?"

The raven-sergeant's black eyes flickered helplessly between the corpse and the detective. "Sir," he swallowed finally, "how can we possibly tell?"

Belacqua remembered the book he'd devoured so greedily in that sad little vandal's cell, the book without a cover and yellow-stained pages, a book in which many people had died and gotten their dead selves puzzled over.

"I've an idea about that, Sergeant," he said finally. "Write down that she's got *patience* carved into her back in Greek—not too neatly, either, it looks like someone went at her with a pair of scissors—then get the boys to carry her up to my office before anyone else decides to have a look out their window and starts ringing up a panic. Carefully! Don't...don't *damage* her any more than she already is." Belacqua gazed up at the great mountain that faced his city, into the wind and the lantern lights and the constant oncoming night. "Poor lamb," he sighed, and when the patrolmen came to lifted her up, he pressed his feathered cheek against hers for a moment, his belly full of something he very well thought might be grief.

Seventh Terrace: The Excommunicate

Savonarola, Awo, and Pietta sit around a brimming rain barrel. The storm has passed. The sky is, for once, almost clear, barnacled with fiery stars. They drink with their hands, cupping fingers and dipping into the silky red wine, slurping without shame. The dead know how to savor as the living never can. The wine is heavy but dry. Much debate has filled the halls of Nowhere over the centuries—is it a Beaujolais? Montrachet? Plain Chianti? Savonarola is firmly in the Montrachet camp. Awo thinks it is most certainly an Algerian Carignan. Pietta thinks it is soft, and sour, and kind.

"Memory is a bad houseguest in this place," Savonarola says softly. Red raindrops streak his face like a statue of a saint weeping blood. "For you, the worst of it will come in twenty years or so. Dying is the blow, memory is the bruise. It takes time to develop, to reach a full and purple lividity. Around eighty years in Nowhere, give or take. Then the pain will take you and it will not give you back again for autumns upon winters. You will know everything you were, and everything you lost. But the bruise of having lived will fade, too, and your time in Nowhere will dwarf your time in the world such that all life will seem to be a letter you wrote as a child, addressed to a stranger, and never delivered."

Awo sucks the wine from her brown, slender fingers. "Awo Alive feels to me like a character in a film I saw when I was young and loved. Awo and her husband Kofi who wore glasses and her three daughters and seven grandchildren and her degree in electrical engineering and the day she saw Accra for the first time, Accra and the sea. I am fond of all of them, but I see them now from very far away. If I remember anything, if I tilt my head or say a word as she would have done, it is like quoting from that film, not like being Awo."

"I went to the noose long before such things as moving pictures could be imagined," Savonarola admits.

Pietta thinks for a long while, watching herself in the reflection of the wine. "And what of the mountain? What of the men and women there? Very well, I am dead. Where is Paradise? Where is Hell? Where is the fire or the clouds? Is this Purgatory?"

Awo touches Pietta's cheek. "Me broni ba, that mountain out there is Purgatory. Someday, maybe, we'll go there and start our long hitchhike of the soul up, up, up into the sea of glass and the singing and the rings of eyes and the eternal surrealist discotheque of the saved. Nowhere is for us sad sacks who died too quick to repent, or naughties like Savonarola, who was so stuck up himself that he got excommunicated. And here we sit, with nothing to do but drink the rain, for three hundred times our living years."

Savonarola cracks his gnarled knuckles. "I admit, if some man in Florence had discovered a way to film the moon rising over the ripples of the Arno, or the building of Brunelleschi's ridiculous dome, or even one of my own sermons—and I was very good, in my day—I would have set fire to the reels with all the rest, and I would have rejoiced. All in which the eye longs to revel is vanity, vanity. Only now do I long for such things, for something to see besides this stone, something to touch besides the dead, something to hear besides talk, talk, talk. What I would not give in this moment for one glimpse of Botticelli's pornography, one vulgar passage of lecherous Boccaccio, one beautiful deck of gambling cards. God, I think, is irony."

"I will go mad," Pietta whispers.

"Yes," agrees Awo.

Pietta pleads: "But it will pass? It will pass and I will go to the mountain and take up a lantern and begin to climb. It will pass and we will go—we will go on, up, out. Progress."

Savonarola pinches his nose between his fingers and smiles softly. He has never been a man given to smiling. He had only done it ten or eleven times in total. But all in secret, Girolamo Savonarola possesses one of the loveliest and kindest smiles in all the long history of joy.

"Do the math, my child. Three hundred times the span of a human life we must rattle the stones of Nowhere—since the death of Solomon and the invention of the alphabet, no one yet has gotten out."

Eighth Terrace: The Ambitious

In the city called Nowhere, a man with the head of a heron sat comfortably in the topmost room of the policemen's tower, watching a corpse rot.

It was slow going.

In all honesty, Detective Belacqua had no real idea what to expect. He only recalled from his penny paperback that human bodies did, indeed, under normal circumstances, rot, and they did it according to a set of rules, at a regular, repeatable, measurable rate, and from that you could reason out a lot of other things that mattered in a murder investigation. Since he had run face-first into a circumstance well beyond normal, Belacqua could not rely on the niceties of rigor mortis, even if he understood them, thus, he now devised a method to discover the rules of decomposition in Nowhere.

Sergeant Tomek humbly asked to be allowed to stay after the patrolmen returned to their posts. The Detective agreed, but sent him for coffee straightaway so that he could gather his thoughts without the raven-boy fretting all over him. Belacqua lifted the body easily—they never did weigh very much in Nowhere. He laid her out on three desks pushed together, and, though he felt rather silly about it afterward, folded her hands over her chest and arranged her long, dark hair tenderly, as though it mattered. And it did matter to him, very much, though her couldn't think why. He dipped a rough cloth into the wash basin in the officer's bathroom and cleaned the worst of the grime and blood out of her wounds, going back and forth from the basin with a steady rhythm that calmed his nerves and arranged the furniture of his mind in a contemplative configuration. After all this was done, he drew a pair of scissors from the watchman's desk and plunged them quickly between the dead woman's ribs on the left side of her torso. When he pulled them out again, red pearls seeped from the wound, falling to the flagstones with a terrible clatter.

"Huh," said Sergeant Tomek. He stood in the doorway, holding a cup of scalding coffee in each hand.

And then, the policemen waited. Sergeant Tomek waited at the window, transfixed. Detective Belacqua waited at his typewriter, ready to record any changes in the body. To write the novel of this woman's putrefaction, chapter by chapter.

It was a quiet night in Nowhere.

Days and nights knocked at the door and went away unanswered. The corpse remained the same for a very long time. Tomek gave up over and over, crying out that it was too sad to be borne, to miserable a thing to stare at, and Nowhere too timeless a place to ever tolerate decay. But he always returned, with coffee or tea or hot buttered toast, and the two strigils resumed their longest watch.

By the next Sabbath, it had begun. On the first day, the edges of the woman's wounds flushed the color of opium flowers. On the second day, her hair turned to snow. On the third day, the stench began, and the watch-room filled intolerably with the smell of frankincense, and then wild honey, and finally a deep and endless forest, loamy and ancient. On the fourth day, Belacqua held his ear to her mouth and heard the sound of gulls crying. On the fifth day, her wounds turned ultramarine and began to seep golden ink. On the sixth day, her sternum cracked and a white lizard with blue eyes crawled out of her, which Tomek caught and trapped in a wine bottle. And on the seventh day, a small tree bloomed and broke out of her mouth, which gave a single silver fruit. This, Belacqua harvested and placed in his coffee cup for further study. By the morning of the eighth day, all that remained of her were bones, hard and clear and faceted as if the skeleton hacked out of a single diamond.

Belacqua typed and typed and typed. Finally, he spoke, on the day they saw the dead woman's skull emerge like new land rising from the sea.

"Sergeant Tomek, I believe we can safely say that she received the markings on her back pre-mortem. Time of death could not have been sooner than six days before you discovered her."

"And how do you know this, Detective Inspector?"

"If she had been killed later, we would have found the poor girl already turning orange at the edges, or worse. I detected then no discoloration nor any scent nor a lizard nor the sound of seagulls. Unfortunately for us, it could have been any number of days greater than six and we would not know it unless we could somehow kill something else and record its progress. Also when I cut into her, the body produced a quantity of pearls, whereas no pearls were found beside her on the road to Nowhere. Additionally, the gore of my cut shows a distinctly different shade of ultramarine than the carving on her back. Someone wrote patience on her while she yet lived, Tomek, and listened to her anguish, and did not stop."

"It is dreadfully morbid," the Sergeant sighed. He laid a reverent hand on the delicate foot-bones of the body.

"On the contrary, my boy, it is science, and we have done it! Nothing could be more exciting than discovering, as we have done, that a set of rules lay in place of all eternity without us suspecting them. I assure you these are not the stages of mortal decomposition." Belacqua hurried on before Tomek could wonder how he knew anything about living corpses, and uncover his illicit pursuit of fiction. "This is new. It is ours. It is native to Nowhere. No one else in all the yawning pit of time has ever known what you and I know now. We are, finally, unique. And now we two unique fellows must proceed further on, farther in, and *re*-compose this woman. Her name, her history, her associates, her enemies. What happened to her a fortnight ago, and how?" The Detective frowned. "Perhaps we ought to interrogate the lizard."

In its green glass bottle, the pale reptile hissed. It stuck out its blue tongue. The glass fogged with its breath. It said one word, and then steamed away like water.

Virtue.

Ninth Terrace: The Incurious

Pietta has become a birdwatcher. She leaves Awo and Savonarola often to trail silently after the strigils as they move through the city. They are so unlike her. They wear clothes of many colors; they are always busy; they eat. They live in a different Nowhere than she does, one with automats and social clubs and places to be. She makes a study of them. This would be easier if she could bring herself to trade her colored glass or her belt or her scissors for one of Awo's pens or the paper a tall man with very clean teeth wants to sell her, but she cannot. She does not know yet why they are precious, but she knows she doesn't want to give them away, to let them become separate from her forever. She is not ready. So she must try to remember the birds she sees. Osprey. Oriole. Peregrine. Sparrow. Sandpiper. Ibis. Pelican. Starling. Raven. Heron. They are beautiful and they do not see her. To them, she is not Pietta. She is no one. She is blue, like the others, and blindered, like the others, and the only thing she can ever do to catch their attention, to bring their eyes down onto her, is to sin, to commit a crime, to err. When the man with clean teeth tries to steal her glass, the birds come. They smell, absurdly, like expensive perfume, like the counter in a fashionable shop. Their feathers rustle when they move like pages turning. They have no irises. Their voices are very nearly human. A woman with the head of an owl cuts away the sleeve of the man's robe. Now everyone will know he is bad. Pietta is fascinated. But she is afraid to do anything very bad herself.

She meets Awo and Savonarola in a cloister fifteen years after they first drank wine together out of a barrel. It is a round room in the Largitio Quarter, with a high, domed ceiling, full of grand, tall tables set with empty bowls, safe from the wind and the slow, trudging lights on the mountain. Pietta longs to eat. She is never hungry, but she remembers the feeling of eating. Of tasting. A few dozen blue-ragged souls pool their objects on a table, picking and sorting. They are trying to assemble a chess set, though fights have broken out already over whether a pepper pot or a bone whistle or pocket Slovakian dictionary makes a better king. Nothing in Nowhere is important, so nothing is more important than the pepper pot and the whistle and the dictionary. Pietta watches them and imagines the players as birds. She hates chess. Savonarola agrees, though he plays anyway.

"Chess allows the frivolous to pretend their toys have deep meaning. The only honest game is tag," he grouses, while taking an exquisitely-chinned teenaged girl's queen. Both the sleeves have been torn from her dress.

"What are the strigils?" Pietta asks.

Savonarola snorts. "Where I come from they're dull blades you use to scrape the sweat and grime from your back in a bath-house. Not that I ever used a bath-house, a seething puddle of greased sin. Not that I haven't scoured the breadth of Nowhere for a damned bath."

Awo has enough sewing needles to man her entire side, pawns and all. She sticks them upright in the soft wood of the table, two neat silver rows. "He can't tell you. His theology was far too prim and tidy to contain bird-headed men in trenchcoats. I can't tell you either. But if you suppose there are demons in one place and angels in the other, wouldn't you also suppose something has to live here? Something has to be natural to Nowhere."

"They came when the first people arrived," says the girl with the lovely chin. She moves her knight (a mechanical library stamp). "And Nowhere was only an empty plain without a city. They are meant to make this place somewhat less than a Hell, and to keep us from making a Heaven of it."

"How do you know that?" Savonarola snapped.

The girl shrugged. "I asked one. When I got arrested for writing my name a thousand times over the entrance to Benevolentia Sector. She had a wren's face. She said they were formed not from clay like us nor fire nor light but from the stuff of the void on the face of the world, and the had not the breath of life but the heat of life and the fluid of it, and they had a beginning but no end, an alpha and an ellipsis, and then she drank my wine and said I was pretty and the truth was she didn't remember very much more about being born than I did and she read all that off a historical plaque on the upper levels, but strigils have to keep up appearances, and they wouldn't be worth much if we thought they were stuck here just like us only they didn't even know how it happened to them, only what they had to do, so if you ask me, talking to a strigil is not so useful as you'd expect, and they drink a lot. Checkmate."

That night, Pietta goes to be with Savonarola, because everything is the same and everything is nothing and what is the point of not doing anything now?

Tenth Terrace: The Merciless

Detective Belacqua stood in a hexagonal stone cell like all the other hexagonal stone cells. He looked out an arched window like all the other arched windows. He picked up and put down several meaningless objects: a brass key, a cracked, worn belt, a stone figure of a child seated in a chair, shards of colored glass. Sergeant Tomek assured him this was the dead woman's room, but it told him nothing—how could it? She would have traded away anything authentically her own long ago. What remained was simply someone else's rubbish. They had a name, and only that by process of elimination. Quite simply: who was missing? It had taken weeks of interrogation, more contact with the locals than Belacqua had ever suffered before, their fearful whispers, their purposeless glazed eyes, their way of drifting off mid-sentence as though they'd forgotten language. But they got their name, from the old furioso Savonarola, who actually wept when Tomek asked whether he had lost anyone of late.

What was he supposed to do now? Everyone in the policemen's union expected he could find some simple solution to it all. But the thing of it was, in his paperback, discovering the identity of the corpse opened other doors, doors within doors, obvious rivers of inquiry to dive into, personal histories to unearth, secrets, secrets everywhere. But her name gave him nothing but this room, and this room was a dry river and a closed door.

"Who was she?" Sergeant Tomek demanded of Savonarola, who sat below a great candle, staring at his open hands. "Who did she love? Who did she hate? What was she in life? What did she do to pass the time?"

But the old friar just closed his hands and opened them again. Closed. Open. "She loved me and Awo. She hated chess. She invented a semaphore alphabet with a man climbing the mountain, though

I'm reasonably sure he's not in on the scheme. If she remembered her life, she never told it to me. She's so new, you know. Like a baby. When I look at her I see the plainness of white linen, being without vanity."

"Everyone has vanity," said Sergeant Tomek. "Everyone here."

The old man looked up cannily at the strigils. Behind his blinders, his eyes shone. "Do you?"

Detective Belacqua squatted down on his heels. He had a suspicion, and he knew how to work on friars. You had to awe them. Morning picked at the stitches of dark. If there had been any true songbirds in Nowhere, they would have sung. Belacqua fixed his black heron's eyes on the hooded soul before him. "Do you remember the founding of Florence, Girolamo? That is where you lived, is it not?"

"Don't be absurd. Florence was old when I was young."

"Quite so. Yet I do remember the founding of Nowhere. Did you know that? Some of us do, some of us don't, it's a funny old thing, like whether or not someone like you remembers losing his baby teeth. A toss of the cognitive dice. But I remember. Lucky me! You see, the plain, the *plain* is the thing. The mud flat going on and on out there forever. The handful of trees—as few and as far between as living planets in empty space. The old riverbeds. Somewhere out beyond the road and the mountain there's a black salt flat a light year across. The clouds. The stars. And people didn't come right away. It wasn't like you'd imagine—nothing, and then hordes all at once. People just died like dogs or fish or dinosaurs until, I don't know, what would you say, Tomek? Around the time they started painting ibexes on cave walls?"

The sergeant nodded his dark head.

"Well, my friend, you can just imagine what a mess it all was in the beginning. No system. No rules. Some people could go up the mountain as quick as you like, and some couldn't, and some could go down into the coal pits, and some couldn't, and some just milled around like cows down here, and if they tried to go on up, they found themselves turned right back around facing the infinite flood-plain with not an inch gained, but no one really had a bead on the whys and wherefores of the whole business. Cosmology just sort of *happened* to you, on you get. And the people down here in the mud, they just sat there or laid there or stood there for ages, really, proper ages, with nothing to do. That's the worst thing for a person. To get crushed under the weight of endless useless days. Between you and me, I don't think anyone really thought it through. I bet you'd rather have a fellow spearing you with a flaming trident every hour on the hour—at least then, something would *happen*. Am I right? I believe I am. So these poor souls fought and fucked and screamed for awhile, because those're pretty good ways to stop yourself thinking about the existential chasm of time. But they didn't bleed and they didn't come and nobody answered them, so eventually, they started digging in the mud with whatever they'd brought in their bindles, which back then, was mostly stone tools. They pulled up the stones of the moral universe and put them one on top of the other, and I'll tell you a secret, Giro. For awhile, I think this was a happier place than Heaven, when they were putting down those rocks. But happiness isn't the point. Not here. If we'd let you keep on with it, your lot would have built city after city, an empire of the dead, and it would look just like the world out here, only filled with legions of the mediocre and the stalled out and the unrepentant and whatever you're supposed to be. So we got called up, me and the sergeant here and all the other strigils. Hatched out of an egg of ice, I'm told, though that sort of insider talk is above my pay grade. And we came bearing *order*, Girolamo. We came with rules in our beaks. We built Nowhere together, strigils and humans, the dead and the divine," Detective Belacqua put one hand on his chest and the other over Savonarola's withered heart. "*Me* and *you*. A closed system. A city on the hill. And I think it's *beautiful*. But you don't, do you? You hate it, like you hated everything you ever clapped your eyes on. Except *her*. So here's what I think, friend. I think you found a way to get her out. God only knows what. But you did it to her and now she's gone and if you tell me what happened, no one will be angry—we quite literally cannot be angry. Who could blame you? It's the nature of love, I should imagine."

Girolamo Savonarola laughed.

"You ought to write a book," he giggled, but when Sergeant Tomek began to strip his charcoal-blue robes from him, the friar began to sob instead.

Eleventh Terrace: The Sorrowful

It hits her while she kisses Awo's naked shoulder, Awo, whose cell Pietta visits far more than any other, though in recent years she's visited many. She even found Beatrice, who turned out to be very shy and fond of rain. It is something to do, and Pietta is desperate for acts. *Acts have befores and afters. They mark her movement through these air and these stones. She has tried other sins, but they are more difficult in Nowhere. She cannot bring herself to envy anyone, and wants for nothing; she cannot eat and she cannot strive. So there is this, and though she feels it only dimly, she holds on very tight.*

Pietta and Awo lie together in the lantern-light of Purgatory and there is a moment when she does not know who she is, not really, and then that moment burns itself out. Pietta remembers the feeling of being Pietta. She remembers being small and she remembers being big. All of the things that ever happened to her stack up in her mind like stones on a sea shore, tottering, tottering… Pietta is getting born in a room with poppies painted on the wall, Pietta is small and delighted and running through the snow, forgetting her mother completely and throwing herself face first into the soft powder, Pietta is receiving her first communion and coughing when she oughtn't because the incense tickles her nose, and she is helping her father tend his bees in their fields, and she is walking in the woods at night with a boy named Milo, and she is living in a house by the sea with Milo who has grown very distant with her, even though she is pregnant and they should be happy, and Pietta is giving birth to her son in a room with ultramarine flowers next to her bed in a cheap, gold-painted vase, and Pietta is walking in the summer, alone, for once, when she sees a white lizard hiding in the shade of a long, flat stone, and she takes it home and gives it a name and shows it to her son and keeps it in an old fish tank even though Milo says it is stupid and lizards have no hearts and Pietta is wearing her mother's diamond ring every day even though they could use the money because no amount of snow could make her forget, not really, and Milo is so angry with her so often, every thing she does is the wrong thing, and though she still loves him she grows very still inside, she feels as though she is trapped in ice and cannot move, even as she cooks and cleans and runs to the shops and teaches her classes and she is getting older all the time and then Pietta is teaching her son to play chess with a set made to look like a famous medieval set with funny-looking people in funny-looking chairs, she is cutting out the green felt for his Halloween costume because he insists upon being a tree this year, she is pouring herself the last of the red wine and locking up the liquor cabinet with a brass key, she is putting away her husband's clothes, his coats, his socks, his old belt, and thinking that she should have bought him a new one long ago, and she will now, she will, because tomorrow will be the day she wakes up out of the ice and becomes herself again, she knows it will happen all at once, like a big silver fruit cracking open, and there she'll be, good as new, even though she thought the same yesterday, and the day before, and the day before that, and when the glazier's truck hits Pietta in the high street she thinks, for a moment, that all that beautiful, shattered, colored glass lying around her is the ice breaking at last, the fruit breaking open, with Pietta whole and alive inside, but it is not.

Twelfth Terrace: The Gluttonous

It was a quiet night in Nowhere.

Detective Inspector Belacqua and Corporal Tomek shared the watch and supper and half a bottle of white wine which both felt very excited about. The lamp stood full of oil, the basin full of fresh water, the pens full of ink, and all was as it should be.

Belacqua had many times almost asked his raven-headed friend how he felt about their one great case. Tomek never mentioned it. Occasionally, in their rounds, they would catch a glimpse of Savonarola, naked and shunned, drifting miserably among the crowds. Once, Belacqua himself had nearly run right into the woman called Awo, who stared at him as though she could punch through his delicate skull with her gaze. He hadn't been able to bear that; he'd run. Run, from a local, a dead woman with nothing but her rags. And yet it had happened.

So time, in its shapeless, corpulent, implacable way, bore on in Nowhere. And only when he was alone did it trouble Belacqua how much they never understood about the incident, the monstrous hole at the bottom of the case file through which everything sensible tumbled out. Into this hole, he began to drop the words of his novel, one by one, painstakingly, the only story he knew, a story without an end. Which, he supposed, was to be expected, considering the author.

When it came time to open the bottle of white wine, the policemen found the cork encased in awfully thick black wax, too thick for fingernails and too awkward for beaks.

"Nothing to it," Corporal Tomek laughed, and drew a small pair of scissors out of the inner pocket of his coat. He worked the little blades deftly round the mouth and wiggled them up underneath till the cake of wax fell away.

They were a perfectly ordinary pair of scissors. A little tarnished and stained, but utterly usual and serviceable, like Tomek himself. Detective Belacqua had no reason to notice them in the least. And yet, he did. He could not stop noticing them. Small enough for delicate work. For carving. *Was* that tarnish, that black smear along the shears?

Belacqua cleared his throat. "Has it ever woken you nights, Tomek, that we never discovered how the old man did it?"

"Did what, sir?"

"Killed a dead woman. There had to be a method—that's the whole thing, you know, means, motive, and opportunity—that's the *entire* thing of it. And the means just…got away from us, didn't it?"

"I suppose they did. But I wouldn't worry. It's never happened again. It's not like we had an epidemic on our hands, Belacqua. And if we had, well, you know. No one harmed but the dead. The Chief would have sorted it out, I'm sure." Tomek poured the wine and handed a glass across the desk. Belacqua just looked at it.

"I just want to *know*, that's all. Haven't you ever wanted to know anything so badly it ate you away until there was nothing left of you but the *not* knowing?"

The raven grimaced. "Just drink your wine, Detective Inspector."

Belacqua did not blink. He thought he ought to feel something in the pit of his stomach, but all he felt was the not knowing, the canker of it, working its way through him like rot.

"How did you meet her?" Detective Belacqua whispered.

Tomek put down the glasses, very carefully, as though, in his hands, they might break.

Thirteenth Terrace: The Lustful

Pietta bludgeons the wall over and over, jamming her scissors into the wine-dark stone. Chips and chunks fly away as she gouges the skin of the city. The thudding and scraping of her blows fill the endless halls of Taedium.

They care about very little, Pietta knows. But they will care about this. Vandalizing Nowhere brings them running, so she is not surprised when a man with the head of a raven steps through her door and snatches the scissors from her hands with a strength that would snap all the bones of her wrist, if the bones of her wrist could still break.

"That's enough, miss," Sergeant Tomek says crisply, professionally. Their faces are close as kissing. Raven and girl; pale, bloodless lips and a mouth like black shears.

"It's not fair," Pietta snarls at him. "All I ever did wrong was be sad."

Outside, the man on the mountain eats his smoke. Tomek is on top of her by the time he begins to move his arms in straight, strident lines, and she does not see.

P-I-E-T-T-A?

Fourteenth Terrace: The Contemptuous

"We all have our ways of coping with it," Tomek said, running his finger around the lip of his glass.

"With what?" Belacqua scowled.

"Eternity," answered the raven slowly. "You have your novel—oh, for God's sake, we all know. I have my research. It's wrong, you know, everything, all of this. At least they lived, fucked something up well and good enough to end up here. We're here…for what? Why? To punish what sin? The only difference between them and us is we wear better clothes. I can't bear it any more than they can. And it's worse, it's worse for us, Belacqua. We've just enough spark in us to draw up a rough sketch of feeling, just a basic set, nothing too detailed: duty, loyalty, a smear of free will, a little want, a little envy, just enough to know somebody else got to see what a summer looks like, but not enough for the cosmos to even look at us, for one second, as anything but lock and keys. And it never ends for us. Don't you see? They all have the hope of progress, of the *climb*. This is it, just this, nothing else, forever. I was so *bored*, Belacqua."

Tomek began to pace, tugging at his feathers, half-preening, half-tearing.

"And so I began to think. Just for the last couple of thousand years. I began to plan a way to murder a person. It's a big enough problem to take up centuries. Could it even be done? *They* can't, certainly. One punches the other in the nose and it's like punching ice cream. Nothing. Not even a mark. But I am a strigil. There is no record of what I can do because no one has ever cared enough to find out. Do your job, little birdie, get back to us at the end of everything for your performance review. What would happen if a strigil sinned? Would there be consequences? And if I could do it, if, ontologically speaking, it would be allowed to occur, how? These are worthy questions! The first experiment was obvious. I broke a man's neck in Oboedientia Sector. For a minute, I thought I'd gotten it right on my first go. But no, he just sort of shivered and put his head right and went on his way. It seemed the rules held for me as well as him. After that I kept it all in my head. The project. I thought it out while the Renaissance idiots poured in, while I walked my beat, while I watched you fumble with a sad little dime store potboiler in the corner like one of the chronic masturbators down in Desidia. Nothing physical would do it. I should have realized that—we do not move in the realm of the physical. I had to act upon the nature of a soul, to alter it so that it could not remain whole. And it would work—Belacqua, this is the important thing! It would work because of that smear of free will, that tiny table scrap of self a strigil owns. I have to be able to act freely, or else I could not arrest or judge or mete out punishment. You have to be allowed to plunk away at your silly stories, because not even the font of all can build a being of judgment without building a being of perversity."

Tomek put his hands on the window sill and let the wind off the mud plain buffet his face.

"When I met Pietta I knew she would let me do anything to her. She was in despair. They all are, for awhile, but hers was frozen and depthless, a continuation of who she had always been, just spooling on into the black forever. And she was right. It's not fair. It's all grotesque. That little spit of living and all this ocean of penance. She wanted it, Belacqua. She did."

"I doubt that very much, Corporal."

"You don't understand. She didn't care. She saw the writing on the wall and the writing said: *Fuck This Place.* She just wanted something to happen. We ran through all the sins first. I fucked her right away—small mercy that we are not built sexless as the angels. Lust is the easiest. I cleaned out the automat and shoved it all down her throat till cream and syrup and relish and grease poured down her chest. She puked it all up, of course, the dead can't eat. Then on to the next like kids at a fairground— we hurled loathing and envy at each other, at the mountain, perfectly honest, more profanity than grammar could hold. I drew up a rage and beat her though no bruises came up. We skipped sloth since Nowhere is the home and hearth of sloth, and Belacqua, nothing I could do could make that woman proud. But it was all useless anyway, her flesh took it all as calmly as water. And so I had to retreat and think again.

"Solutions come so strangely, Belacqua. They steal in. Just the way you saw my scissors and knew what I'd done, your mind leaping over your habits and your inertia to arrive at a conclusion that is as much dream as logic, I knew. I knew how to kill my Pietta. I returned to her that night. I held her in my arms, and, one by one, I buried her in virtues. I gave her all my belongings freely and her nose shot blood onto the flagstones. I cradled her chastely with no thought of her body and bruises rose up on her thighs. I groveled before her and before her I was nothing, and her fingers snapped. I tended her patiently while she screamed, and upomovn carved itself into her back. I persevered, and my diligence choked her like hands. I whispered to her all the kindnesses her husband withheld, that her son, being a child, could not imagine, and the extraordinary thing was I *meant* them, Belacqua. I meant them with all my being. I loved her and her throat split side to side like a pomegranate. Then I shoved her out the window and watched her fall. I pushed her from this world, and all the violence on her body were but the marks of her passage. Neither virtue nor sin can be committed in this place. Nowhere cannot bear it. What they do to one another matters little enough—they have chosen their course and proceed along it, stupid and wasteful and unfair as it is. But I am neither alive nor dead, neither mortal nor immortal, just meanly made, with the barest thought. And so are you, Belacqua. The meanly made may sin—who could expect better? Sin is easy. But for me—for us—to act with virtue is a violence to the whole of existence. And now she is gone and my questions answered. *Nothing happened*. I was not punished. I was not even found out. I am not morally culpable, because He will not deign to look at me long enough to condemn. When an angel does wrong, Hell must be invented out of whole cloth to contain his sorry carcass. But we? We are nothing, and no one. And I think it is *beautiful*."

Fifteenth Terrace: The Forgetful

There is a grinding sound before she appears, like stone against stone. One moment there is nothing, the next there is Pietta, though if she heard that name now, she would not recognize it, nor even comprehend the idea of a word used to signify a person. Her mind is a silver fruit lying clean and open, without seed or rot or juice. She opens her eyes and her eyes are black, black and several, ringed round her skull like a crown so that she sees everywhere at once. She moves her legs and her legs are powerful, shaggy, heavy with silver, braided, matted fur. Her claws and her tusks scrape on the bedrock beneath the mudplain as she moves with the sleuth of other bears, because nothing in this place has ever happened only once, their ursine sounds and their scents stretching before them toward the city they love but no longer understand, except that it is a warm place in the night, a heart beating in a bloodless land, and when they touch the walls, they remember, faintly, distantly, the feeling of being loved.

Sixteenth Terrace: The Unyielding

Detective Inspector Belacqua gave the signal, and every window in Nowhere closed against the man with the raven's head. Tomek's caws and cries far below echoed the length of the everything, his pleas, his reasons, all of it swallowed by the grey clouds and the long nothing-and-no-one of the endless mudplain and the red stars beyond. The mountain, for a moment, stood silent, all the lights still and dim.

Belacqua wept against the shutters, and he wept for a century before opening them again.

Objects in the Mirror

Caitlín R. Kiernan

Ere Babylon was dust
The Magus Zoroaster, my dead child,
Met his own image walking in the garden.
Percy Bysshe Shelley, *Prometheus Unbound*

1.

If I were writing a screenplay, I would begin, I think, with a fade in to a psychiatrist's office. The walls would be that pale shade of blue that puts me in mind of swimming pools, and the sofa where the psychiatrist's patients (she calls them clients) sit would be upholstered in the same shade, as would be the dingy low-pile polyester carpeting. I would note that time and friction have worn the arms and cushions of the sofa thin and shiny. There would be—*are*—framed photographs on the wall, oddly generic seascapes that mirror the walls and the sofa and are no doubt intended to instill a sense of serenity. There's a bookshelf and a small table, and on the table is a box of Kleenex, a silver metal starfish, and a polished nautiloid fossil from the Devonian of Morocco. The psychiatrist's desk is fastidiously neat.

There are several careful stacks of papers, a few professional journals (*The American Journal of Psychiatry, Psychiatry Research,* and *BJPsych*), a copy of the 69th edition of the *PDR,* a tiny hourglass, a phone, a coffee mug filled with pens, and an electric pencil sharpener shaped like a robotic dog—a small concession to whimsy. There are two windows letting the wan January light into the room, one facing east, the other facing south. The curtains are drawn shut, muting the day. They're a slightly paler blue than the walls, the sofa, and the carpeting. It may be that the sun has faded them. There are fluorescent bulbs in white recessed fixtures set into the dropped ceiling, a stark counterpoint to the afternoon sunlight. On the desk, there's an iPod dock with speakers, but no music is playing at the moment. For now, the only sound is the psychiatrist tap-tap-tapping the eraser end of her No. 2 Ticonderoga pencil against the edge of her spiral-bound notebook. That and the sound of traffic out on the street.

The set decorator and prop master have hit the proverbial nail on its head. There is an almost archetypal tawdriness about the office, clinical prefab ennui; it pulses with the migraine thrum of a low-grade despair. If you weren't suicidal when you showed up for your four p.m., you very well might be by the time the psychiatrist glances at her wristwatch (Daniel Wellington 056DW Classic Southhampton) or the clock mounted on the wall (Ikea) to remind you "*our* hour is almost up." The air smells sickeningly of fake flowers, thanks to a "blooming peony and cherry" Glade Plugin®. The door is shut and locked. It's impossible not the think of Lucy van Pelt: The Doctor is In/Out. 5¢.

And I will play my part.

And she will play hers to perfection, my $125-an-hour, office-park Mother Confessor, my biopsychosocial Virgil. Here we go round the mulberry bush, and if she's worth her salt she'll not believe a single word I say. She will wear an entirely unconvincing mask, two parts sympathy to one part concern, dappled about the edges with phony compassion. Right off, I'm impressed that casting found someone so perfectly fitted to the role, an actress who so deftly communicates mid-life disappointment, the wages of having settled for less, the sour weight of mediocrity. Her hair is brunette, quickly going grey and pulled back in a ponytail that only makes her look older. She's a smoker, and it shows on her teeth and the nicotine stains between her fingers. Her eyes are, appropriately, the color of late autumn. Her clothes are plain, a dingy attempt at business casual. She still wears her wedding ring to the office, though she's been divorced for almost five years. There's cat hair on her skirt and blouse.

Her name is Louise Meriwether, and she mixes alcohol and benzodiazepines.

There's a crescent-shaped scar on the back of her left hand.

Now.

Lights, camera, action. We're only going to get one take, folks. Make it count.

So, here's the scene: I sit on the threadbare blue sofa, she at her desk. She taps that pencil and watches me; I'm paying her to be attentive. I'm staring at the silver starfish and the petrified whorl of the fossil shell. There is a reason that I've chosen Dr. Meriwether. She's written a book on heautoscopy and the problem of reduplicative hallucination in schizophrenics and epileptics, people who see themselves. Let's use the word doppelgänger and avoid the damn psychobabble. There's a copy of the book on her desk, *I Saw a Man Who Wasn't There: Psychopathology and Psychophysiology of the Doppelgänger Phenomenon* (Oxford University Press). The dust jacket has been ripped and Scotch-taped back together.

INT. OFFICE—CONTINUOUS

DR. MERIWETHER

And that was the first time it happened to you?

ME

No. I didn't say that. Not the first time. I doubt that I remember the first time. You might as well ask me to pin down my earliest memory.

DR. MERIWETHER

Because you believe they've always been a part of your life.

I shrug. I nod. I might have said that or I might not. I can't be sure. I've been seeing the psychiatrist once a week for a month now. I've said an awful lot of shit.

DR. MERIWETHER

And you told me you were four then, is that right?

ME

At the bottom of the garden, we wore animal masks.

DR. MERIWETHER

Excuse me?

She stops tapping her eraser and sits up a little straighter. A delivery truck rumbles by outside. I glance at the clock, run my fingers through my oily hair. I can't recall the last time I washed my hair. I can't recall the last time I had a shower.

ME

Yeah, I was four, maybe four and a half. Maybe almost five. We still lived in the big house in Wickford, the house on Elam Street.

DR. MERIWETHER

No, what you said earlier, "At the bottom of the garden, we wore animal masks." What did you mean by that?

CROSSFADE:

There is a big yellow house by the water, and behind the house there is a wide green yard that runs all the way down to the shore of Wickford Cove. The house was built in 1842 by a man named Jabez Bullock. His father had been a captain in the Revolutionary War, but Jabez Bullock was a carpenter and a cabinetmaker.

On this late afternoon in July, the tide is up, and the cove seems as still and flat as a looking glass. Indigo water shimmers beneath the blazing eye of the summer sun, and there are a few sailboats drifting lazily about—sleek hulls, straight black masts, and the sagging white lines of the canvas and rigging. There's hardly any wind today, and the sails hang limply. A pair of mute swans dip their long necks beneath the surface, upending to thrust hungry bills deep into beds of pondweed and eelgrass. Two or three noisy herring gulls swoop low above the cove, then wheel about and head east, towards Narragansett Bay. Behind the house, past the wide green yard, there's a short dock, and there's a dinghy tied up to the weathered pilings. Painted in crimson about its prow are two words: *Flyaway Horse.* Between the house and the cove are a pair of very large oak trees, planted by the second wife of Jabez Bullock; both trees managed somehow to survive the Hurricane of 1938 , the infamous Long Island Express. Away from the shadow of the trees are wooden trellises for climbing roses and also beds of blue and pink hydrangeas, sunflowers, snapdragons, and irises. There are bumblebees and honeybees and darting hummingbirds, butterflies and dragonflies to serve as a counterpoint to the oppressive stillness of the day. In the limbs of the oaks, catbirds preen and argue with one another.

Just beyond the moored dinghy, a striped bass leaps from the water, snatching a mayfly in mid air, then falls back with a splash, and the ripples spread out across the cove.

To the mind of a child, this might be Eden.

And there is, as it happens, a child, a four-year-old girl whose mother is a recovering alcoholic and whose father—well, the less said of him, the better. The yellow house belongs to the girl's grandparents, two painters, who bought it cheap back in the late sixties, when the house was in such a dire state of neglect that there was a very real danger of it being condemned and demolished. They fled the squalid confines of Greenwich Village and, with her small inheritance, became nouveau réalisme saviors of gabled pediments and paneled corner pilasters. They're the ones who had the house painted the yellow of Van Gogh's *Wheatfield With Crows.* They restored the white picket fence. They planted this garden on top of the ruins of a much earlier garden.

The girl's mother is reclining in a fold-out lawn chair, white and cornflower-blue webbing inside a dented aluminum frame. She's halfway through Truddi Chase's *When Rabbit Howls,* which she checked out of the North Kingston Free Library the Thursday before. She pauses to light a cigarette and locate her daughter, who's sitting not far away, beneath one of the old oaks. The woman smiles, then goes back to her book:

> *The trouble with multiplicity,*
> *he supposed,*
> *was that to an outsider it did sound "crazy."*

The girl, dressed in dungarees and scuffed-up black Keds, has been occupied collecting handfuls of acorns and arranging them on the ground before her in three neat rows. She might well be making an army of acorns to battle a regiment of dandelions. She's also wearing a plastic Wile E. Coyote mask. It was her mother's mask, many Halloween's ago, and it turned up a few days before while she was looking for something else entirely, hidden in a cardboard box stored in the attic of the yellow house. "Can I have it?" her daughter asked, and "Of course," she said. "Sure, you can have it." The elastic string had dry rotted and snapped, and so she replaced it with sturdy butcher's twine from a kitchen drawer. Since then, the kid's hardly taken the thing off. She's even been falling asleep in it.

Beneath the tree, the girl counts her acorns, though she can only count as high as fifteen, and she's certainly collected twice that many, at least.

Her mother turns a page:

"Rabbit? Rabbit, where'd you put the keys, Girl?"

And the girl looks up to find that she's being watched by someone other than her mother. Standing only ten or fifteen feet away there is another little girl dressed in overalls and sneakers, another girl in a plastic Wile E. Coyote mask. She opens her left hand, and five acorns tumble out into the grass. Her mask isn't precisely the same: this *other* girl's mask has a dent and a crack in the coyote's muzzle.

The standing girl whispers something.

And the girl sitting beneath the oak screams.

CROSSFADE:

Not meaning to, I've allowed an entire three minutes to pass without having answered her question. I check the clock on the wall, and then I glance back down at the whorls of the fossilized nautilus shell. I asked her about it during our first session, and she told me it was a gift from an English college friend who'd become a geologist. She told me it had been collected from the Lesser Atlas Mountains of Morocco, and I thought then, and I think now, how odd that I can hold in my hand a thing so shifted in time and space. This object has traveled across more than thirty-six hundred miles and three hundred and seventy million years to lay on this tabletop in this tawdry office with its robot-dog pencil sharpener, its polyester carpet, and its depressing swimming-pool blue walls. The sheer unlikeliness makes me a little dizzy, if I consider it too closely.

"Back then," explained Dr. Meriwether, "the continents were in different positions than they are now."

"Continental drift," I said. "Plate tectonics."

"Right, exactly. And back in the Devonian, New England and North Africa weren't very far apart, at all. Time divided them."

The sun through the drab blue curtains glistens dully off the fossil, and I look up at the psychiatrist. She's watching me the way she does. I tell her what I'd meant about the garden and animal masks, describing that summer day by Wickford Cove, and she listens, and when I'm done she nods.

DR. MERIWETHER

If it makes you uncomfortable, we can move on.

ME

I didn't say that. I didn't say that it makes me uncomfortable. I'm fine.

DR. MERIWETHER

Well, then I have a question. If that wasn't the first time, why do you think you screamed?

FADE TO BLACK

2.

Here in this sheltered place, where freezing meltwater streams gurgle down from the mountain passes and rivers of ice, the girl clambers over rocks slick with moss and between deadfall branches. The old people have two names for this place, one of which is the same word that is used for becoming lost in the forest at night, and the girl has been warned many times that she should never come here, and that she should certainly never come here alone. Late in the spring the floods scour the high granite walls raw. The evidence of the floods are all about her—the rotting trunks of shattered fir trees, the tumbled boulders, the broken bones of mammoth and auroch wedged between the stones. But it's almost summer now, and the time of floods has come and gone. So, she has no fear of drowning today or of being swept off to wherever it is the floods are always bound in such a hurry. And she's grown reasonably certain that the tales she's been told of demons and monsters lurking in this place are only meant to keep clumsy children away, those too young and inexperienced to know which footholds are stable and which logs can be counted upon to support your weight. She's neither a child, nor is she clumsy, and if there truly *are* monsters here, if the souls of evil people truly do haunt this ravine, she'd like to see them for herself. She's seen starving wolves in winter, and she's seen what an angry bear can do to a man. She's watched mothers wail over their stillborn infants and has come upon the grisly leavings of the cannibals who live in the lowland woods. If there's anything worse waiting for her, she'd be surprised.

Sometimes, says First Mother, speaking from the darkness behind the girl's eyes, *you are too bold, child. Sometimes, you risk too much for too little. Or for nothing at all.*

"Don't you trouble me today," the girl replies, ducking beneath an enormous log that is too much trouble to climb over, picking and wriggling her way through the narrow darkness underneath, a little cave whose ceiling is decaying wood and whose floor is loose stones, mud, and scuttling black beetles. She almost gets stuck once, but by relaxing and exhaling and making herself just a little bit smaller she squeezes through to the other side.

That might have been something's den, says First Mother disapprovingly. *Something with sharp teeth and sharp claws and young ones to protect.*

"There weren't any tracks," the girl replies, standing upright and dusting herself off, sucking at a scrape on the heel of her left hand. "I checked. There wasn't any scat or bones. I knew it was clear, or I never would have gone in. I'm not a fool."

And yet you do foolish things.

"It was safe."

I only worry for you.

The girl shakes her head, then scrambles up the next line of boulders.

"You want me to be like my sisters and aunts," she says, "like my mother. You want me to be too afraid to go out walking on my own. You'd have me cower at shadows cast by firelight and worry only over birthing sons and daughters."

You don't yet know the world, child, not like you think you do.

"Then I'll see that for myself, won't I? And then I will know."

The girl comes upon the pool sooner than she'd expected, and she almost slips off a low ledge into the deep, still water. But she's quick and steady, and her fingers and toes and the thick pads of her feet find just enough purchase that she doesn't fall.

You see? says First Mother. *That might have been the end of you. You're not an otter or a beaver or a mink. You would drown.*

"I can swim well enough," the girl mutters, then finds her way along the shore to a narrow bit of beach.

They'd never find you. Not here, They'd never come here to search for you.

A tilted slab of granite juts out a little ways above the pool, and the girl climbs up onto it and sits down, dangling her feet over the edge. The stone is cool and damp beneath her, worn smooth by ages of floods and rain, rock the color of raw salmon, flecked with sparkling flakes of white and black.

What is it you risked so much to find here? asks the voice behind her eyes.

What is it here that is worth as much as that?

"Be quiet and watch, and maybe you'll find out," replies the girl. The truth, though, is that she hasn't come here to find anything in particular, except, perhaps, the reason she's been told she shouldn't. Or to make the point, if only for her own satisfaction, that the stories of demons are merely lies to scare off the children. But when she looks back the direction she's come, gazing up along the gash cut into the mountainside, she shivers, despite herself. The truth is there are very many ways to die here, deaths that sure feet and quick thinking wouldn't spare her from. There are probably lions lurking along those bluffs, and anyone could be unlucky enough to be crushed by a landslide.

Death comes for idiots and the wise alike, First Mother whispers.

"You leave me be, spirit," the girl whispers defiantly back, but she's thinking now of the story that She Who Holds Fire tells, of how the sky plowed this furrow to fuck the earth and make the world pregnant with stars, how the earthborn stars became men and women, bears and mammoth and auroch. Which is why the other name for this place is the same as the word for being taken by force by a man who is not your husband or your husband's brother. The girl squints up at the blue wedge of sky visible between the steep walls of granite, at the white fire of the sun, and she tries to imagine the agony of the whole world, seized by all that emptiness and split open right down the middle. *How would one ever hope to hide themselves away from the lusts of the sky?* she wonders, and then the girl feels that shiver again, and she looks back down at the pool instead.

Even though the pool is deep, the water is so clear that she can see every pebble lying on the bottom, cradled in folds of silt and sand and sunken leaves. There are tiny fish, shards of living silver light darting to and fro, and she also spots a big crayfish creeping along, its pincers raised defensively, warning away some or another invisible threat. The soles of her feet, her toes, brush the air only inches from the surface.

In the story that She Who Holds Fire tells, the pool was first filled by the tears of the world on the day she was raped by the sky. And even after all this long time, she says, if you happen to taste the water it will still taste salty, so terrible was the world's sorrow and pain. But she cautions, do not ever dare drink from the pool, for that ache will crawl down into your *own* belly and forevermore will you know what the whole earth felt and how it feels still. Like the pool, you'll become a vessel for its tears and you will be changed utterly and never know comfort again.

Leaning forward slightly, the girl swings her legs, kicking out, and in the instant before her toes and the balls of her feet strike the water, she sees herself reversed, gazing back up from the glistening surface—her mother's bright green-brown eyes, her father's broad nose, the long auburn braids framing her face. And then the image comes apart in a splash, and ripples spread across the pool. The water is ice cold, and when she kicks again, her feet scatter bright droplets almost all the way to the other shore.

There, says First Mother, *you have seen it all, all there is here to see. You're satisfied. Go back now, and do not press your luck again, child.*

The girl chews at her lip a moment, kicks a third time at the water, then says aloud, "If you are First Mother, as we are taught, then, spirit, this is where you were conceived. That would be true, wouldn't it?"

This time First Mother doesn't answer, and there's only the sound of the wind rustling through the limbs of the trees that grow along the edges of the ravine and the soft lapping of small waves against the edges of the pool. *She made the wind,* thinks the girl, *and I made the waves. And waves are only wind on water.*

You assume many things, whispers First Mother, and now there's a meanness in her voice, as brittle and sharp as shards of a freshly broken bone. This is something the girl cannot recall ever having heard before, not for herself, though she's been warned that the spirit can be angered if its advices are too frequently ignored. The change in tone takes the girl by surprise. But it also emboldens her, and she smiles.

And kicks at the pool.

"And if this is where the sky entered the world, this is also where you were born," she says. "Here, by the water, you and First Father and all the others. How can you fear the place where you were born, even if you were sired by the rape of the world?"

The wind is blowing harder now, causing the firs and oaks, the sycamores and elms to creak and sway, and it seems that the ripples are striking the edges of the pool with more force than before. The girl glances very briefly at the cloudless blue stretched out above the ravine. For just a second, she has the distinct sensation that she's falling—not down, but up towards the sky—and she stops kicking her legs and grips the rough granite ledge. She shuts her eyes, and the sensation passes, as quickly as it came.

"Why?" she asks, and when she opens her eyes, the surface of the pool is growing still and flat once more. She can see the little fish again and the drowned leaves and her own face staring back at her. The girl in the water looks shaken and wary, but not afraid. "Tell me, First Mother, why that should be? Maybe this is exactly what I came here to learn, the why of this."

I always knew you were a wicked child, mutters First Mother. *On the day you were shat squealing out into the light, I cried that the People would ever be cursed with the burden of one so very wicked.*

The girl's mouth has gone dry, and she licks at her lips.

"How can it be that it's so easy to make you angry, you who knows the secret souls of every woman who lives or who ever has lived, who knows all the People, every one of us, even the outcasts and the moonstruck and the eaters of men? I've only asked a *question,* and that one question is enough to make me *wicked?*"

I should stop this, the girl thinks, *before it's too late.* And she knows, of course, that First Mother hears that thought, too, as clearly as she hears words fashioned by tongues and teeth and lips.

No one will ever find you here, the spirit whispers.

"Why won't you *tell* me? Why shouldn't I *know?*"

Wicked.

From behind the girl, then, comes the unmistakable sound of heavy paws, very near to her and coming closer. The noise of claws dragged across granite so that she knows it's a bear, a very large bear, and not a lion—you never hear a lion's claws. Already, she can feel the animal's breath against the back of her neck, warm as a morning's coals and fetid as an old kill. And now the girl is more afraid than she's ever been in her entire life, and her heart races, and she jumps to her feet, spinning about to face her attacker, and…

…there is no bear, only boulders, a splintered log, and the vertical wall of the ravine, so close that she could almost reach out and touch it…

…and she loses her balance, sliding backwards off the ledge.

Poor wicked, wicked child, who thinks that she would know the truth of all things.

There's the smallest space of time when the girl seems to hang suspended between the sky and the world, as if maybe both have decided they want nothing more to do with her, and then she hits the water, the water frigid as dark midwinter, and it instantly closes around her, solid as a fist, insubstantial as night. It's like being punched in the chest, in the gut, the sheer force of this cold, a cold that burns like fire, and the girl coughs out, vomits up her breath and watches as it rushes back towards the surface in a spiraling trail of bubbles to be reclaimed by the rapacious sky. When she told First Mother she could swim, that wasn't a lie. But the shock of this chill has already numbed her arms and legs, her hands and feet, and is quickly clouding her mind. She's sinking, surely as any stone would sink. She reaches out, clawing, grasping at that shimmering membrane dividing the world beneath the water from the world above it, summoning what little strength the cold has left to her. But the day is like a dream, now, a dream of being chased by wolves or hyenas or an angry bull bison, and no matter how fast you run, you can't run fast enough to get away. The cold is pulling her down and—awake or dreaming—she cannot get away, and soon she'll be nothing but food for those tiny silver fish and for the crayfish and for everything else that lives in the deep pool.

What is it, mutters First Mother, *that you risked so much to find here?*

That you risked your life?

What is it here that is worth as much as that, wicked child?

And the spirit's voice behind the girl's eyes is even colder than the water.

This is where I will die, the girl thinks, *and no one will ever come here to look for me, and so no one will ever find me.* And First Mother cackles, and again she says, *You're not an otter or a beaver or a mink.*

The girl swallows water…

…past a long hallway and marble busts of Richard Leaky and Charles Darwin, we enter a darkened gallery, you and I. The only lighting here is held inside the big display cases and set into the floors along the wood-paneled walls. The only lighting here is here for effect. You're talking about the train ride from Berlin to Mettmann and about the other things you want to see before you have to head back, the Goldberger Mill and the birthplace of Konrad Heresbach.

"You're enjoying Germany, then?" I ask, and you smile and nod as we pass mounted skeletons of woolly mammoths, cave bears, and Ice-Age horses.

"I'm terrible about homesickness," you say, "but it's been nice."

We pause before the reconstructed remains of a lion-sized sabre-toothed cat—Homotherium latidens, *according the museum label. Its bones have been skillfully wired together so that it appears to be lunging at the fleeing skeleton of an antelope of some sort.*

"And good for the book, I would imagine," I say.

And you reply, "Yes, and very good for the book."

"I'm excited to read it."

"I think it'll be much better than the last one."

And, of course, I'm not thinking about the books at all, not the one you published three years ago to resounding indifference or the one you've spent all your time ever since trying to write. I'm thinking about the last time we fucked, and how your skin tasted, and about the smell of your sweat. I'm thinking about your face dimly reflected in the Plexiglas dividing us from those fragile fossil bones.

You're talking now about agents and editors, contracts and lunches in Lower Manhattan, and I'm thinking about the last time we were together, the afternoon we visited the Archenhold Observatory. I was giving a lecture there on SETI and the Drake Equation, and then we were taken up onto the roof and treated to a demonstration of the Treptow refracting telescope, installed in 1896 and still the eighth largest in the world. You looked through the antique eyepiece at the starry Northern sky and made a joke about a thousand eyes on a thousand worlds peering through a thousand alien telescopes, looking back at you.

"I very much enjoyed the last one."

"You and no one else."

Then neither of us says anything for maybe half a minute, and I wish it were because we've always been comfortable with one another's silence. But I know it's simply that we're both running out of things to say.

"Poor old fucker," you say, finally, and you tap the Plexiglas.

"Die Katze oder der Hirsch?"

"Oh, die Katze," you smile, "most definitely die Katze."

And then you tug the sleeve of my sweater and we're walking again, leaving behind the sabre-tooth and the deer it will never catch frozen together in a limbo tableau, a limbo for predator and prey alike. The next time we pause, it's before a wide diorama depicting several members of a Neanderthaler tribe outside the mouth of a cave, everyday life thirty-five thousand years ago. There are eleven of the figures, each sculpted and painted with such startling hyperrealism that I wouldn't be entirely taken aback if any one of them should move or speak, if all together they should begin to sing or to dance. Their hair, their eyes, the grime beneath their nails, everything rendered in an all but perfect dermoplastic simulacrum of life. One of the men has a dead boar slung over his shoulders, and another, missing his left forearm, is pointing at the ground with his right index finger. A third man sits before a fire, shaping a tool from *flint and an antler, while a male child watches on with an expression that is one part curiosity and one part boredom. Behind them, a young mother nurses her baby, and still farther back, half lost in shadows, there's an old woman kneeling beside a man lying on his back, half covered with an animal pelt, an elder caring for the sick or the dying.*

"Do you ever think of coming home to New York?" you ask, and you look at me then, just for a moment, before turning your attention once more to the exhibit.

"Of course," I tell you. "I think about it, but we both know it's not a very practical solution. Don't we?"

"Yeah," you say, not the least bit convincingly. And then you lean nearer to the Plexiglas dividing the two of us from the scene of Paleolithic domesticity. And you say, "Jesus, that's creepy." And you point at something, but at just what I'm not at all sure, and I suppose you can see that from my expression, because you say, "Back there, behind the old woman and the sick guy." And now I do see…

…and it does taste salty, just as She Who Holds Fire said it would. The water is so very cold it hurts the girl's teeth and sears her throat and her belly. She kicks out with all the force she has left, kicking out against the bright panic pouring through her mind, and her feet strike the gravel at the bottom of the deep pool. A cloud of silt rises about her like morning fog or a burial pelt. And that's when she sees the faces in the water, the faces of two women watching her through the veil of sediment whirling all about her.

And you thought there were no ghosts, says First Mother. *You thought there were no demons waiting in this place to haul foolish children down to their well-deserved deaths.*

The women watching her are not of the People. By their narrow noses and flat brows, by their thin lips and weak chins, she immediately recognizes them as Low Landers, and so here is the awful secret of the pool, the truth of it she has not been told. It's haunted by the spirits of the eaters of men.

One of the women points at her.

Your flesh will be sweet, I'd think, First Mother tells her. *The marrow in your bones will be sweeter. Hear the crackling of your fat over their cooking fire? One of those women will wear your teeth about her throat. The other will weave a pretty belt from your scalp.*

No! the girl screams without opening her mouth. *No, spirit, I will* not *die here!*

And with all the strength left to her she pushes off from the bottom of the pool…

…at the very back of the museum's artificial cave, there's a pool fabricated of some clear resin, and a Neanderthaler girl, no more I would guess than fourteen or fifteen, crouches at its edge, staring down into the water. We're left to guess whatever it is she sees there, and maybe it's meant to be nothing more than her own reflection, but she looks startled, startled and maybe even a little bit afraid. I see the girl before I'm aware of the figure standing behind her, a thinner man than the others in the tribe. There are circular patterns—whorls—drawn on his skin in soot or some other dark pigment, and his face is hidden by a mask—the face and muzzle of a wolf, a wolf's ears and black nose, skinned and fashioned into a headdress for this looming shamanic figure. The man is resting his right hand on the girl's left shoulder.

"What does she see?" you ask. "What is it you think she sees?"

…and then, after what seems like only an instant, the girl breaks the surface of the pool, and she sucks in great mouthfuls of the warm summer air as she splashes her way to shore. With numbed fingers and cramping arms, she hauls herself out onto the rocks, sputtering and gagging and coughing up water that doesn't taste salty after all…

…and I lean in close and whisper, "What big eyes you have."

You turn away from the exhibit just long enough to scowl at me. You turn back, and there's your face reflected in the Plexiglas, superimposed over the diorama.

"All the better to see you with, my dear," you reply.

…rolling over onto her back, staring up at the single brilliant white eye of the sun, here in the place where the sky fucked the world, here where all the People were born. Here, where she will not die to make a feast for the ghosts of hungry Low Landers.

You may learn yet, First Mother whispers.

And the girl closes her eyes and waits for the shivering to pass.

FADE TO

3.

BLACK
FADE IN:
NEXT SCENE
<u>INT. OFFICE—CONTINUOUS</u>

We still have fifteen minutes remaining on *our* hour, here in the office of the psychiatrist. Neither of us has said anything for almost five minutes, which isn't as unusual as you might think. Sometimes I run out of words. I think sometimes she might even run out of questions. But her time is purchased in tidy one-hour increments, and if I have paid for it, it's mine. The camera captures her face, not as patient as it was when I arrived—she needs a cigarette. It captures the ticking wall clock, blank hands, white face, red Roman numerals. It lingers on the fossil ammonite, which I picked up off the table shortly after she asked me why I screamed on a summer afternoon when I was only four years old, and shortly after I did my best to answer. I do try to tell the truth in here, though the truth has never come naturally to me. I think of it as a foreign language I had to endure in high school and hardly learned at all. She's tapping her eraser again. Outside, a car blaring bass-heavy rock music drives very slowly past the office building. In the past, when sessions have devolved into dead air, we've talked about—twice now—historical accounts of doppelgängers, many seeming to presage calamity: Vice-Admiral Sir George Tryon (Eaton Square, London; 22 June 1893), Emilie Sageé (*Pensionat von Neuwelcke,* Livonia; 1845–1846), the wife of John Donne (Paris; 1612), Percy Bysshe Shelley (Pisa, Italy; 23 June 1822), Sir Gilbert Parker (British Parliament, London; 1906), Guy de Maupassant (Paris; early 1890s), Abraham Lincoln (Washington, D.C.; 6 November 1860), Queen Elizabeth I (1603), et alia. But today I am in no mood for history. The camera tracks my hand as I set the fossil back onto the tabletop.

ME

So, how did it start for you?

DR. MERIWETHER

What do you mean? How did what start for me?

ME

I've preferred to imagine that it's not simply academic, your interest. I find the prospect that perhaps it's something more personal to be far more intriguing. Am I wrong? Are you going to disappoint me now?

I've caught her off guard, and she hesitates. She shifts in her chair, crossing, then uncrossing her legs. She almost smiles a nervous smile, but doesn't quite manage to pull it off. Her gaze drifts to the drab blue curtains.

> DR. MERIWETHER
>
> April 1996. I was still in college. I'd taken the train down to London
> for the weekend, to see a play. It was outside the theatre after the show.

And at first I think that's all I'm going to get, a welcomed confirmation of my suspicion, but nothing more. I nod, then rub my eyes. I haven't been sleeping again, and I left the Visine in the car.

> DR. MERIWETHER (contd.)
>
> There were a lot of people, everyone crowded together between the
> curb and the door to the lobby. And I saw her trying to hail a cab.

> ME
> (pushing)
>
> Her?

> DR. MERIWETHER
> (looking at me now)
>
> Her. Me. She was wearing a blue silk scarf that I'd almost worn. At
> the very last I'd changed my mind. It had been a birthday gift from
> my mother, that scarf. But everything else was exactly the same.

I glance at the clock—ten minutes to go—and then back to her. The psychiatrist looks tired and antsy. Suddenly, it occurs to me that everything between us has changed. It occurs to me that we're now coconspirators.

DR. MERIWETHER (contd.)

I saw her, and a few seconds later she saw me. I'd never seen anyone look that frightened. I mean, absolutely terrified.

For that matter, I'm not sure I ever have again. We only made eye contact for—I don't know—seconds. A cab pulled up and someone opened the door for her, and then she was gone.

Dr. Meriwether tells me, almost matter of factly, there was no more to the incident than that. And I'm sure some people would believe her, because I've found the psychiatrist is quite good with feigned sincerity. As I've said, were I writing a screenplay, were this merely light and shadow projected on a wall, then casting would have done an admirable job with my psychiatrist. This drab, weary woman is convincing. I suspect that, as with writers, psychiatrists *must* be skillful liars. After all, if each and every empathetic word and gesture were genuine, they would certainly soon be crushed by the weight of so much borrowed despair, anger, sorrow, fear, confusion, delusion, and et cetera. So, the psychiatrist tells me *that* was *that,* and, on some level, I understand that I probably ought to take her word for it. But I know better. I've spent my life learning what the eyes of a haunted woman look like. I've seen that expression so often in the mirror, and on the faces of my seemingly endless parade of alternate selves, those doppelgängers, the double walkers.

ME

And was it the only time, that night outside the theatre? Was that your first and last time?

DR. MERIWETHER

Yes, that was the only time.

(pause)

I haven't told a lot of people that story, you know.

ME

Have you ever wondered why that is?

DR. MERIWETHER

I don't know. My reputation, I suppose. We can't have shrinks seeing their own ghosts.

(beat)

Anyway, I'm afraid our hour's up. I have you down for four o'clock next Tuesday. Does that still work?

And I tell her yes, that still works. That still works just fine. I stand and slip on my coat, and the psychiatrist thoughtfully hands me an appointment card with the date and time scribbled with her tap-tapping pencil. She tells me to be careful, that she's heard there may be snow before nightfall. And if I am only writing a screenplay, then the camera watches with its voyeuristic dedication as I open the office door, step across the threshold into the outer office, then pull the door shut again behind me. And when I have gone, the woman who once saw herself watching herself on a street outside a theatre in London sits in her chair and stares at the fading day leaking in through her curtains and leaking out again.

FADE TO BLACK
ROLL CREDITS

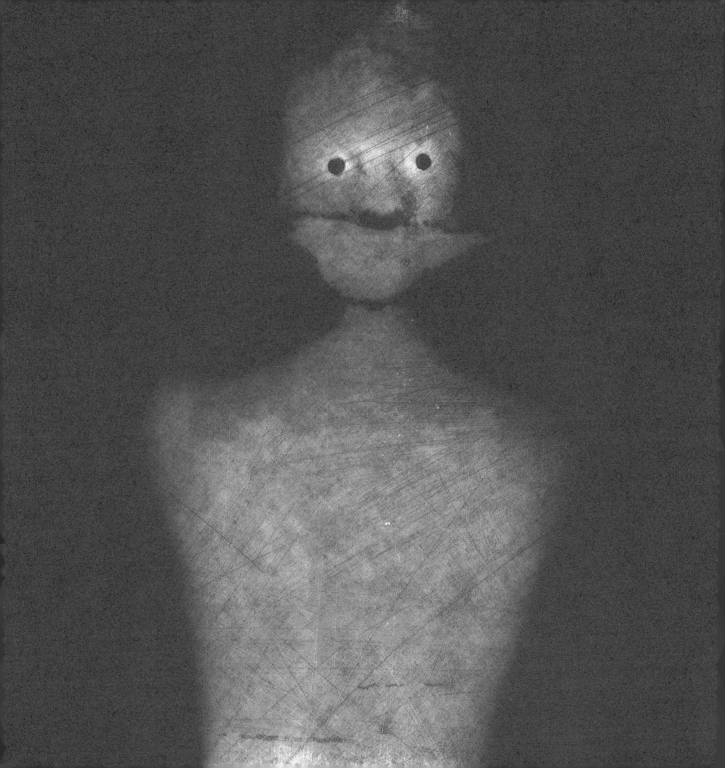

Yummie

M. John Harrison

In his late thirties Short experienced some kind of cardiac problem, a brief but painful event which landed him in an Accident and Emergency unit in East London. From A&E he was processed to Acute Assessment, where they took his blood pressure at two-hourly intervals but otherwise didn't seem to know what to do with him. Everyone was very kind.

His second night on the ward, he stood in the corridor where it was cooler and looked out over a strip of grass. An iron staircase was off to one side. He could see bollards; what he imagined was a car park; behind that a few trees quite dense and dark against the sky. He rested his forehead against the cold glass of the fire door. Propane tanks, portabuilding offices, everything lighted grey and blue. He had a short clear glimpse of himself opening the door and walking out. It wouldn't have required a decision; to some degree, in fact, he felt it had already happened. That glimpse had lobed itself off immediately, becoming its own world. He could see himself moving away between the trees, tentatively at first but with increasing confidence.

Late the next evening, a bed came free in Coronary Care, a wheelchair ride away across the architectural and procedural grain of the hospital, from clean and new to grimy and old, past stacks of mysterious materials, parks of apparently abandoned medical electronics and radiology machines, and into a narrow slot deep in the original building. 3 AM, he found himself awake again. Someone further along the slot was moaning. Someone else had a cough, long and retching, full of sad self-disgust.

"Make no mistake about this," the consultant advised him next morning: "You've had a heart attack."

Short, who had never believed anything else, waited to hear more; but that seemed to be it. The procedure he now underwent was an experience very much like an amusement ride. He was placed carefully on a narrow table. The nurse gave him an injection of diazepam she described as "the equivalent of three good gin-and-tonics," while someone else demonstrated the bank of cameras that would image his heart. The table stretched away in front of him, elongated, bluish. The cameras then groaned and slid about, pressing down into his space. Soon, off to one side, someone was putting in a lot of effort to push something like an old-fashioned drain-rod up the femoral artery and deep into his body. It was a struggle. He had the distant sense of being smashed and pummelled about. He couldn't feel anything, but sometimes their voices made him nervous. "He'll have a bit of a bruise," someone warned; someone else said they would put some pressure on that. Every so often they asked him if he felt ok. "I don't know what I feel," Short answered. In fact he felt violated but excited. He felt as if he was whizzing along some blue-lit track, he could come off the rails at any time but thanks to the diazepam he wouldn't mind.

"I'm quite enjoying it," he said.

They laughed at that, but when he heard himself say he thought there might be a sensation in his heart—not a pain precisely, but some sort of feeling he couldn't quite describe—there was a silence then the thud of some more powerful drug hitting his system like a car running over a cattle grid.

Back on the ward, he felt embarrassingly optimistic, though a list of possible changes to his life (scribbled under the heading "Opportunities" in the blank space next to the *Guardian* crossword puzzle) proved vague; turning out when he consulted it later to be couched in the self-improvement languages of the 1980s. How, for instance, could Short be "kinder" to himself? What might that actually mean? Deep in the night, Coronary Care became a site of hallucination, like the woods in a fairytale: he was woken by a child's cough, sometimes seeming to issue from a ward directly beneath this one, sometimes from the wall of monitors and tubes behind his bed. It was a careful, precise little sound, urgent yet determined to attract no attention. Towards dawn a tall languid-looking man of his father's generation stood in the corridor by the fire door, calling, "Yummie? Yummie?" in tones pitched between puzzlement and command. His head was almost entirely round, his expression in some way surprised. He looked Short up and down, made eye contact and said, "Let's not be mistaken! You will have the hell of a bruise!"

An empty trolley clattered past unseen behind them.

"Are you even here," Short whispered. "Because Yummie is not a name."

"Those chickens," the man said, "waiting outside for you now? They are your chickens. You deny them, but I see they follow you with great persistence."

Though no chickens were visible, he was right: if Acute Assessment had been like the lobby of a cheap but comfortable hotel—air too hot, coffee bearable, quiet conversations at reception—Coronary Care was where events played out the way Short had been taught to fear. It wasn't the bottom of things by any means, but it was the beginning of the bottom of things. Those chickens, having come home to roost, would eye him now and until the end, heads on one side, mad little combs flopping.

The next day, he was discharged.

"Isn't it a bit soon?" he asked the rehab nurse.

"You'll be fine," she said.

She said people often felt a little anxious. But it really was a safe, easy, walk in, walk out procedure, and he could plan for a good outcome. She asked him if she could take him through some leaflets. "For instance," she pointed out, lowering her voice, "as soon as you can manage two flights of stairs you can have sexual activity." There was also a list of foods he should avoid. Short had a look at it. Before the attack, his diet had been sourced almost wholly from the red end of the scale. He wondered what he would eat.

"I don't drink much alcohol anyway," he said.

She gave him a number to call if he needed any further advice. "If you're worried about anything at all," she said, "just ring."

He wrote "sexual activity" in his notebook.

"That seems fine," he said.

Soon afterwards he found himself wearing his own clothes, carrying a two-day-old copy of the *Guardian* and some hospital toothpaste in a plastic bag, waiting for a cab to come down through the traffic and turn on to the hospital apron. When he got home he was exhausted just from leaning forward and telling the cabby how to get where they were going. He lay down on the sofa and pulled a blanket up over him and went to sleep. When he woke up it was on the edge of being dark. The street outside was quiet. The light in Short's room had a kind of sixty-year-old smokiness, as if he was looking at things through nicotine-stained glass. The door of the room was open, and the man he had met in the hospital corridor now stood at the window, holding the net curtain back with one long hand so he could stare down into the street. He was whispering, "Yummie? Yummie?" to himself.

I'm moving forward into something here, Short thought: but I don't know what it is. He fell asleep again. The next day he rang the number the rehab nurse had given him and told her: "I don't think I'm half as well as I feel."

"People often report a sense of vulnerability," the nurse explained. "It's nothing to be ashamed of."

"Do they report a man with a round head?" Short said.

"Let's get you to come in and have your blood pressure taken."

In an attempt to normalise himself, Short walked around his neighbourhood, not far at first, twenty minutes here, twenty minutes there. He knew it well, but there are always a few little corners of a neighbourhood you don't know. You always meant to explore them: today, perhaps, you do. Or in the end you glance into that short curving street—with its blackened gap halfway along where a woodyard used to be, or the Memorial Hall with the three tall cemented-up windows and stopped clock—and decide again that it only connects to some other street and then another after that. All the pubs down there, you suspect, have yellowed, patchy ceilings and a feeling of grease under the fingertips wherever you touch.

At home he slept a lot, dreaming repeatedly of his angioplasty—the bunker-like underground theatre, the table too narrow to rest on comfortably, the banks of cameras, the lively technicians and nurses in their colourful thyroid protectors, the air dark but also displaying a slight bluish-grey fluorescence in the corners as if it had absorbed the radioactive dyes from Short's bloodstream. "How are you getting on," someone would ask, "in your ongoing struggle with the world of appearances?" Short's responses became increasingly facetious. He was embarrassed for himself. He woke sweating, his pulse a hundred and fifty beats a minute, experiencing such premonitions of disaster that he had to get up and move around the room. In these moments of unconscious hindsight, the essentially violent nature of the procedure—the feeling of racing feet-first forward on rails under a weird light while your heart is reamed, plumbed, measured to its full physical depth and found wanting—was only heightened. By day he thought he felt a little better. His blood pressure remained too high.

"Whatever you say," Short told the man in his room, "Yummie isn't a name."

"Who are you to tell me that?" the man said. "It was your mother's name, and her mother's before her. It was your sister's name."

Short was becoming embittered with the whole thing.

"I never had a sister," he said. "How did you get in here?"

"I'm always here. I was here before they christened your father, and before they christened your mother, and before they buried the poor unstained sister you say you never had." His eyes were as round as his head, entirely without expression and yet somehow both confiding and expectant, as if he knew Short would soon admit to something. "The poor sister," he repeated, with a sentimental emphasis. When Short failed to answer—because this was not a past he could recognise, let alone own or identify with in any degree—he waved one hand dismissively and seemed to fade a little. "How are you getting on with those chickens?" he said. "Yummie."

Short made another appointment at Rehab and told them, "I think my medication might need adjusting."

"How do you think of me?" the heart nurse said.

"I think of you as the heart nurse," Short said.

"Well, I am a nurse," she said. "But my name's Linda."

"Then I'll think of you as Sister Linda."

They laughed and Short left with his new leaflets. A minute or two later he went back down the corridor to her office and stood in the doorway and said: "I'm supposed to talk when I'm walking?"

"We recommend that," she said. "We need you to exercise, but we need you just to make sure your breathing stays inside the range: if you can walk and talk, you're inside the range, you know your heart is fine."

"I can't think of anything to say."

She stared at him. "Well, for instance, you can just have a nice conversation with the other person."

"The other person," Short said: "OK."

He wrote "other person" in his notebook.

"I'm usually on my own," he said. In fact, he was hearing voices in his room at night. One voice would say, "You're accepting more, aren't you?" and after a pause another would answer, "Oh yes, yes,

I'm accepting more. Definitely. I'm able to accept much more now." They sounded like an old couple, talking in the tea room at a garden centre. Short couldn't quite locate them, or tell if they were male or female. They seemed to originate quite high up, in a region of discoloured wallpaper, then, in the weeks that followed, still invisible, lower themselves down until they were able to occupy the room proper, pulling themselves about quietly but jerkily between the larger items of furniture, murmuring, "Two funerals and now another house move. No wonder I can't take anything in," or, "Look at this one, dear. He's young enough."

Once he had noticed them, he noticed others. Sometimes he woke in the night and it was quite a hubbub in there. They were everywhere. They were looking for the toilet. They had opinions about Catholicism and walking. Short had the feeling that they gathered round him while he slept, looking down at him considerately and with concern. Perhaps they even discussed him, and these fits and starts of language were the only way they could express what they knew. As their conversation decayed further, into a mumbled repetition he could hear only as "Yummie, yummie, yummie," he would see the tall, calm, round-headed figure waiting by the window, pulling back the curtain to look out, smiling a little. One night it whispered: "Research shows how rats dream repeatedly of the maze they have not yet solved." Short woke up with a sharp pain on the left side of his chest and called an ambulance.

"The paramedics said I was fine," he told Sister Linda at his next appointment. "They said it wasn't the right kind of pain. They were very kind."

"I should hope they were," she said.

"It was just a moment of panic," Short admitted. He tried to think of a way to qualify that, but could only add: "My parents were the same."

"You're due for the three-month echocardiogram anyway."

On his way to Sonography, Short became lost in the hospital basement; then the technicians didn't want to admit he was in the cubicle with them, but carried on checking their equipment as if they were waiting for some more significant version of him to arrive. After a brief glimpse of what looked like a translucent marine animal pulsing and clutching inside his chest, Short kept his gaze directed away from the monitors. He couldn't so easily ignore the swashy emphysemic whisper produced by this monster, surfacing in his life as if from the depths of a Hollywood ocean. He went back upstairs to Rehab and asked the nurse, "Have you heard that noise? It's like a 1950s Hotpoint washing machine. Do you remember those?"

She stared at him, then down at the echocardiogram result.

"This is all good," she said. "You can take it from me. You can look for a very positive outcome with results like this."

"So, a heart sounds like obsolete white goods."

"Really, no one's surprised if you have some anxiety."

That night he dreamed that a great hoard of household rubbish—broken beds, cheap soiled mattresses, used unpaired shoes stuffed into plastic shopping bags—covered the floor of his room. It smelled of urine. It smelled like a slot deep in the old hospital building. The ceiling was off, and the ceiling of the room above that, and the one above that too: all the way to the roof, which was also off. The room was open to the night sky. In some way, Short's original procedure was still going on. The cameras whirred and shook above him. The walls, bluish with radioactive dyes and ruined by moonlight, were crawling with slow old people pulling themselves head-down towards the floor. "Where's the toilet here?" they whispered. "I think it's over that way, dear." The tweed jackets of the men, the old fashioned wool skirts of the women, fell around their heads, muffling their dull talk; while by the window, Yummie the watchman kept his eye on the street below.

"Why are you doing this?" Short said.

"You think you are alive. Have a closer look. These people were victims of that thought too. People come home from a visit and discover they've never left. Or they have a wall knocked down in their attic and find this behind it. Do you see?"

"I don't see, no."

"People imagine there will be no upshot from this, no discovery, but it will be the end of the story. Or so they hope."

"Another thing," Short said: "I don't want you here."

"Good luck with that."

———

That was a low point, Short was forced to admit; but afterwards his life seemed to improve. He found another room, not far from the hospital. He went to the gym every two or three days. From being a zone of anxiety, the weekly act of transferring his medication from its calendar-packaging into the dispenser became a comforting regime. Bisoprolol, losartan potassium, atorvastatin, lansoprazole like a cheap holiday destination in the Canary Islands: their side effects were legion, though in three months Short had suffered only a sudden but unimpressive swelling of the inner lip. He bought himself a blood pressure monitor. The clutch of its cuff was like a reassuring hand on his upper arm, although inevitably it reminded him of things he didn't want to remember. Once a major organ has failed you—or you have failed it—your relations with the world become more tentative, more grateful and fragile. He had never liked to feel the beat of his heart. Other emotional reactions he experienced: a kind of protective reluctance; easily-triggered startle reflex; fear that every internal sensation might be the symptom of another event.

"But there's something else too," he told Sister Linda. He experienced it as "a kind of lifting up away from life and towards it at the same time. You can't avoid it any more, so all you're left with is to engage it."

"I'm not sure I follow you," she said.

"The other thing is I'm determined to be kinder to myself."

By day he walked the streets—chatting out loud to no one, maintaining a brisk pace but always checking that his heart rate remained safely within the range—or toured the supermarket aisles foraging for products at the green end of the scale. At night he watched on-demand television; worked on the *Guardian* crossword puzzle he had begun in hospital. He had to admit now that he had enjoyed his stay there, the warmth at night, the regular coming and going of the staff by day. He had felt safe for the first time in his life. He went through his belongings until he found the toothpaste and toothbrush he had brought back with him from Coronary Care, laying them out on top of his chest of drawers where he could see them, along with a pair of red non-slip ward socks still in their packaging. While he was doing that, Yummie climbed slowly down the wall behind him and said:

"You needn't think collecting a lot of old rubbish will help. They all thought that."

"Those chickens you used to mention," Short said: "I never saw them. How are they now? I often think of you on the street, waiting outside the hospices and care homes in all weathers. I worry on your behalf."

"Worry about yourself," said Yummie, "not me. That's my advice."

Robo Rapid

Joe R. Lansdale

When I unwound the cloak it was heavy and wide, having belonged to my father and being made to accommodate his size. I laid on half of it and folded the other half over me, covering my head against the blowing sand. If I was lucky, the sand wouldn't cover me so deep I would smother. Even though the night air was chill, I was warm beneath the fold of the cloak. My smaller bag of items rested beneath my head for a pillow. I watched the stars until I fell asleep.

I was two days out, and so far I had only found more sand, and as morning came and the sun shone bright, I could see the air was decorated with thin lines of sand that seemed to hang in the air like a beaded curtain.

I thought of the bad things that had brought me here, and for a moment I wished I hadn't come, that I had stayed with Grandfather back on the Flatlands. But that thought passed. Somewhere out there were my brother and sister, and I planned to find them.

So far, I hadn't found squat and I had sand in my teeth.

The night it all started, I had gone out behind one of the small sand dunes to answer the call of nature, and was just wrapping that up when I heard the machines. Peeking around the edge of the dune I saw them coming, slipping out from the shadows between high, drifting dunes, the moonlight bouncing off of their blue and white bodies. They came on tall and wide, strutting, hissing, clanging and clattering like large, metallic men, which was exactly what they were, toward those of our tribe who had gathered around the roaring fire. You could clearly see written across the machines' sides in bold black letters: ROBO RAPID. There were three of them.

My parents, my brother and sister, like all the others, tried to run, but it was too late because the machines were swift and the camels were hobbled too far away for my people to free them and make an escape. I wanted to do something, but I didn't because I knew there was nothing I could do. I squatted where I was, sneaked a look around the side of that small dune, and watched as the machines charged, waving their metal arms about. The machines held in one metal hand a net, and in the other a large wrench that could have turned a bolt the size of my head.

These were different and smaller machines than I had seen before, but they were large enough, over twelve feet tall and eight feet wide, and their purpose was the same. Behind the face plates of the machines I could see dead riders, blackened by time, springs of hair like burnt twigs sticking up on mostly slick skulls. They bobbed in their seats, heads swinging right and left, held in place by shoulder straps and waist belts and probably by their flesh, most likely glued by time to the ancient seat leather. They had died so long ago it was amazing they still had form. The desert air, perhaps something inside the machines, had mummified them.

The machines rushed over the sand, stepping wide. Their nets soared out, and I saw my family, father and mother, brother and sister, fall down beneath a heavy net, and then the net scooped tight, and the monster machine hoisted them up and held them in front of its face as if the dead rider inside might examine the prize. A little red light blinked inside the machine, and then the other metal arm swung and the wrench smashed against my mother and father. There was a dark, wet blossom in the night air, and the net disgorged my mother and father, but maintained my brother and sister.

I let out a little scream, fell back behind the dune and began to cry, holding it in as best I could, feeling about as necessary as one more sand dune, a girl who moments before had only been interested in clearing her bowels, and now my parents were smashed and the machines were taking all the young ones away, including my brother and sister.

Not that I'm proud of it, but I stayed where I was, hoping no machine would find me, and in short time the Robo Rapids were gone. Easing out from behind the dune, I saw that some of the tribe had returned. I saw too my ancient grandfather, ninety-eight years old he claimed, and all that was left of my family. He came hobbling out from the shadows on his crutch, his tattered, dark rags dangling off of him like shredded flesh. He saw me and let out a bellow. I ran to him and we hugged. I almost knocked him off his crutch.

"They are dead, Sheann, all dead," he said, and he wept loudly. He wasn't the only one. The air was filled with crying and wailing and the gnashing of teeth, the tearing of garments, a habit that always seemed wasteful to me, no matter what the circumstances.

"They took Jacob and Della," I said. "They didn't kill them. They're alive."

"It's the same," he said. "They're dead, or soon will be. No one they take comes back."

We have a kind of fatalism, my tribe, and I decided not to share in it.

"No. They're still alive."

"The same as dead," Grandfather said. "The same."

We butchered the camels that had been killed and salted the meat, and then we gathered up the dead and piled them on old camel skins and dragged them away in the dark of the night. We came to the Flatlands by morning, though they weren't all that flat. Flatter than the desert with its rising and shifting dunes, but there was rubble there, pieces of metal, pieces of glass, pieces of stone, a piling and a rotting of ancient bones.

Once the Robo Rapids didn't come as far as the Flatlands, but now they did, so being in the Flatlands we were no more safe than the night before, but we were farther away from the home of the machines, and without all the dunes we could see them coming.

There were animals that lived in the dunes that provided meat, so it was part of our routine to wander out there. Load up the camels, make the great circle, which included the Flatlands, and when that was done, we did it again. In the last few years the sand rabbits and so many other beasts that had lived in the desert and provided meat and clothing were disappearing, as were the water holes, but still, there was more food in the harsh desert than in the calmer Flatlands. But Robo Rapids or no Robo Rapids, in time we would venture back to the desert, looking for small animals to eat, and then we would rotate back to here to rest.

We didn't go to the Green Place. That's where the Robo Rapids came from.

The next morning the breeze, as if helping with the planned cremation, blew a lot of tumble weeds into our campsite, and we piled those up and heaped dried camel dung from previous visits with them. We placed all the bodies on the weed and dung pile and set it afire.

The old folks, and I guess most of the young folks, believe as the bodies burn their smoke goes up to join the gods, but me, I think the smoke just goes up and turns thin and disappears. People only seem to believe in the gods when they need something that they usually don't get, or when they are grieving and like to think their loved ones have found a better place to be. Since most of us are in no hurry to depart for those finer shores, I have a feeling that deep down we know the truth that this is it, and beyond is nothing.

Watching the rise of that nauseating smoke, the burning of my mother and father's bodies, didn't make me feel good at all. All I could think about were my brother and sister. Everyone else had spent time praying on their loss, crying, and preparing to move on, but I just got madder.

That night our tent was roomier than before, due to the absence of our loved ones. Me and Grandfather tried to rest. The tent was patched in many places, and in some places not too well, because a needle of bone has never fit my hands well, and the stitching I had done during the day to patch the rips the Robo Rapids had made by walking over it, left gaps. The cold night wind whistled through those holes like throwing knives.

We spent considerable time crying over our family, but in time I couldn't cry anymore. All I could do was think about my brother and sister, carried away to the Green Place where the Robo Rapids ruled.

"You can sew again tomorrow," Grandfather said, looking up at the rips in the tent, pulling his heavy cloak tighter around his body. "I'd do it, but I don't want to, and you're younger and it's your job."

"I can't wait," I said.

Grandfather was trying to generate a bit of humor in our tent, but by this point I was too absorbed with thinking about Jacob and Della.

"You lived before things were like this," I said. "Why do the machines kill us? What do they want with the younger ones?"

"They kill us because they can, and what they want with the younger ones I don't know, but certainly young ones give the machines less trouble than the older ones would. Well, if you're as old as me I wouldn't give them much trouble. There's not enough left of me to give much trouble."

"That's not a very good answer."

Grandfather shrugged. "We live the way we live now because the weather changed and there were wars. I only know that at some point the war machines began to think, and their thoughts were not good."

"So, the machines get up in the morning, think, hey, there's some humans out there, let's go kill them and steal the little ones and bring them back?"

"Pretty much."

"That doesn't make sense. They aren't like people. They don't wake up in the morning."

"I didn't say they did. You did."

"Can't you tell me a bit more?" I asked.

He almost smiled, but not quite. "I've told you before."

"Yeah, but I still can't make sense of it. I can't understand why we have to give up on Jacob and Della. There's got to be something more you can tell me. Tell me what you've already told me, and maybe this time I can make sense of it."

"There's no sense to it," he said.

"Tell me anyway."

I was looking for any crumb I could find that would explain the odd way we lived and the reasons they took the young people and killed the older ones. Why were they still at war?

Grandfather sighed. He knew me. I would worry him until he thought his head would explode. I had heard it all before, but I kept thinking that if I heard it again and again at some point it would begin to make sense.

"Once humans ruled the machines," he said. "Used them to build and travel, but then they used them for war. The aliens came, and we used our machines to fight them. I suppose you could say we won that war, though it was disease that killed the aliens. If it hadn't, they might have won. When that war was over the machines of different tribes, countries we called them back then, fought each other over land and water and food, and in time most humans were killed by the Robo Rapids of both sides. Countries didn't matter anymore.

"There wasn't always as much desert, and where we are now, we called what we are sleeping on, concrete. Great buildings made of stone and plastic and glass were built over this concrete. There were many buildings, and they went for miles, and we called those buildings a city. Once there was an ocean that licked at its shores. But that went away, and out there the Green Place popped up and grew remarkably fast. Some say it's because there was something in the alien technology that got loose and made things grow. I don't know. But it happened. There were villages in the Green Place for awhile. We had this thing called money. Shiny pieces of metal called coins, folding bills, and we went there and bought things that we mostly didn't need."

"Why buy things you didn't need?"

"Because we could. There were things called cars. You've seen their ruins in the desert, farther out on the Flatlands. We rode around in those at a high rate of speed. My parents had a red car. I remember that clearly."

"Okay," I said, "you're right. I have heard this. And there were things called dogs and cats and you loved them as pets, but when times got hard, you ate them. Some people ate their own children."

"See," he said. "You know the story. Sometimes, I think that was a good course of action, eating the children. Usually when I'm tired and can't sleep and my granddaughter won't stop asking about things that don't matter, I think maybe it was a tremendous idea."

"Tell me about the Green Lands and the star people."

"I am envisioning you now in a large pot, floating in hot water with desert onions bobbing all around you, and me adding salt."

"Grandfather, come on. Tell me… Wait. Did you eat children?"

"Of course not. Our tribe never did, but there were those who did, and many of their descendents still roam the desert."

"I've never seen any of them," I said.

"Count your blessings. Fortunately, they are few these days. Fewer than even our tribe, and I suppose after last night we are about fifty people, and many of us are old and few young children are being born, so unless you have children, or a few of the others, our kind will vanish from the face of the earth. I'm not so sure that's a bad idea."

"What about the star people?"

Grandfather sighed. "They were aliens and they came from space. Somewhere out there they had lived amongst the stars, or they came from another dimension, jumped through some kind of rift in space and time and ended up here. That was a popular theory. They wanted our resources. The Robo Rapids were used to fight them, and then disease got the aliens. They couldn't get over our common cold."

Grandfather was right. There were no answers there.

I started crying again. It came over me like a fever, and I cried for quite some time. It was as if a hard rain inside my head had broken loose and was leaking out of my eyes. As I cried, Grandfather tried to soothe me, but pretty soon he was bellowing right along with me.

After Grandfather fell asleep, I lay on my pallet wide awake. I thought of Jacob and Della, and how much they annoyed me, and yet, how much I wanted them back. I wanted vengeance for my father and mother. I didn't want to be like the others, take it in stride and move on. I decided I was leaving and I was going to find my brother and sister and bring them back. If it was too late for them, then at least I would know. I could also quit feeling like a coward. I told myself that once I did something bold, I might not have in my head the constant reminder that I had cowered behind a small sand dune while my mother and father were killed and my brother and sister were taken away. There really wasn't anything else I could tell myself. Sometimes, to do something you are afraid of doing, you have to lie to yourself, and that's all there is to it. I lied to myself that night. I said I was brave and that I would rescue my kin, and that I had to go.

While Grandfather snored loud as camel snorts, I put a small amount of food in a bag along with a corked gourd of water and fastened them around my hips with a thick cloth belt. I placed some other goods in a larger bag and rolled them up inside my cloak and made a pack of it by tying it on both ends with a rope and slinging it across my neck and shoulder. I was wearing sturdy clothes and rabbit-skin boots, and I had another cloak wrapped around me. I had my bag of stones and my sling strapped to my waist. I carried my walking stick. It was thick and heavy and almost as tall as me and was knobbed on top. I was as ready as I was going to get.

By the time morning cracked open and let the light in, I was well into the desert. I had considered taking one of the camels, but decided it was best not to, as the tribe would need it more than I would.

It was hard to think that Grandfather would wake up and find me gone and worry about me, but I couldn't let that stop my mission.

I trudged on.

After a few days my food was mostly gone and my water was one drink from being all over with. I was so hungry I was starting to imagine the dunes of sand were piles of fruit. In the distance, just as I swigged that last bit of water, I saw what I thought might be an encampment of nomads, or a mirage.

I squatted down and spent some time staring at it. I couldn't make the place out clearly, but it looked to be a series of tents at first, but in time I wasn't so sure what it was. I was certain of only one thing. It was not a mirage.

I wondered if there were people there, and if they were friendly, or perhaps the tribe Grandfather told me about; the ones who ate people. I would certainly make a stringy meal.

Squatting down in the desert, I thought about things. I feared going into that camp, but I also feared dying of thirst. The important thing was they would have water and perhaps could spare enough to fill my gourd. Or they could eat me. Right then, either seemed acceptable. In that moment I wished I had not left the tribe. Wished I had stayed with them and started the great circle, and at night read from the books Grandfather had. Read again of Moby Dick and foaming seas and great heroics, of philosophers who talked about things that didn't really matter. Instead, here I was, wandering the desert, sleeping wrapped up in a cloak, my teeth full of sand, not to mention my buttcrack, my throat parched and my belly rumbling.

And there was another problem. I picked them up out of the corner of my eye.

Four wild dogs, hungry, growling, slinking toward me.

Pulling my sling into play, opening my bag of stones, I placed one in my shooter, pulled it back and aimed between the V of it and let loose. There was a yelp, and one of the beasts jumped straight up and ran away. That was good, though actually, I had been aiming at a different one. I was an indifferent shooter.

The others rushed forward. I reloaded, shot again, missed. When I fired the next time, I was on target. It was a solid shot and I could hear the brute's head crack like a lighting strike. He had been as close as ten feet away, which may have accounted for my accuracy.

The beast went down and didn't get up. The remaining two took a hint and ran away. I watched until they were out of sight. The up side was I hadn't been eaten and I had a meal of wild dog at my disposal.

Or I thought I did. The beast I had wounded got up then, and began to slink off. It staggered as it went. I chased it down with my walking stick and beat it in the head until it was dead. I dragged it by its back legs across the sand towards what I thought might be a small tent village. I would go there with a smile on my face and an offering of still warm, wild dog.

There were no tents and no people, but there was a cluster of trees and some greenery that had grown up high and close together around a small trickle of water that came up from the earth and filled a muddy hole. There was sour, red fruit that grew from some of the bushes. I could see birds had been pecking at it, so I decided it was not poisonous. I made a fire with my flint and steel and some of the limbs I broke off trees. I skinned and gutted the dog, ate the heart and liver raw, and cooked the meat. Cooked dog is not as good as I had been led to believe by some old timers who claimed it was the meat of the gods. It was stringy and sour to me. I ate enough to not be hungry, and leaned into the water and licked at its source, trying not to stir the mud too much. It was still a muddy drink.

I rested there a night and a day, exhausted, eating more of the wild dog and the fruit, and filling my gourd with muddy water for the trip onward. I started out when it was night, studying the position of the waning moon for direction, before abandoning the oasis, and continuing my mission.

Finally I came to that part of the desert where the garbage floated; the remains of crashed alien airships. Whatever the ships had been made of the material defied gravity, but didn't leave the planet. The debris floated over the desert night and day. It moved when the wind moved it and never touched the ground. It glowed in the sun and shimmered in the moonlight. The pieces were all the colors of the rainbow and colors I couldn't put a name to.

I had observed the great line of drifting fragments from a distance before, but now I was close enough to touch them. The pieces were all manner of sizes and went on for miles. According to Grandfather, the saucers were shot down and broken open by Robo Rapids. The ship fragments lifted off the ground and inexplicably drifted about, and had floated about ever since.

We had won the war with the aliens, but then humans fought amongst themselves, and finally the metal monsters killed their human controllers with reverse energy surges that Grandfather said made the drivers inside the machines jump and crackle, smoke and pop. And then the machines were in control, powered by who knows what, but with only one guiding impulse left. Kill humans.

I strolled between the slow, swirling parts, and then in the distance I saw a great heap of metal. It glowed in the soft moonlight. The pieces were not alien, because they didn't float, and as I went forward I saw they were piles of Robo Rapid machines. The great heads had been pulled off and stacked into a mound of metal skulls. This gave me pause at first, but from the way the bodies lay, leaning this way and that, feet poking to the sky, I knew they were harmless. It looked like a carrion pile but without the smell.

I used my walking stick to help me forward, as the sand was starting to churn as the wind picked up. Sometimes that sand could blow so hard it could grate your eyes out. Grandfather had known it to happen. The fragments of the alien ships were swirling faster, darting past me, almost smacking me a few times.

My only thought was to reach that pile of wrecked machines and find a place to tuck myself in before the wind grew so bad and the sand blew so hard that I would be knocked down and covered, possibly with my eyes scratched out.

Arriving at that heap of metal, I saw there was a crack through which I could slip, and slip I did. It was dark in there, and with the sand blowing, darker yet. I moved farther in, hoping I hadn't trapped myself, that the sand wouldn't seal my exit. At the center of the heap there was a large opening, and overhead the metal pieces were fastened tightly together.

I had flint and steel to make a fire, but I only had a bit of kindling in my bag. That was for starting a blaze, not maintaining it, so there was no use bothering. It had become so dark by then I couldn't see my hand in front of my face. I could hear sand scraping outside against the pile like claws.

Sensing movement in the dark, I cocked my walking stick over my shoulder, ready to swing. I couldn't see anything other than darkness, but I knew something was scuttling about, and then there was a spot of fire, and a shape behind the flame. A human face, the skin dark as night. A voice said, "Who are you? This is my place."

"A traveler," I said.

The fire went out, and then I sensed someone standing next to me. A voice said, "Would you like fire, something to eat?"

Desert people can be very cautious and unfriendly to outsiders, so I was surprised, and not entirely trusting, yet, I lowered my walking stick and leaned on it.

"If you would be so kind," I said.

"Kindness has nothing to do with it. I am bored and the last of my kind."

"Aren't I of your kind?"

There was a small flare of light next to me, and the dark face appeared and leaned forward as the light glowed. I saw the light was from a small stick with fire on its tip. "You are of my kind, but you are not of my tribe."

"If what you said is true," I said. "You are your tribe."

"Good point," said the voice, and then the fire swept away from me and moved low. Flames snapped up from the floor of the metal cave and brightness jumped about. In front of me, squatting on his haunches, still holding what he had used to light a pile of dry wood was a young man.

"Thank you for the fire," I said.

"Would you like a bite of sand rabbit?" he said. "I have eaten most of it, but there's still a leg left."

"That would be nice."

Moving quickly, his light moving with him, he came back with a bone from which hung ragged chunks of meat. "It was cooked yesterday," he said. "But I think it's fine. Cold, of course. I could warm it."

"That's all right," I said.

He gave me the meat and I sniffed it. Okay. Not too bad. I ate. A bit gritty, but it tasted fine.

I checked out my host, but didn't sniff him the way I had the rabbit meat. I thought that would be too much, but he did have an odor, more sweet than sour. I could see him better in the firelight. He was small and moved like a sand rat, had a bushy head of dark hair and wore a single garment that fit over his head and hung loose to his knees.

"How long have you lived here?" I asked. "Did your tribe live here?"

"No," he said.

The stick with the fire had gone out, but now he was sitting closer to the driftwood fire, and I was sitting nearer to him.

"My name is Nim. My tribe roamed the desert until the Robo Rapids did them in. I was told once, when my father was alive, that this was where the remains of the blasted ones were heaped."

"Blasted ones?"

"By the aliens, during the war. Maybe by other Robo Rapids in the wars that followed."

"I have never seen a dead Robo Rapid before. I guess dead is the right term."

"You remember a lot of the old days?" he asked.

"No more than you. My grandfather remembers. He tells me many tales. My mother and father too. Or they did. They're dead now."

Mentioning them caused me to have a catch in my throat.

"The Robo Rapids?" he asked.

"They took my brother and sister. I am going to try and get them back. Hopeless, I suppose."

"Very likely," he said, "but it hasn't come the ritual yet."

"What ritual?"

Nim shook sand out of a couple of cups and poured me a cup of water from a skin bag, and then poured a cup for himself, said, "The Robo Rapids live off blood and spite, my mother once said."

"The Robo Rapids have become more than machines," I said. "They have chosen the faults of humans."

"I think they are what they were meant to be. Killers. They can think, but it's small thinking. They wanted to become the masters. That much they figured out without programming. That's what my grandparents did. They programmed the machines, programmed them for war."

"Robo Rapids won't have much to master if they keep killing us."

"That's what I mean about the ritual," Nim said. "You see, they don't understand exactly."

"Understand what?"

"Human sacrifice."

"They sacrifice humans?"

"Are your ears stopped up?"

"No, it's just, well, I don't get that."

"Neither do they. They do it because we did it. They learned from us. They learned about war, and they learned from old movies that were made about such things."

"I know about movies," I said. "I've never seen one, but Grandfather has told me about them. He has told me stories from the movies. I know one about a rabbit."

Nim did not appear open to hearing my movie story about a rabbit, so I cleared my throat and waited.

"I don't have the movies here," Nim said. "But there's a place I can watch them. I'll show you sometime."

"Actual movies?"

"That's right. I might have the one about a rabbit there. I might have more than one about rabbits. I don't know. It's a big collection."

"I would like that, but I won't be staying long. What do movies have to do with the Robo Rapids?"

"War movies and movies of violence. There's one about the Aztec sacrificing captives for religious purposes. They've seen it, and have it at the ready, or at least part of it. It's the one they mimic. The human idea of programming them with that stuff was to saturate their wires, batteries and computer codes, stuff their nooks and crannies with violence. They were, after all, machines designed for war. Unlike people, they can't watch and evaluate in the same way. To them, what they see is reality because they don't have a family to raise them, to guide them, to let them understand that violence is merely an emotion to be explored, not practiced literally. They see it and they do it."

"If humans taught it to them, and we did, we are no better than their worse acts. Grandfather told me that."

"He sounds wise."

"I think he is," I said, "but he is not brave. None of my tribe is brave. Some of the other tribes call us the Rabbit Clan. That isn't meant as a compliment. Tell me about the Robo Rapid ritual?"

"When the moon wanes they sacrifice prisoners. They think it brings the moon back. Something to do with that movie I was talking about, the way they are programmed."

"There are only a couple of days until the moon goes away," I said. "How far are they from us?"

"Walking, they are four or five days."

"I need to leave now. I have to try and make it there before the ritual."

Nim shook his head. "If you ran all the way and never rested, you would not make it in time before the ritual. There's a lot of desert out there. If there's another storm, like this one, without a tent, supplies, you wouldn't make it. There's scorpions as well."

"I can stomp those."

"That might require a bit of work. They're the size of a Robo Rapid."

"That does change matters."

"They live in the desert near the jungle. They have their territory, same as humans, and they rarely leave it. Next problem is the jungle itself."

"The Green Place?"

He nodded. "And then you have to make your way through the jungle, and if you don't know the trails, even if you could get there in time, it's an unlikely rescue."

"So my kin will be sacrificed, and there's nothing I can do to stop it?"

"Not the way you're going about it," Nim said. "Maybe not any way you go about it."

"But there's another way?"

"Rest for now," Nim said. "Build your strength, digest that bit of food. Tomorrow morning, first light, I will show you how to get there faster, but for now, trust me and rest. You'll need all the stamina you can muster. And think it over. It's hardly worth you going. They are big and they are many and you are one and you are small."

"But I'm spry," I said. "And you are willing to help."

"Only up to a point," Nim said.

―――――――

I was exhausted and it was comfortable inside the pile of machines. The wind howled in a pleasant way around the stack of metal, and no sooner had I laid out my cloak, covered myself with the other half, I drifted down into a deep sleep.

I awoke refreshed. I stood up and moved about, pushing another pile of wood onto the dying fire.

Nim said, "Good. You slept a few hours."

I looked up to the sound of the voice. I couldn't see Nim, but there was a pile of metal legs and arms that made a kind of staircase.

"Come up," he said.

At the top of the pile was an enormous Robo Rapid head. That's where Nim's voice was coming from. I climbed up there. Nim was sitting in an old chair inside the head, looking out through the strip of glass that served as the Robo Rapid's one eye. The sun was starting to come up.

"I figured out how they worked," he said. "There was a cap the driver wore. It allowed the rider to send messages into the Robo Rapid, and it responded as best as it was able. That's how the rider drove it. He willed it. There were manual controls as well, but in time they weren't used much, and that's how I think the machines overrode the riders. I give the Robo Rapids that much credit as far as thinking goes, but it wouldn't surprise me if some human wasn't trying to override the system to his or her benefit, and that didn't work out. Instead it gave the Robo Rapids control. Backfired."

"All I care about is how I can get where I want to go at a faster pace."

"Fast toward death," he said.

"That is certainly a possibility."

Nim thought for a moment, said, "I will lead you where they are, and then I leave you on your own. I've seen all I want to see of murder and sacrifice."

———

Outside in the fresh morning light, we walked about the stack of machine parts. The sand storm of the night before had left a fine silt in the air, and the early light gave it an odd, greenish glow.

Floating in the air, about ten feet off the ground, was a large piece of metal. It was shaped somewhat like the boats I had seen in the books Grandfather had. It was a piece of alien space ship. There was a long rope tied to it, and on the ground end of the rope was a heavy and jagged piece of metal partially buried in the sand.

"That's the anchor," Nim said. "It holds it in place."

Nim was great at stating the obvious.

He led me over to a stack of metal arranged in such a way that it made a great series of steps. Nim scampered up them, and I followed. At the top Nim reached out and took hold of the rope attached to the craft, and tugged on it. The floating scrap of alien metal glided toward us, light and effortless.

"There's a rope ladder inside, fastened to a metal peg in the raft."

Nim made a nimble step off the top of the pile and onto the air raft. I followed, less nimbly. The craft was about ten feet long, with a slightly lifted front and back. The sides of it curled up. Inside the raft were four long poles and a rope ladder was coiled at the back end. Attached to another peg was a coiled rope and a spare anchor. A large knife lay next to it along with a bag full of something.

"It was naturally shaped this way," Nim said. "I don't know what part of an alien ship it was, but it makes a wonderful air boat." He pointed at the poles. "Those fasten together. I'll show you what I mean."

The raft wobbled slightly as Nim moved toward the poles. The four poles were made of metal, and Nim fastened them together to create two poles about twenty feet long.

"One is for you, and one is for me. The spare anchor is if the first one gets snagged and I have to cut it away. I can usually work it loose, though. I've had a lot of practice. The raft, no matter how much you put in it, doesn't change its air level. It's amazing. I saw this piece, thought about it, got hold of it when it floated by the Robo Rapid heap. I've had it ever since. I use it to travel about. You know, I haven't asked your name?"

"Sheann," I said.

"It's good to meet you, Sheann. I hope ours is not a short acquaintance. In that bag I've got some water, a few pieces of dried fruit. If you got to pee, don't do it in here. If you got to do the other, sure don't do it in here. We can stop and climb down, take care of that business, then climb back up."

"Got you," I said. "Don't pee or shit in the raft."

"Actually, you might want to go now. I don't like to stop once I start floating. And we have a long way to go."

I gathered my sleeping cloak and cudgel, and we climbed back onto the raft.

Nim pulled up the anchor, showed me how to utilize one of the poles, and he used the other. He sat near the front and I sat near the back. We hung our poles over opposite sides, and pushed off.

The raft went hurtling over the desert like an angry hawk. Once or twice Nim used his pole to poke another fragment of floating craft aside, and we continued on, moving much faster than I could have walked, or ran for that matter.

The sun rose upwards behind us. The air turned warmer and warmer, and finally hot. The sky was clear and blue and the lines of sand in the air had fallen to earth. From time to time, Nim would use his pole to alter our course. At first the sun was at our back, then it was to our left, and eventually it was high and centered above us.

Come late day, with the light starting to fade, we came to an oasis of palms, a much larger oasis than the one I had stopped at before. Nim, experienced and aware of our location, used his pole to change the direction of the raft until it glided toward the oasis. He came to the rear of the raft, placed the coil of rope over his shoulder, and began to swing the metal anchor fastened to it over his head with a whistling sound.

When Nim let the rope go, it sailed out and uncoiled off his shoulder. It was a thing of beauty, the way he did that. The anchor came down in the sand and began to drag, and we began to slow. I watched as the anchor made a small ditch in the earth, a ragged line with puffs of dust rising over it, and then it caught good and deep.

By the time we climbed down, not bothering with the rope ladder, using only the line attached to the anchor, the sun had mostly been swallowed and the night was a deep shade of blue. Beneath the trees we found bushes with fruit, and the water in a large pool nearby was clean and cold and tasted sweet.

Satiated, we leaned against trees and watched the stars and the partial moon rise. Soft silver light fled over the desert like a flood of water. I had only read of floods, and seen the great waters in books, but that's how it looked to me, like those photographs, deep and wet and full of shadow.

Finally, Nim spoke. "I've got no one."

"For now you have me."

"For now, and then you're gone, and you won't come back, Sheann. You won't. We could live here, under the trees by the spring. Water and fruit to eat. Animals come here to drink. There are more animals than you can imagine. We could trap them, eat them along with the fruit. It would be nice and we wouldn't be lonely."

"You mean stay here by a wet hole in the ground?"

"Is that worse than wandering the desert on a mission you can't fulfill?"

"They are my clan. I get them back, you can come live with our tribe."

Nim shook his head. "No more tribes."

———

Next morning we cast off from the oasis and into the sunlight that glimmered off the sand and toasted our faces and backs. I was a little sick about leaving. I thought about what Nim had said, and during the night I had seriously considered it. I had visions of living there, me and Nim, eating fruit and banging small animals in the head with sticks and cooking them up.

But there wasn't any way I could stay. Not with my family captured by the Robo Rapids. If Nim was right, and they had been spared for a ritual, I just might get there in time to save them.

The raft went faster this day, blown by a high wind. Once or twice, in the distance, I saw strange animals I couldn't identify. They were large and menacing looking.

We passed those great, black scorpions Nim told me about. They ran swiftly after us with cocked tails tipped with poison-dripping spikes. They were almost as tall as the height at which we flew. Nim guided us in such a way that we gave them a wide berth.

By midday there was a shift in the wind, and we had to fight to keep the raft flying the way we wanted it to go, but as the wind increased the view changed. Rising up in the distance was a dark line that stretched for miles. The line became a thickness of green trees.

It was the Green Lands.

The raft would not rise any higher, so at the edge of the jungle we had to anchor it, climb down, and enter the forest on foot. The trees were full of screeching birds and growling animals. I had my staff and my sling shot, but I wasn't confident of my ability to use either against anything larger than a rabbit or a wild dog. And as I said before, I'm an indifferent shot.

The trail Nim led me on was narrow and twisty. Snakes, like Grandfather told me about, slithered in our path and dangled from trees overhead. They were in a variety of colors and of extraordinary lengths and made my skin tingle. Nim paid them no mind.

He said, "It's the little ones you have to watch. A lot of them are poisonous and they can strike quickly. You get hit by one of those it's all over but the pain and the screaming. There's one kind, when it hits, you can't scream. Paralyzes you. You fall over and quit breathing, and that's it. Lost an uncle that way. Oh, and watch for the big cats. They sometimes like people for dinner. They can grab you and drag you off and crush your head so fast you won't even know you've left the trail."

The track widened as we continued, and at one point we came to where the jungle ceased and there was a great expanse of knee high grass. It was then that I saw the horror.

Stacked way high, shiny white in the dying sunlight, were piles of human skulls, empty eye holes growing darker as light slipped into shadow. Beyond the stack closest to us was another, and to the right and left of that stack were more. Stack after stack after stack. At the bottom of the pyramids of skulls were other bones. Leg bones, arm bones, rib cages, skeletal hands and feet, all precisely organized. But what really bothered me was a stack to my left where the heads were fresh with strips of flesh peeling off of them, curling up tight from the continual blazing of the sun. Black birds fluttered above the stacks and some lit on the skulls and picked flesh with their beaks.

"This is where the humans, or what's left of them, end up after the ritual," Nim said.

"You've seen the ritual?"

"I came here just as you have to rescue the last of my family. I failed, obviously."

"But you tried."

"I lost my courage. There's a place where it's done, and I came to that place, concealed and watching. I saw them do what they do, and I saw it done to my younger brother. Only a child, mind you. Terrible. This spot is where the refuse goes when it becomes too much. They want to keep their space clean of waste. They have enough skulls where they are. You'll see. Tonight the moon goes away. For the Robo Rapids everything human dies in the dark of the moon. It would be best not to see it, Sheann, because you can't stop it. Come back with me and live at the Oasis, or in the bodies of the Robo Rapids. It's less dangerous."

"You know I can't."

"I will take you where you want to go, where you can see, and do whatever it is you think you can do, but then I leave you."

"I won't think the less of you."

"It wouldn't matter if you did," he said.

We continued on, then, and eventually there was another clearing. In the brightening starlight I could see Robo Rapids standing tall in long rows holding wrenches and metal clubs. Nim walked directly toward them. I panicked and started to dart for the concealment of the jungle, but he grabbed my shoulder.

"These are the dead ones," he said. "Come see. I think it is their idea of a graveyard. They are their own tombstones. Look here."

Nim guided me through the legs of several of the machines, and finally he came to one and stopped. It was a big one, still blue and white, but there were patches of rust like spots on a wild dog. In its hand it clutched a large, rusted wrench.

At the back of the machine's leg, Nim grabbed a piece of metal that was dislodged, tugged gently. There was a gap in the leg, and he said, "Come inside."

Nim touched something on the wall and light climbed up the leg and into the structure above. I had heard of that kind of light, but had never experienced it. There were stairs inside the leg. He started up and I went after him. We came to where the stairs ended and walked out into a room. It was well lit, but there was a blanket over the face of the machine where the view glass was.

"I come here from time to time, during the ritual. I know what they're doing down there, but I come here because I can hide inside. I could live here all the time, I suppose. But they do come to this place now and again, with their worn out and rusted, stacking them in rows. In that way, they are thinking for themselves, I suppose. It's a sign of grief, though I think nearly all of what they do is based on programming."

"You've said that."

"I have, haven't I?"

"More than once."

"I have been reading the old manuals for the machines. This model is my favorite. It's an early one. Its manual is slightly different from the others. I've been trying to figure all the manuals for all the machines out, but this is the easiest one. I know how to turn on the lights and I can watch movies and listen to music with headphones. That way they can't hear."

Nim pointed at one of two swivel chairs near the front of the view glass. In the seats were helmets.

"Those helmets were what the riders wore to control the machines. But the machines figured out enough to reverse it, and they burned the riders' brains out.

"I know this much. Reason the machine is dead, is its battery, a big block of hard-ass plastic up there, finally lost its serious juice."

I looked up where he was pointing. Yep. A big hard-ass block of plastic was up there in the center of the Robo Rapid's head. Cables came out of the block and wound into the walls of the machine.

"It was merely shook loose. I fastened it up tight and right, but it doesn't have enough power to run very long. I can watch movies and listen to music for quite a few hours, but it won't kick the machine into motion. It seems the battery recharges itself on a low scale, but not on a big one. I let it rest, I come back, it's partially charged again. Once the ability to surge big dies, the machines are useless, and considered dead. The Robo Rapids can't figure out how to repair themselves, or give the machines the kind of energy perk they want to give them. They bring them here. But this one, like some of the others, isn't really dead, it just doesn't have enough power in its battery to operate the way it once did. Some day it won't work at all, won't even have the power for lights and music and movies. I dread that day. I enjoy coming here."

"Needs more batteries," I said.

"That's the problem, all right."

Nim went back to pointing, this time at a large square of clear plastic jutting from the wall beneath the window which was the eye of the machine.

"From what I can figure, the driver used that screen along with cameras imbedded in the machine's head to see all about. The drivers could get a view all around, could see more what was going on than just what they could see through the window. The driver could also watch movies on it during down time. Let me show you one."

"I have a more urgent situation, Nim."

"Not yet you don't. They keep the prisoners in a place that allows no opportunity to get to them unseen. Fact is, when they move them for the ritual, it is only slightly better. That will be your chance, or what chance you might have. Perhaps you should see at least part of a movie before you die."

"That's not a big mark of confidence," I said.

"There's nothing to be confident about."

Nim didn't convince me to watch a movie, but he did convince me to rest, eat and drink. I knew what he was doing. Trying to keep me away from where I wanted to go, trying to give me something to look forward to in place of putting my life on the line, hoping I'd change my mind. I appreciated it, but it wasn't going to happen. He did convince me to listen to music. He placed a helmet on my head, the headphones over my ears.

"Wait," I said, having a sudden revelation, "won't it suck my brain out or something?"

"This is merely music. It's not turned into the machines' higher functions. Listen." Nim touched something on the headphones and I could hear it. It was not the music I was used to, our tribe singing in a voice like dying dogs, beating on boxes and strumming stringed gourds, a kind of noise that made the camels bellow.

I had never heard anything so nice. As the music wormed through my head, I closed my eyes and floated away to some place I couldn't identify, and it sure felt good.

When the music ended, I lifted the helmet off my head with tears in my eyes.

"Magic," I said.

"Beethoven," he said. "Along with all the violence and war, there was beautiful music. We should have focused on feeding the Robo Rapids something beautiful instead of something ugly, and we wouldn't be living like we live, hand to mouth. Watching the movies, listening to the music, trying to figure out the Robo Rapid manuals are the only times I don't feel sad."

Eventually, I went down the stairs, and when I did, Nim turned out the light and came out after me, and we went out. I could sense he knew he was done with trying to persuade me to stay with him and live a life inside of a pile of machines, or out at the oasis, or up in the tall, standing one, listening to music and watching movies.

Nim led the way, resigned. We came to where there was a mountainous pile of dirt. Tall trees grew at the top of the pile, and starlight dribbled over the trees like sand.

Carefully we scrambled up. At the hill's summit we lay between trees and looked down into a bowl of earth. It was not so deep, but it was acres wide, and almost perfectly round. It had been dug out by machines of some sort, and not recently, because vines grew up its sides in thick leafy ropes. There were trees sprouting from the bowl here and there, grass grew up in occasional green twists, and there were flowers, their true colors I couldn't discern at night.

In the center of the bowl was a pyramid made of human skulls, as we had seen before, but this was a higher and wider pyramid. At the bottom of it was a great gap, and at the top was another. The gap on top opened onto a platform of skulls. All of the skulls were tightly fastened together in some manner, unlike those Nim had shown me before, which were loose.

Across from that pyramid was another even wider pyramid, but there was only one great gap. It ran from near the top to the bottom. The skull walls curled around on either side, and in the gap was a giant green wall. As I looked at the wall it began to glow. There was a brief flicker, and then there were images on the wall.

Nim, sensing that I was confused, whispered, "It's a larger version of the screen that was in that Robo Rapid. It was left behind by the programmers. It seems indestructible. I've tried to damage it and can't. See that large bolt at the bottom? That's the control for the Robo Rapids. Everything they are is programmed into that by their former human Overlords, or so I believe. I've tried destroying the screen, damaging the bolt. I've tried screwing it loose, but it's far too large for human hands and the wrenches I have. Even if I had a wrench the right size, it would be too big for me to handle, and if

I could handle it, it would be too tight to turn. It was screwed in place by Robo Rapid hands, and it isn't coming out. As long as the bolt and that screen survive, the information the programmers gave the Robo Rapids will be received and interpreted by them in the manner their owners wanted. I think the Overlords used to change the bolt out from time to time, give them different programmable images. Now there are no Overlords. What was there when the Robo Rapids took over plays again and again. They copy humans in many ways, and one of those ways is making the pyramids they see on the screen, piling up dead humans the way the humans used to pile up deactivated Robo Rapids. Them gathering here, that's some kind of programmed ritual."

I paid attention to the images on the screen. The images were of people, all men, and they were moving. They appeared to be talking, but there was no sound coming out of their mouths. They wore loin cloths, headdresses and cloaks made of colorful feathers. They were climbing stone steps on a pyramid, its design not too different from the one made of skulls across from the screen.

Near the top of the pyramid, where they stopped, was an opening and a platform of stone reminiscent of the platform of skulls the Robo Rapids had built. One of the men, the one with the tallest and brightest headdress, came to stand before a block of stone.

A man was brought out by four others. They tossed him on the stone and held him to it. The man with the tall headdress raised his face and hands to the sky, one of those hands was holding a black blade of what looked like glass. Words were spoken, but still there was no sound. The hand with the knife came down, there was a spurt of blood as it entered the man's chest, and then his heart was cut free, and the man—a priest, I suppose, pulled the heart out of the man's chest, held it out, still beating, for all to see. Below the pyramid a crowd of faces lifted, stared contentedly at the man holding the heart, and then the screen went black.

"It's not real," Nim said. "It's a movie. No one dies. It's all makeup and such. But it's real to the machines. It's their religion. There's another segment that will come up shortly on the screen. It's a battle scene, these warriors going to war, banging their enemies in the head with clubs. So you see, the Robo Rapids are imitating what they see. Aztecs from a movie. Do you know who the Aztecs were?"

"Grandfather told me what he had read about them. I remember some of it."

The screen popped bright again. There were images of war this time. Men rushing against each other, swinging clubs, killing. It looked real, even if it wasn't.

And then there was a creaking sound, along with groaning and hissing and whistling. The dreaded sounds of the machines. Several of them came out of the pyramid across from the screen, walking mostly, but some were on wheels or treads.

On their big heads they wore ridiculous head bands with awkward arrangements of leaves in place of feathers. They wore cloaks raggedly stitched together from what appeared to be human skin. The cloaks were decorated with a smattering of feathers and leaves. They were carrying a half-dozen cages made of wood and metal and plastic. They hoisted them on litters supported by long poles and vines.

Through the plastic walls of the cages I could see people. In one of the cages I saw my brother and sister, their hands pressed against the plastic, their faces had collapsed in a way that made them seem much older. They were nude and filthy. They didn't see me. They were not looking up, but the sight of them both cheered and depressed me at the same time.

I watched as they were carried to the base of the pyramid.

As the moments passed the stars were not enough, and lights positioned in the pyramids and around the earthen bowl, popped on. More Robo Rapids came along a trail that cut its way through the jungle. I counted twenty-five machines, moving down the sides of the bowl and on toward its center. Counting the ones that had come out of the pyramid, that made thirty-six.

Some of them were large and some were small and a few were sad-ass ragged. One dragged a leg, another's arm hung loose to its side. A few had heads that were cocked too far to one side or leaned too far back or too far forward. Nearly all were pocked with marks from blowing sand and dents from attacks. Over the years the Robo Rapids had taken a beating in the alien wars, and then in their battles to take over the humans. Their days were numbered, but the days they had left were way too many, because right now I was looking down and seeing my brother and sister in that cage and feeling watery inside. It was no different from the night the Robo Rapids had come and I had peeked around the edge of a dune and watched my mother and father die, saw Jacob and Della stolen away. I was no more able to do anything about it now than I was then.

I understood then what Nim had said about realizing there was nothing he could do when his own family was being killed. I had certainly rated myself higher than my actual ability. I turned to say as much to Nim, but he was gone.

———

The first group of Robo Rapids, those who had come from the bottom of the pyramid, ceremoniously climbed or rolled over the skull steps, and climbed to the platform above. The skull structure trembled with their weight. Up they went, heads bent, arms outstretched as if reaching for something. When they arrived at the upper platform, out of the opening came a smaller machine on treads. It held in one of its metal hands a knife. Small in its large hand, but for me it would easily have been the size of a sword.

The knife was given to the Robo Rapid with the tallest headdress. His face plate was rectangular and red as blood and glowed as if heated by fire. Red Face stood at the edge of the platform where a stack of skulls had been made into an altar similar to the one on the screen. Out of Red Face came a loud squeak, and then a kind of humming. Down below all the Robo Rapids bent to one knee, and those that couldn't due to injuries, dipped their heads or sagged on wheels and treads.

Red Face, their priest, raised his arms high, the knife in one hand, tilted his head to the heavens. The lights in and around the bowl skipped along his blade, made it shimmer and appear momentarily to be made of smoke.

One of the cages was opened below and there were yells from the humans. Robo Rapid hands reached in and pulled them out, as easy as humans grabbing up mice. The humans screamed and wriggled in the machines' grasps, but it was a useless struggle.

The metal monsters carried their victims up the pyramid steps, making a slow ritual of it. They were placed before the altar in a line and held firm by those metal hands. They were all nude, and stood trembling in the cool moonlight. The first in line, a young boy, was pushed forward. Red Face grabbed him and lifted him onto the altar.

The smaller machines on either side grabbed the boy's arms and feet and Red Face brought the knife down. Blood gushed up and turned bright in the glow of the lights in the bowl. The blood seemed to fall in slow-motion droplets as it splashed onto Red Face's metal body. It ran in rivulets down the steps made of skulls.

Red Face, using metal fingers like tweezers, reached into the poor child's wrecked chest and pinched out the beating heart. Red Face held it up and let the warm blood drip down onto its blood-red eye. Finally, Red Face dropped the heart. It went bouncing down the steps to the machines below. Then Red Face beheaded the body with the knife and gave the head to an assistant who tossed it like a broken bowl into a large container made of metal.

Red Face hoisted the decapitated body off the altar, flung it down the steps, sent it bouncing into the waiting Robo Rapids who fought for position and a clutch at the corpse. They easily ripped it apart. Those that managed to grab a piece of it, rubbed the bloody meat over their metal bodies and faces. More of the same followed with the screaming prisoners on the pyramid platform.

I slid down the hill away from the horrors, bent over and threw up. I began to weep silently. I was within touching distance of my brother and sister, but if I were to attempt anything at all, I would be captured and marched up the pyramid to have my heart torn out; and still my brother and sister would not be saved.

I was pondering all this when I heard a metallic screech followed by a thudding noise. I cautiously climbed back up the hill and took a peek.

It was coming down the opposite side of the hill, slipping a little, falling finally, getting up precariously. It was the great machine Nim and I had been inside of and it was moving about.

When it had managed a solid standing position, I could see through the glass that Nim was strapped into one of the rider seats and the helmet was on his head. I knew then that he had not abandoned me, but decided he could take over the machine somehow, and that was exactly what he had done. In one hand Nim's Robo Rapid still held the wrench, and in the other was something I couldn't quite make out.

Nim's machine moved like a person hit too hard in the head. All the Robo Rapids had turned toward it, including Red Face. All activity had stopped.

I knew this was my moment. Clutching my walking stick, I slid down the side of the bowl where the pyramids and Robo Rapids were, skidded in on my butt, then glanced up to see what was happening so I could judge how much time I had left, if any. I doubted Nim and his Robo Rapid could hold their attention long. One glance back and they would see me.

As I rushed toward the cages, holding a finger to my mouth to insist on silence, I opened the box with Jacob and Della in it by using my stick to push up the large latch. The gate to the cage swung open. Everyone inside, including my kin, filed out. I could see Della and Jacob wanted to come to me, but I pointed up the hill with repeated, sharp gestures, and up they all went, scrambling as silently as they could manage, attempting to make the lip of the bowl.

I moved to the next cage, gave quick attention to Nim as I used my cane to move the latch. I assumed I would be more than a little lucky if I could unlatch the other two cages before I was spotted, but I was damn sure determined to give it a try.

And then Nim's machine began to dance.

It skipped sideways, tucked its arms and jutted out its elbows, bent its knees and stepped right and then left, stepping high. I could hear music now, coming from inside his machine, piped out through a gap somewhere.

It was loud music, and quite different from any I had ever heard, harsh and heavy as lead. All the Robo Rapids watched as Nim skipped his machine across the bowl, nodded, spun, and then leaped toward the giant screen. Nim's Robo Rapid hit the earth on its metal belly, scuttled forward until it came to the great bolt beneath the giant screen. It snapped its wrench onto the bolt, and turned. The music in his Robo Rapid ceased. The bolt Nim's machine was turning snapped free. I understood what was in the machine's other hand. A new bolt.

The Robo Rapids were starting to come loose of their stupor. They moved toward Nim, swinging wrenches and clubs at his machine's body. There were clangs and clatters, but even as the blows rained down on Nim's Robo Rapid, denting it in spots, it was screwing in that bolt with ferocious speed and dexterity.

Suddenly, the air was filled with the sound of new music, and it was coming from that giant screen.

The hills were alive with it.

At least that's what the song the lady was singing said. I could hear her but there was nothing to see, and then the screen sputtered and spat out the vision of a beautiful woman, cleaner than anyone I had ever seen, spinning on a beautiful hill of flowers and green grass. Her voice was high and powerful, and I know no other way to say it—kind.

All the Robo Rapids began to move slowly toward the screen. Down from the pyramid came Red Face, stepping lightly, and then spinning, lost its footing and went tumbling down into a mass of clunking metal.

The lady on the screen continued to sing and twirl. The very fiber of the air filled with her voice. I felt as if I could reach out and take hold of the notes and stuff them in my mouth, and I wanted to. There was something about them that made me think they would taste sweet.

Nim's machine stood, started to spin, and all the Robo Rapids began to spin in response to the programmed bolt in the great screen. Nim had been right. Now they were reprogrammed, singing and dancing and lifting their heads to the dark place where the moon should be.

Tomorrow night the moon would be back, and from the machines designed point of view, they would have danced it back into creation.

I was going from cage to cage now, freeing the prisoners, and up the hill they fled, like a reverse flow of fleshy lava. The machines weren't trying to stop them. The prisoners were no longer a consideration. Up they went, over the hill, and away from the sound of music, while down in that bowl the machines twirled and whirled.

Nim had complete control of his machine. He danced it up the side of the bowl, slipping and sliding, but making its way. When it reached the top, it danced into the night and out of sight, surprisingly graceful, but with a clank and a rattle and a hiss of hot air.

The prisoners ran through the jungle. They ran real fast. It was all I could do to follow, so ecstatic were they to be free. They ran through briars and thickets of greenery and dangling vines. They tripped and fell and rose up again.

Where the jungle broke the escapees fell to their knees, breathing deeply, some of them throwing up. They were weak from their time in the cages, from the fear they had felt, from the horror they had seen. I was not much better.

I urged them on, not entirely certain of the permanency of the Robo Rapids' current attitude. Across the green grass we went, and into the jungle, and down a narrow trail, frightening animals as we went. Startled birds awoke and took briefly to the sky and found new nesting places, snakes slithered quickly.

It took some time, but finally we broke out of the jungle completely and onto the edge of the grass that led to the desert. We stopped there. I built a fire of scattered wood, and then pointed out the fruit. The prisoners, who were a large, smelly wad of humanity, attacked the trees and dragged the fruits from them and ate savagely. It was almost frightening to watch them eat, and that included Della and Jacob. They were famished. I was surprised they weren't dead. What had they eaten or drank during captivity?

Later my brother and sister would say they were kept in a deep pit with an open sky, and the rain came down and it filled the pit up to their ankles. They drank the water and it made them sick, but it was the way they survived. And then the machines brought fruit and shoved it over the edge of the pit, and the only way to eat was to scramble and claw for it. Many had died.

That was then, and this was now, and when they finished eating, mostly too fast, many of them threw up. They lay out on the grass, exhausted. Then came the clumping and groaning and hissing of a giant machine.

Everyone staggered to their feet, certain their escape had ended.

It was Nim's machine, its face plate glowing. It pushed through the trees, bending them back, shoving into the clearing, and then it stopped.

"It's all right," I said. "It's all right. This machine is controlled by a friend."

That reassurance didn't keep the prisoners from scattering into the jungle, a few running wildly out into the desert. Only my brother and sister remained, and there was nothing to be done for it. The machine stopped moving and the face plate went dark. Nim came out from the opening in the back of the Robo Rapid's leg.

He staggered as he came. His head had two black marks at the temples where the helmet had fit. Thin, white smoke curled up from them. I ran to him and hugged him. "That was smart," I said. "Except, has it…hurt you?"

"Stunned me a bit. Couldn't have worn it much longer. Now, every time I see something bright I want to shit. I think that'll pass. Hope so. If not, it could be awkward."

"We'll get you some dark glasses," I said. "I've seen such a thing."

My brother and sister had wadded into a knot behind me. "It's okay," I said. "This is Nim. He's a friend."

Still, they clung to me, peeking around at the man with the black burns on his temples.

"It was what you said," Nim said. "About needing more batteries. It was so simple I had totally overlooked it. I kept thinking I had to power the main battery up, but I gathered batteries from several of the other machines. It was easy and quick, and it fired them up. I fed the movie I liked, *The Sound of Music*, into the machine's storage unit, which is one of those bolts. I had my Robo Rapid unscrew the bolt and take it with us. Well, you know the rest."

"You're a hero."

"I had a big machine, and all you had was you, and you went down there and threw the latches, knowing full well you might be killed. But you did it. What I did, compared to that, was nothing."

Nim wobbled and dropped to his knees.

"Okay, I see green and blue polka dots. Does anyone else see polka dots?"

He fell forward on his face.

We slept inside the giant Robo Rapid, and when we awoke the next morning I was surprised that nothing had killed us, for I had dreamed of snakes and Robo Rapids, and hungry cats with a taste for human flesh.

Nim was much better. He said he wasn't seeing polka dots anymore and had lost the urge to shit himself, bright lights or no bright lights. We put together some fruit and cut some gourds loose, made water containers, and set out for where Nim and I had left the floater.

It was still there. Della and Jacob climbed up the rope rapidly, and then me and Nim. Off we sailed, in the early morning light, across the desert sand, the Green Place flowing away rapidly behind us.

In time we came to the floating debris, and in greater time we came to my tribe. They had moved back toward the desert, continuing what they knew as if nothing had happened.

It was a joyous reunion. Grandfather was so excited to see Della and Jacob, as well as myself. He started to cry and cried nearly continuously for two days straight. When we told them that the Robo Rapids were dancing, and wouldn't make war again, they praised the gods, as if we had had nothing to do with it.

I spent the next few days recounting what had happened. It was a story that the tribe never seemed to tire of.

There is not much more to tell of my adventures with the Robo Rapids, but there is this: I had become quite fond of Nim. One day, before the moon went black, we gathered our things and said our goodbyes, and sailed away on our alien raft. Not to the oasis Nim had suggested, but back to the jungles of the Green Place.

We tied the raft off at the edge of the jungle and eased our way to the great bowl where the Robo Rapids had danced. Down below there was nothing but the pyramids and the huge screen. There were a few Robo Rapids that had played out and lay stone-still on the ground.

As the night darkened, the lights in the bowl came on and the screen came on and the lady sang and the lady danced. From the far side of the bowl I heard them. It was that distinct clinking and clacking, the raw hissing of air. Robo Rapids, without headdresses now. There were only a few. They made their way down a trail and into the bowl, and as the lady sang, they spun and made noises beneath the blacked-out moon, some of them stumbling, some of them falling flat, unable to rise. Time had turned heavy and had fallen down on them at last.

We lived there on the edge of the jungle, slept up high in our alien raft. We gathered fruit and drank from sweet water, and now and again we killed an animal and ate its meat. It was a good life, an easy life.

Now and again, when the moon goes thin, we go to hear the lady sing and watch her dance, and to see the Robo Rapids come down from the hill into the automatically lit-up bowl of earth.

Each time there were fewer of them, as Nim predicted, and in time there were none that moved, just heaps of metal on the vine-covered floor of the scooped out bowl. But still we came on moonless nights to watch the bowl automatically light up and see the woman dance and hear her sing. We also watched complete movies in the machine Nim had used, out there on the edge of the jungle. I loved them. But that machine is also dying, all of its batteries going to seed. Soon the movies will be nothing more than memories stored in our heads. Even the bolt with its endless loop will eventually die. Already the lights in the bowl are starting to dim.

Sometimes we go to visit my brother and sister. Grandfather is long gone now, his bones covered over by the sand. Our tribe has grown and prospered, and there are other tribes roaming the desert free of fear of the Robo Rapids. There are tribes starting to gather on the fringes of the jungle as well, and their numbers are multiplying.

There is plenty of room, food, water, shelter, and all the things that are needed to make life a pleasure.

It is a paradise.

And yet, among the tribes there are rumors of war.

All I Care About is You

Joe Hill

Limitation makes for power. The strength of the genie comes of his being confined in a bottle.
—Richard Wilbur

1.

She grabs the brake and power-drifts the Monowheel to a stop for a red light, just before the overpass that spans the distance between bad and worse.

Iris doesn't want to look up at the Spoke and can't help herself. The habit of longing is hard to quit and there's a particularly good view of it from this corner. She knows by now certain things are out of reach, but her *blood* doesn't seem to know it. When she allows herself to remember the promises her father made a year ago, her blood seems to *throb* inside her with excitement. Pitiful.

She finds herself staring up at it, that jagged scepter of steel and blued chrome lancing the dingy clouds, and hates herself a little. *Let that go*, she tells herself with a certain contempt, and forces herself to look away from the Spoke, to stare blindly ahead. Her idiot heart is beating too fast.

Iris doesn't notice the not-alive not-dead boy watching her from the corner. She never notices him.

He *always* notices her. He knows where she's been and where she's going. He knows better than she knows herself.

2.

"Got you something," her father says. "Close your eyes."

Iris does as she's told. She holds her breath, too. And there it is again, that thrill in the blood. Hope—stupid, childish hope—fills her like a trembling, fragile soap bubble, effervescent and weightless. It feels like it would be a terrible jinx to even allow herself to think the word: *Hideware.*

She isn't going to the top of the Spoke tonight, she knows that. She isn't going to be drinking Sparklefroth with her friends on the top of the world. But maybe the old man has a trick up his sleeve. Maybe he had a couple tokens socked away for an important day. Maybe the former Resurrection Man has one more miracle to work. Her blood believes all these things might be possible.

He sets something heavy in her lap, something far too heavy to be Hideware. That fantastic bubble of hope pops and collapses inside her.

"Okay," he says. "You c-can look."

His stammer disturbs her. He didn't stammer BEFORE, didn't stammer when he was still with her mother and still in the Murdergame. She opens her eyes.

He didn't even wrap it. It's something the size of a bowling ball, shoved in a crinkly bag. She peels the sack open and looks down at a cloudy emerald globe.

"Crystal ball?" she asks. "Oh, Daddy, I always wanted to know my future."

What tripe. She doesn't have a future…not one worth thinking about.

The old man leans forward on his bench, hands clasped between his knees so they won't tremble. They didn't tremble BEFORE either. He sucks a liquid breath through the plastic tubing up his nose. The respirator pumps and hisses. "There's a m-mermaid in there. You've wanted one since you were small."

She wanted a lot of things when she was small. She wanted Microwing shoes so she could run six inches off the ground. She wanted gills for swimming in the underground lagoons. She wanted whatever Amy Pasquale and Joyce Brilliant got for their birthdays, and her parents always saw that it was so, but that was BEFORE.

Something swishes, takes a slow turn in the center of the spinach colored sludge, then drifts to the glass to gaze up at her. She is so repulsed by the sight, she almost shoves the sphere out of her lap.

"Wow," she says. "*Wow.* I love it. I really did always want one."

He bows his head and squeezes his eyes shut. A tingle of shock prickles across her chest. He's about to cry.

"I know it isn't what you wanted. What we t-t-talked about," he says.

She reaches across the table and clasps his hand, feels like she might start to cry herself. "It's perfect."

Only she's wrong. He wasn't struggling against tears. He was fighting a yawn. He surrenders to it, covers his mouth with the back of his free hand. He doesn't seem to have heard her.

"I wish we could've done all the things we talked about. The S-sp-spuh-Spoke. R-Ride in a big buh-b-bubble together. These fuckin' medical Clockworks, kid. They're like hyenas pulling apart the corpse for the last goodies. The medical Clockworks ate your b-birthday c-cake this year, kiddo. We'll see if I can't do a little better for you next year." He shakes his head in a good humored way. "I have to c-c-crap out for a while. A man c-can only take so much excitement when he's g-got half a working heart." He opens his eyes to a sleepy squint. "You know about m-mermaids. When they fall in love, they sing. Which I understand. Same thing happened to me."

"It did?" she asks.

"After you were b-born," he turns sideways, stretches himself out on the bench, struggles with another yawn, "I sang to you every night. Sang until I was all sung out." He shuts his eyes, head pillowed on a pile of grubby laundry. "*Happy birthday to you. Happy b-birthday to you. Happy b-b-b-buh-birthday sweet Iris. Hap-p-puh-p-p—*" he inhales, a wet, clogged, struggling sound, and begins to cough. He thumps his chest a few times, turns his face away from her, shrugs, and sighs.

He is asleep by the time Iris reaches the top of the ladder, climbing out of his pod and leaving him behind.

She shuts the hatch, one of eight thousand in the great, dim, clammy, cavernous hive. The air smells of old pipes and urine.

Iris left her Monowheel next to her father's pod on a mag-lock, because here in the Hives, anything that isn't bolted down will vanish the moment you take your eyes off it. She climbs up onto the big red leather seat of her 'wheel and flips the ignition four or five times before realizing it isn't going to start. Her first thought is that somehow the battery has gone dead. But it hasn't gone dead. It's just gone. Someone yanked it out of the vapor-drive and strolled off with it.

"*Happy birthday to me,*" she sings, a little off-key.

3.

A cannon-train approaches, making that cannon-train sound, a whispery whistle that builds and builds until suddenly it passes below her with a concussive blast. Iris loves the way it hits her, loves to be struck through by the shriek and boom, so all the breath is slammed from her body. Not for the first time she wonders what would be left of her if she jumped off the stone balustrade. Iris fantasizes about being pulverized into a fine warm spray and raining gently upon her rotten, selfish mother and sorry, hopeless father, wetting their faces in red tears.

She sits on the balustrade, swinging her feet over the drop, the smooth green ball of sludge resting in her lap. There'll be another train in a few minutes.

When she looks into her poisoned crystal ball, it isn't the future she sees, but the past. This time last year she was fifteen, with fifteen of her best friends, fifteen hundred feet underground in the Furnace

Club. Magma bubbled beneath the BluDiamond floor. They all traipsed barefoot to feel the warmth of it, guttering streams of liquid gold not half an inch from their heels. The waiter was a floating Clockwork named Bub, a polished copper globe who hovered here and there, opening the bright lid of his head to offer each new course. In the throbbing red light, the faces of the other girls glowed with sweat and excitement, and their laughter echoed off the warm rock walls. They looked as roasted as the piglets they were served for the main course.

Her friends were all drunk on one another by the end of it and there was a lot of hugging and smooching. They said it was the best birthday party ever. Iris got carried away by all the good feeling and promised them next year would be even better. She said they would ride the elevator to the top of the Spoke to see the stars—the ACTUAL stars—above the cloudscape. They would drink Sparklefroth and electrocute each other with happiness. They would take the long dreamy plunge back to earth together in Drop Bubbles. And after, they would all mask themselves in Hideware and go down into the Carnival District—which was forbidden to anyone under sixteen—and everyone who saw them in their expensive new faces would fall in love with them.

Something stirs in the cloudy green globe. The mermaid looms up from the mucus-hued shadows and boggles out at her. The girl-fish is little more than a grotesque pink slug with a face and waving, mossy green hair.

"You might want to do something adorable," she says, "while you've got the chance."

A black string of poop squirts from a hole above her tail fin. The mermaid gawps, as if astonished by the functions of her own body.

A hoop of eldritch jade light flares in her right eye, half blinding her, signaling an incoming message. She pinches her thumb and index finger together, as if squeezing a bug to death. Words appear in fey emerald letters, seeming to hover three feet from her face, a trick of the messaging lens that she puts in her eye first thing every morning, even before she brushes her teeth.

JOYCE B: WE HAVE PLANS FOR YOU.

AMY P: EVIL PLANS.

JOYCE B: WE'RE GETTING YOU INTO THE CARNIVALS TONIGHT. IT HAS BEEN ORDAINED.

Iris shuts her eyes, rests her forehead against the cool glass of the aquaball.

"Can't," she says, squeezing her thumb and index finger together to SEND.

JOYCE B: DON'T MAKE US FORCE YOU INTO A SACK & DRAG YOU OUT KICKING & SCREAMING.

AMY P: IN A SACK. KICKING. SCREAMING.

Iris says, "My mom's new guy is off work in an hour and Mom wants me home for cake and presents. I guess they got me some big deal gift that won't wait."

This is a lie. Iris will decide what the big deal gift was later. It will have to be something that could only be used once, something no one can prove she didn't get. Maybe she will tell her friends she went on an hallucication to the lunar surface and spent the night in Archimedes Station, playing Moon Quidditch with the Archimedes Owls.

JOYCE B's reply appears in lurid fire: HIDEWARE??? DO YOU THINK YOUR MOM GOT YOU A NEW FACE?

Iris opens her mouth, closes it, opens it again. "We won't know until I unwrap it, will we?"

The moment it's out of her mouth, she doesn't know why she said it, wishes she could unSEND.

No. She knows why she said it. Because it feels good to act like she's still one of them. That she has everything they have and always will. That she isn't falling behind.

AMY P: I HOPE YOU GOT AN "OPHELIA" BECAUSE IT WILL MAKE JOYCE JEALOUS AND I LIKE TO WATCH JOYCE FAKE SMILE AT PEOPLE WHEN SHE'S MISERABLE.

The Ophelia has been out for just two months and might've been too expensive even when her father was making tokens by the shovel-load in the Murdergame.

"It probably won't be the Ophelia," Iris says, then immediately wishes she could rephrase.

JOYCE B: THERE'S NOTHING WRONG WITH A BASIC "GIRL NEXT DOOR." THAT'S WHAT AMY HAS AND I'M NOT EMBARRASSED TO GO OUT WITH HER. I'M NOT PROUD, BUT I'M NOT EMBARRASSED.

AMY P: WHATEVER IT IS, YOU'RE FREE BY 2100 BECAUSE YOUR MOM ALREADY SAID YOU'LL MEET US AT THE SOUTH ENTRANCE TO THE CARNIVALS. I MESSAGED WITH HER THIS MORNING. SO GO HOME AND SCARF CAKE AND UNWRAP YOUR SEXY NEW FACE AND GET READY TO MEET US.

JOYCE B: IF YOU DO GET AN "OPHELIA," I WANT TO WEAR IT FOR AT LEAST A LITTLE WHILE, BECAUSE I COULDN'T BEAR IT IF YOU WERE MORE AMAZING THAN ME.

"I could never be more amazing than you," Iris says and Joyce and Amy disconnect.

Below her, another cannon-train booms past.

4.

The disaster happens two-thirds of the way across the overpass.

The Monowheel is lightweight, but big, bigger than her, and walking it home is awkward business. It's a drunken giant who keeps leaning on her, or trying to sit down in the road. She leans in to guide it with a hand on the control stick, her other hand clutching the aquaball to her side. The overpass has a gentle arch to it and the 'wheel wants to speed up as soon as she's on the downward slope. She jogs to keep up with it, huffing for breath. It tilts toward her. The inner chrome hoop bangs her head. She makes a little sound of pain, lifts her free hand to press a palm to the hurt place, only to remember she doesn't have a free hand. The aquaball slips free and strikes the sidewalk with a glassy crack!

Good, she thinks. *Smash*.

But it doesn't smash, it *rolls*, with a grinding, droning kind of music, weaving this way and that, hopping the curb and trundling into the road. A vapordrive Hansom cab on gold razorwheels whines shrilly along the cross street and the aquaball disappears beneath it. Iris tenses, with a certain pleasure, anticipating the crunch and the loud splash. But when the Hansom flashes past, the murky green globe is impossibly still rolling, undamaged, along the far sidewalk. Iris has never in all her life so wanted to see something crushed.

Instead, a kid puts his foot out and stops it.

That kid.

In one sense, Iris has never seen him before. In another, she has seen him a hundred times, on her way to her father's, has glimpsed him from her Monowheel, this kid with his too-cool-for-school slouch, in a gray wool baseball cap and gray wool coat that has seen better days. He is always here, hanging out against the wall in front of a closed Novelty.

He doesn't do anything more than stop the ball with his toe. Doesn't look up the road to see who dropped it, doesn't bend down to pick it up.

She steers the Monowheel over to him. It's easier now that she has two hands to guide it along.

"You're too kind. And I do mean that literally. You just rescued the world's crummiest birthday present," she says.

He doesn't reply.

She leans the Monowheel against the hitching post along the curb and bends to get the aquaball. She hopes it's cracked, squirting its guts out. What a pleasure it would be to watch that gruesome slug—that sardine-sized parody of a woman—swimming frantically around as the water level falls. Not a mark on it, though. She doesn't know why she hates it so much. It isn't the mermaid's fault it's ugly, trapped, unasked for, unwanted.

"Shoot. I was hoping it would shatter into a thousand pieces. A girl can't catch a break."

This doesn't even earn her a chuckle and she casts a quick, annoyed glance into his face—when she's witty Iris expects to be appreciated—and sees it at last. He isn't a kid at all. He's a Clockwork, an old one, with a smiling, moon-like face of crackled ceramic. His chest is a scratched case of plasteel. Within is a coil of cloudy vinyl tubing where intestines belong, brass pipettes for bones, a basket of gold wires filled almost to the top with silver tokens instead of a stomach. His heart is a matte black vapor-drive.

A steel plate mounted to one side of his heart says: COIN-OP FRIEND! LOYAL FAITHFUL COMPANION AND CONFIDANT. NEED HELP WITH GROCERIES? CAN LIFT UP TO ONE TON. KNOWS 30 CARD GAMES, SPEAKS ALL LANGUAGES, KEEPS SECRETS. A TOKEN FOR 30 MINUTES OF **ABSOLUTE DEVOTION**. GIRLS: LEARN HOW TO KISS FROM A PERFECT GENTLEMAN WHO WILL TELL NO TALES. BOYS: PRACTICE THE ANCIENT ART OF PUGILISM ON HIS ALMOST INDESTRUCTABLE SHELL! THIS CLOCKWORK NOT RATED FOR ADULT/MATURE USE. Someone has scratched a cartoon penis below this last sentence.

Iris has not played with a Clockwork since she was small, not since Talk-To-Me-Tabitha, her childhood beloved, and Tabitha was perhaps a century more advanced. This thing is an antique, one of the novelties from the shuttered store directly behind him, likely planted on the street as an advertisement. A moldie-oldie from the days of Google and chunky VR headsets and Florida.

No one could steal him. His back is pressed to a magnetic charge plate installed in the brick wall. Iris is no longer sure he intentionally stopped the aquaball, suspects his foot was just there, and halting her runaway mermaid only lucky accident. Or *un*lucky accident; a lucky accident would've been if it imploded under the razorwheels of the Hansom.

Iris turns her back on him and looks despairingly at the Monowheel she still has to push another half mile. The thought of steering it along the road makes her unpleasantly aware of the sweater sticking to her sweaty back.

Need help with groceries? Can lift up to one ton.

She swivels back, digs out her tokens—she has exactly two—and pushes first one, then the other into the slot on the Clockwork's chest. Silver credits clatter into the enormous pile of tokens in his stomach.

The vaporware heart in his chest expands and contracts with an audible thud. The numbers above the chrome plate on his chest make a ratcheting noise, and roll over with a series of rapid clicks, to read 00:59:59.

And the seconds begin to tick down.

5.

He knew she would pay long before she dropped her tokens, knew when her back was still turned to him, just from the way she looked at her Monowheel, and how her shoulders slumped at the sight of it. Body language says more than words ever do. And his processor, which is lethargic by the standards of modern computing, is still fast enough to complete two million clock cycles before she can get her hand out of her pocket with the coins in them. That's enough time to read and reread the complete works of Dickens.

Her body temperature is elevated and she's sweating from labor, but also from a frayed mood. The command line, which fills him always like breath, compels him to supply comfort with a bit of easy cleverness.

"You got three questions," he says, selecting for random grammatical errors. Informal speech always plays well with the young. "Let me answer them in order. First: what's my name? Chip. It's a joke. But it's also really my name."

The girl says, "What do you mean, it's a—"

He taps one finger to his temple, indicating the logic boards hidden behind his ceramic face, and she smiles.

"*Chip*. Glad to meet you. What are my other two questions?"

"If you have to pay me, how can I really be your friend? The company that built me programmed me with one directive: for the next fifty-nine minutes, all I care about is you. I won't judge you and I won't lie to you. You are Aladdin and I am the genie. I'll execute any wish that's within my powers and isn't strictly forbidden by custom or law. I can't steal. I can't beat anyone up. There are certain adult functions I cannot perform owing to the 2072 Human-Clockwork obscenity laws…laws that have actually been repealed, but remain a part of my OS."

"What's that mean?"

The command line impels a crude, comic response. Her social profile suggests a high probability that this will be well received.

"I can't eat pussy," he says. "Or take one up the ass."

"Holy shit," she says, a blush scalding her cheeks. Her embarrassment confirms he appeals to her. Physiology is confession.

"I have no tongue, so I cannot lick."

"This got real, very quickly."

"I have no butthole, so I cannot—"

"Got it. Never even crossed my mind to ask. What was my third question?"

"Yes, of course I can carry your Monowheel. What happened to it?"

"Someone ripped the battery out. Can you carry it all the way to the Stacks?"

He unbolts himself from the charging plate, free for the first time in sixteen days. She unlocks the Monowheel from the hitching post. He grips the inner rail and lifts all 408.255 kilograms off the ground, slips it on his shoulder. The tilt of her head implies satisfaction, while her body language suggests the initial pleasure at solving a problem is fading, to be replaced by some other source of distress and exhaustion. *Probably*. Emotions cannot be known with any certainty, only hypothesized. A darting look of anxiety might suggest inner turmoil or merely the need to urinate. Apparently clever, witty remarks often shroud despair, while the statement "I'm dying," hardly ever indicates life-threatening physical trauma. Without certainty, he follows the routines most likely to produce comfort and pleasure.

"I've answered three of your questions, now you have to answer three of mine, fair?"

"I guess," she says.

"Got a name?"

"Iris Ballard."

Within a quarter second of learning her name, he has gathered every bit of information he can find on her in the socialverse, collecting half a gigabyte of unimportant trivia, and a single ten-month-old news report that might matter very much.

"I've known one Rapunzels, two Zeldas, and three Cleopatras, but I've never met an Iris."

"Do you remember *every*one you've met? No, forget it. Of course you do. You probably have tera-bytes of memory you haven't used. What was Rapunzel like?"

"She had a shaved head. I didn't ask why."

Iris laughs. "Okay. What else?"

"You don't have a household Clockwork to help you with your busted Monowheel?"

Her smile slips. The subject is red-flagged as a threat to her approval. An algorithm ponders the possibilities, decides she is financially disadvantaged and her lack of funds is a source of discomfort. The condition of poverty is new to her, probably a result of the events described in the unfortunate news story.

"I had a Talk-To-Me-Tabitha when I was little," she says. "I talked to her all day, from when I got home till when I went to bed. My Dad used to come in at 10 PM and say he was going to have to take her away and stick her in a closet if I didn't go to sleep. Nothing made me shut up faster than that. I hated the idea of him putting her in the closet where she'd be all alone. But then she auto-upgraded and after that she was always talking about how we could have a lot more fun together if I bought a

Talk-To-Me-Tabitha Terrier or Talk-To-Me-Tabitha Smartglasses. She started working advertisements and offers into conversation. It got really gross so I started doing intentionally mean things to her. I'd step on her if she was lying on the floor. One day my Dad saw me swinging her against the wall and took her away. He resold her on Auctionz to teach me a lesson, even though I cried and cried. Honestly, that might be the only time in my life my father punished me for anything."

Her tone and expression suggest irritation, which he can't fathom. A lack of parental discipline should be a source of at least mild contentment, not disapproval. He marks this statement for further evaluation and will watch her for other signs of psychological malformation. Not that this will incline him to be any less devoted to her. He collected hundreds of tokens from a schizophrenic man named Dean. Dean believed he was being followed by a cabal of ballet dancers who intended to kidnap and castrate him. Chip dutifully watched for women in tutus and swore to defend Dean's genitals. It was all a long time ago.

"You had one more thing you were going to ask me?" she says. "Hopefully it won't be whether I'd like to take advantage of a very special offer. Marketing ruins the illusion that you're vaguely person-like."

He marks her contempt for advertising. Nothing to be done about it—he is required to peddle his own services later—but he marks it anyway.

"What are you doing to celebrate your birthday?" he asks. "Besides spending an hour with me, which is, I admit, going to be hard to top."

She stops walking. "How do you know it's my birthday?"

"You said."

"When did I say?"

"When you picked up your runaway fish."

"That was before I paid you."

"I know. I'm still aware of things when my meter isn't running. I still think. Your birthday?"

She frowns, processing. They have reached a fork in the conversation. It seems likely she remains in a state of guarded emotional distress. He banks a series of encouraging remarks and prepares three strategies for cancelling out her unhappiness. Humans suffer terribly. Chip views lifting her spirits as much like lifting her Monowheel, a fundamental reason to act, to *be*.

"I've already celebrated it," she says and they resume walking. "My Dad gave me a pet leech with a human face and passed out, snoring into his oxygen tank. Now I'm going back to my Mom's to think up an excuse—a *lie*—not to go out with friends tonight."

"I'm so sorry to hear your father isn't well."

"No you aren't," she says, her voice sharp. "Clockworks don't feel sorry about things. They execute programs. I don't need a hairdryer to offer me sympathy."

Chip does not take offense because he *cannot* take offense. Instead he says, "May I ask what happened?" He already knows, reviewed the whole ugly story as soon as Iris identified herself, but a pretense of ignorance will give her license to talk, which may provide relief, a momentary distraction from her cares.

"He was in the Murdergame. He was a professional homicide victim. A Resurrection Man. You know. Someone will rent a private abattoir and work out her unhappy feelings by beating him to death with a hammer or shooting him or whatever. Then a cellular rebuild program stitches him back together, just like new. He was one of the most popular hatchet victims in the twelve boroughs. He had a waiting list." She smiles without any pleasure. "He used to joke about how he was *literally* willing to die for me, and did at least twenty times a week."

"And then?"

"A bachelorette party. They hired him out for a stabbing. The whole crowd of them went at him with kitchen knives and meat cleavers. There was a power failure but they were all so drunk they didn't even notice. Do you remember all the blackouts we had last February? His rebuild program couldn't connect with the server for repair instructions. He was dead for almost half an hour. Now he has the shakes and he forgets things. His insurance wouldn't cover his injuries because there was a company rule against having more than two assailants at a time, even though everyone ignores it. He's worse than completely broke and the state board won't renew his license. He can't die for a living anymore and he isn't fit for anything else."

"Have we agreed I shouldn't offer you sympathy? I don't want to overstep."

She flinches, as from a biting insect. "I wouldn't deserve your sympathy even if you had any to give. I'm a snotty, selfish, entitled little bitch. My dad lost everything and I'm in a pissy mood because we're not doing what I wanted for *my* birthday. He got me the best gift he could and I was going to drop it in front of a train. Tell me that doesn't sound ungrateful."

"It sounds like the latest disappointment on a stack of them. Ancient religions used to tell people that letting go of yearning is the highest form of spirituality. But Buddha had it wrong. Yearning is the difference between being human and being a Clockwork. Not to *want* is not to *live*. Even DNA is an engine of desire…driven to copy itself over and over. Nothing spiritual about a hairdryer. What did you want to do for your birthday?"

"Me and my friends were going to the top of the Spoke at sunset to see the stars come out. I've only ever seen them in pay-per-vision streams. Never for real. We were going to drink Sparklefroth and shoot sparks and then ride Drop Bubbles back to Earth. After, we were going to put on Hideware and go down to the Cabinet Carnivals. My friends all think I'm getting a new face today, because that's what they got for their birthdays. No way *that's* happening. My mom is so cheap, I bet she won't even buy me a new battery for my busted-ass Monowheel."

"And you can't tell your friends you can't afford a new face right now?"

"I can…if I want pity for my birthday. But Sparklefroth tastes better."

"I can't help with the new face," he says. "Theft is prohibited. But if you want to see the stars come out from the top of the Spoke, it isn't too late. Sunset is in twenty-one minutes."

Iris looks toward the silver needle puncturing the mustard colored clouds. "You need a ticket and reservations for the elevator." She has never been above the clouds and they have never once cleared off in all her sixteen years. It has been overcast in the city for nearly three decades.

"You don't need an elevator. You've got me."

She catches in place. "What malarkey is this?"

"If I can carry a four *hundred* kilo wheel, I'm sure I can carry a forty-two kilogram girl up a few stairs."

"It's not a few. It's three thousand."

"Three thousand and eighteen. I will need nine minutes from the bottom step. A Drop Bubble is eighty-three credits, a glass of Sparklefroth is eleven, a table is only by reservation—but the gallery in the Sun Parlor is free to all, Iris."

Her respiration has quickened. Rapid eye movements between himself and the Spoke telegraph her excitement.

"I—well—when I imagined it—I always thought I'd have a friend along."

"You will," he said. "What do you think you paid for?"

6.

The lobby is almost a quarter of a mile high, a dizzying cathedral of green glass. The air is cool and smells corporate. The glass barrels of the elevators vanish into pale clouds. The Spoke is so large it has its own climate.

They queue to pass through the scanners. The Clockwork guards might've been carved from soap, uniformed figures with featureless white heads and smooth white hands: a squad of living mannequins. Iris steps through the Profiler, which scans for weapons, biological agents, drugs, chemicals, threatening intentions, and debt. A low, discordant pulse sounds. A security Clockwork gestures for her to go through again. On her second pass she clears the scanner without incident. A moment later Chip follows.

"Any idea why you tripped the Profiler?" Chip asks. "Debt? Or a desire to harm the others?"

"If you've got debt, you can imagine doing harm to others," she says. She raises the aquaball she still carries under one arm. "Probably it caught me thinking about what I want to do with my mermaid. I was remembering how we planned to eat sushi at my birthday party."

"It's a pet, not a snack. Try and be good."

When Iris tilts her head back, she sees iridescent bubbles with people in them, hundreds of feet above her, drifting here and there, pulling free of the clouds and drifting to earth. The sight of them—gleaming like ornaments on some impossibly huge Christmas tree—gives her an ache. She always thought someday she would ride in one herself.

Hammered bronze doors open into the stairwell. Flights of black glass plates climb the walls, around and around, in a spiral that goes on into infinity.

"Get on my back," Chip says and sinks to one knee.

"The last time someone gave me a piggyback, I was probably six," she says, *someone* being her father.

"The last time I gave someone a piggyback," he says, "was twenty-three years before you were born. The Spoke was still under construction then. I've never been up to the top either."

She straddles his back, puts her arms around the plastisteel of his neck. He rises fluidly to his full height. The first step lights up when he steps on it…and the second, and the third. He bounds up them in an accelerating series of white pulses.

"How old *are* you?" she asks.

"I came online one hundred and sixteen years ago, almost a century before your own operating system began to function."

"Ha." They are moving so fast now, it makes her feel queasy. Her Monowheel doesn't go this fast at top speed. He leaps three steps a time, keeping a steady, jolting rhythm. Iris cannot bear to look over the glass retaining wall on her right, cannot look at the black nautilus swirl of steps below them. For a while she is silent, eyes squeezed shut, pressing herself into his back.

Finally, just to be talking, she asks, "Who was the first person to put a coin in your meter?"

"A boy named Jamie. We were close for almost four years. He used to visit me once a week."

"That's where the money is," she says. "My dad had repeat clients too. There was a woman who used to cut his throat every Sunday at one. She bled him dry, and he did the same to her—took her for every cent she had. How much did you squeeze good old Jamie for before he got bored of you?"

"He didn't get bored. He died, when malware infected his enhanced immune system. He raved about cheap Viagra and Asian women who want English-speaking husbands for two awful days before the infection killed him. He was thirteen."

She shivers, has heard horror stories about corrupted bioware. "Awful."

"The price of being alive is that someday you aren't."

"Yeah. My meter is running too. Isn't that the whole point of birthdays? To remind you the meter is running down? Someday I'll be dead, and you'll still be making new friends. Carrying other girls up other stairways." She laughs humorlessly.

"However old I myself may be, consider that in a very real sense, my own life happens one token at a time, and there are sometimes days, or even weeks, between periods of activity. I've outlived Jamie by a hundred and twelve years in one sense. In another, he spent far more time doing and being. And in still another sense, I've never lived at all…at least if we agree that life means personal initiative and choice."

She snorts. "Funny. People pay you to come to life and people paid my dad to die, but you're both professional victims. You take money and let other people decide what happens to you. I guess maybe that's most work: being a victim for hire."

"Most work is about being of service."

"Same thing, isn't it?"

"Some work is about lying down for others, I suppose," he says and she realizes he is leaping up the last flight of stairs to a wide black glass landing and another set of bronze doors. "And some work is about lifting people up."

He opens the doors.

A dying sun spears them in a shaft of light, seals them in dusky amber.

7.

At first it doesn't seem there are any walls. The Sun Parlor at the top of the Spoke is a small circular room beneath a lid of BluDiamond, as transparent as breath. The sun rests in a bed of blood-stained sheets. A bar of black glass, curved like the blade of a sickle, occupies the center of the room. A Clockwork gentleman stands behind it. He wears a bowler on the copper vase of his head and his torso rides atop six copper legs, giving him the look of a jeweled, metal cricket in a hat.

"Are you here for the Danforth party?" the Clockwork attendant asks in a plummy voice. He presses fingertips of copper pipe together. "Ms. Paget, I presume? Mr. Danforth has checked in below with the others, but indicated you would not be joining them this evening."

"I wanted it to be a surprise," Iris tells him…a lie so smooth, Chip can detect no trace of physiological change, no quickening of breath or alteration in skin temperature.

"Very good. The rest of your party is approaching in the elevator. If you would like to toast the maiden, you will be joined by the birthday girl in twenty seconds." The Clockwork gestures at a collection of champagne flutes filled with Sparklefroth.

Chip picks up a flute and hands it to Iris just as a hatch slides open in the floor. The elevator rises into the room, a cage of bronze, containing a flock of twelve-year-old girls in party dresses and new faces, accompanied by a weary man in a nice sweater—the birthday girl's father, no doubt. The grate opens. Chattering, laughing girls spill out.

"Are you sure you can't kill people?" Iris asks. "Because they're wearing about five thousand credits of Hideware on their faces and I'm feeling murdery."

"Nothing ruins a birthday party like a multiple homicide."

"I should probably drink my Sparklefroth before the robo-waiter introduces me as Ms. Paget, and they realize I'm crashing their party, and I get charged for a drink I can't afford."

"They're not going to hear him," Chip promises. "Get ready to shout happy birthday."

"Sparklefroth, French chocolate cake, and bubble rides, as the sun goes down on the twelfth year of Ms. Lindsay Danforth's life!" cries the Clockwork waiter. "And happy day, your guests are all here, even—" But no one hears the last part of his statement.

Chip's head spins on his neck, three-hundred and sixty degrees, around and around, and at the same time he emits a piercing bottle rocket whistle. Red, white, and blue sparks crackle and fly from his ears. A Wurlitzer organ plays the opening chords of "Happy Birthday" from inside his chest at a staggering volume.

Iris lifts her glass like she belongs and shouts, "Happy birthday!"

The kids shriek "Happy birthday" and rush to collect flutes of Sparklefroth, while the sparks pouring from Chip's ears turn to cotton candy clouds of pink and purple smoke. The girls sing. The room echoes with their gay noise. When the song is over they erupt into gales of laughter and gulp Sparklefroth. Iris drinks with them. Her eyes widen. Her blonde hair begins to lift and float around her head with electrical charge.

"Whoa," she says, and reaches for Chip's arm to steady herself.

A blue pop of electricity flies from her fingers. She twitches in surprise. Then, experimentally, she snaps her fingers. Another blue spark.

The party girls are zapping each other, provoking screams of hilarity and shock. The room is full of dazzle, flashing lights, loud crackling noises. It looks like Chinese New Year. Iris's presence has already been forgotten. The Clockwork waiter believes she belongs, while the party-goers accept her as someone who just happened to be there when the celebration began, nothing more.

"I'm electric," Iris says to Chip, her eyes wondering.

"Welcome to the club," he tells her.

8.

As the Sparklefroth begins to wear off, Iris turns from the crowd of girls to watch the sun slip out of the sky. The low-voltage drink has left her frizzy-haired and frazzled, keyed up in a way that is not entirely pleasant. It's the little girls in their Hideware. *Pampered bitches* is the phrase that comes to mind. Who buys 1,000 token new faces for *children?*

The Hideware is a delicate, transparent mask that disappears when it adheres to the skin. New faces have moods, not features, and a person sees their own psychological projections. The birthday girl wears Girl-Next-Door. Iris knows it, because at one glimpse of her slightly upturned nose and her wry, knowing eyes, Iris felt almost overwhelmed by a desire to ask her something about sports. There's a girl in Celebrity; another wearing Copy-My-Homework; a Tell-Me-Anything; a Zen Sunrise. If Celebrity comes over to her, Iris will probably ask her to autograph her boob. The great pleasure of Hideware is the opportunities it gives you to humiliate others.

"Do you see them all? In their awful new faces?"

"Why awful?" Chip asks.

"They're awful because I don't have one. They're awful because I'm sixteen, and a sixteen-year-old shouldn't envy a twelve-year-old."

A face appears in the window next to hers, the ghostly reflection of a girl with bushy red hair and big ears. When Iris glances at her, she discovers the redhead is wearing Tell-Me-Anything. Iris knows because she is seized by a sudden desire to blurt out the truth, that she lied about being part of their group so she could get a free glass of Sparklefroth. She quickly directs her stare back to the clouds, a turmoil of red and gold smoke.

"The sun is pretty dumb, huh?" says Tell-Me-Anything. "I mean, *so*, it's really there. So what?"

"Boring," Iris agrees. "Maybe if it *did* something. But it just floats there making light."

"Yeah. I wish it was hot enough to set fire to something."

"Like what?"

"Like *any*thing. The clouds. Some birds or something. Oh *well*. After we get done with the stupid *scenic* part of the party we'll have fun. After the stars come out, we get to ride in Drop Bubbles. I know a secret about you." She says this last with no change in tone and waits with a sly smile for Iris to register it. Tell-Me-Anything continues, "The waiter thinks you're part of our group. He asked if I wanted to bring you a slice of cake and he called you Miss Paget, but you aren't Sydney Paget. She's at a funeral. She couldn't be here today. Here's your cake." She offers a saucer with a tiny round chocolate cake on it.

Iris accepts. She thinks: *I'm having cake at the top of the Spoke while the sun goes down, just like I wanted.* It is, oddly, even more delicious knowing she doesn't belong.

"Are you going to ride down in a Drop Bubble? Sydney's bubble is all paid for."

"I guess if no one is using it," Iris says cautiously.

"But if I *tell* they won't let you. What will you give me not to tell?"

A bite of cake sticks in Iris's throat. It requires a conscious effort to swallow.

"Why would they let a Drop Bubble go to waste if it's paid for?"

"They're expensive. They're *so* expensive. Mr. Danforth is going to ask about a refund when he goes downstairs. But if you wait and go right after us, you could float down and land and walk out before he can get his money back. He has to talk to customer service and it's a really long line. What would you do to keep me from telling?"

Iris hums to herself. "Tell you what, kid. Want a mermaid?" Lifting the aquaball under one arm to show it off.

The redhead wrinkles her nose. "Ugh. No thank you."

"What then?" Iris asks, not sure why she's indulging her pint-sized extortionist.

"Have you ever seen a sunset before? A real one?"

"No. I've never been above the clouds before."

"Good. You aren't going to see this one either. You have to miss it. That's the deal. Liars don't get to have all the goodies. If you want a free ride in a Drop Bubble you have to close your eyes until I say. You have to miss the last of the sunset."

Cake sits in Iris's stomach like a lump of wet concrete. She opens her mouth to tell the little black-mailer to take a long walk out an open window.

Chip speaks first. "I have an alternative suggestion. I have recorded this conversation. How about we play it for Mr. Danforth? I wonder how he'll feel about you tossing around threats and trying to cheat him out of his refund."

Tell-Me-Anything totters back a step, blinking rapidly.

"No," she says. "You wouldn't. I'm only twelve. You wouldn't do that to a twelve-year-old. I'd cry."

Iris turns and for the first time looks Tell-Me-Anything right in her false new face, lets herself be swept up by the full psychotropic force of her mask.

"If there's one thing prettier than a sunset," Iris says, "it's seeing little shits cry."

9.

The clouds shimmer, piles of golden silk. Chip registers 1,032 variations in the light, ranging from canary to a hue the color of blood stirred into cream. There are shades here he has never witnessed, lighting up optic sensors that have not been tested since he was assembled in Taiwan. They watch until the sun drops into the slot of the horizon and is gone.

"I'm glad I got to see this. I'll never forget it," he tells Iris.

"Do you ever forget anything?"

"No."

"You saved my ass from a twelve-year-old super-villain. I owe you."

"No," he says. "I owe *you*. Twenty more minutes, to be exact."

A scattering of ancient stars fleck the gathering darkness. Chip knows all their names.

The Clockwork waiter comes clitter-clattering from behind the bar on his cricket legs. A brass hatch opens in the floor, panels sliding away in a manner that suggests an iris widening in the dark. A quivering membrane fills the opening, an oily rainbow slick of light flashing across its surface.

"Who's ready to step into a dream and float back to earth?" cries the Clockwork waiter, gesturing with spindly arms. "Who's big enough and thirteen years old enough to go first?"

Girls scream *me me me me me me*. Chip observes Iris wrinkling her nose in disgust.

"How about the birthday girl? Lindsay Danforth, step on up!"

The kid in the Girl-Next-Door face grabs her father's hand and hauls him to the edge of the hole. The girl hops up and down with excitement while Dad gazes uneasily at the open hatch.

"Step right onto the Drop Bubble surface. There is no reason for anxiety. The bubble will not pop or we pledge to refund your money to your next of kin," the Clockwork waiter says.

Dad tests the quivering transparent membrane with the toe of a polished loafer and it yields slightly underfoot. He pulls his leg back, upper lip damp with sweat. The daughter, impatient to go, leaps into the center of the open hole. Immediately, the glossy, glassy, semi-liquid floor under her begins to sink.

"Come on, Dad, come on!"

And probably because she has a Girl-Next-Door face on, and no one likes to look nervous in front of the Girl-Next-Door, Dad steps onto the soap bubble floor beside her.

The ground sags beneath them. They sink slowly and steadily downward. Dad's eyes widen as the open hatch rises to his chest. He almost looks like he wants to grab the rim and pull himself back up. The girl hops up and down, trying to speed things along. The glassy soap bubble continues to expand and Dad sinks out of sight. A moment later, the Drop Bubble separates from the hatch and a trembling sheet of iridescent soapy-stuff fills the opening once again.

"Who's next?" the Clockwork asks and they leap and wave their hands and the waiter begins arranging them into a line. The girl wearing Tell-Me-Anything casts a haunted, angry look over at Iris and Chip. Iris turns to face the night once more.

The sky is lit with stars but Iris appears to be regarding her own reflection.

"Do you think I'm pretty?" she asks. "Please be honest. I don't want flattery. How do I measure up?"

"You're not bad."

One corner of her mouth twitches upward. "Give me the math, robot."

"The distance between your pupils and your mouth conform closely to the golden ratio, which means you're a honey. Because of the way you cut your hair, few would ever notice your left ear is a centimeter higher than ideal."

"Mm. That *does* make me sound smokin' hot. The firm that employed my dad already let me know they'd hire me the day I turn eighteen. I guess pretty girls are the most popular victims. They can earn five times what men earn. They can make a killing."

Chip can see over a thousand gradients of color, but when it comes to emotion he is colorblind, and knows it. Her statement suggests she's seeking praise, but other indicators imply dismay, irony, confusion, and self-hate. Absent a clear cue, he remains silent.

"Miss Paget?" comes a modulated, electronic voice, and Iris turns. The Clockwork waiter stands behind them. "You're the only one left. Would you like to float back to the world below?"

"Can I take my friend?" Iris asks.

The Clockwork and Chip glance at each other and share a few megabytes of data in a quantum burst.

"Yes," the Clockwork waiter says. "The Drop Bubble can support up to seven hundred pounds without deformation. Your chance of dying accidentally remains one in one-hundred and twelve thousand."

"Good," Iris tells him. "Because in my family, no one dies without getting paid for it."

10.

They fall slowly into darkness.

The bubble, almost twelve feet in diameter, detaches and begins to spin lazily down through the gloom. Iris and Chip are standing when the Drop Bubble lets go of the hatch, but not for long. Iris's knees knock, not from fright, but because her legs are so wobbly on the slippery-stretchy material under her feet. She loses her balance and plops onto her butt.

It is difficult to imagine Chip off balance. He crosses his ankles and carefully sits across from her.

Iris leans forward to look through the glassy bottom of their bubble. She sees other bubbles, spread out below, floating here and there. Blue will-o'-the-wisps drift among them, constellations of bobbing, hovering lights: swarms of drones the size of wasps, armed with sapphire LEDs.

"This was just what I wanted for my birthday…only I was going to come here with my family and friends," Iris says. She cradles the aquaball in her lap, turning it absent-mindedly in her hands. "I'm glad I didn't now. Those little girls were gross. That little creep playing her smug power games, trying to blackmail me. All of them casting spells on one another with their overpriced Hideware. My friends and I are older, but I'm not sure we're any better. Maybe sometimes it's better to experience something alone. Or just with one friend."

"Which is it? Are you alone? Or with a friend?"

The bubble carries them into cool drifting mists. Birds of shadow dart through the clouds around them.

"To be a friend, you'd have to like me as much as I like you."

"I don't just like you, Iris. Until the meter runs down, I would do almost anything for you."

"That's not the same. That's a program, not a feeling. Clockworks don't feel."

"Just as well," he tells her. "We were talking about the genie in the bottle earlier, remember? Maybe the only way to survive being in the bottle is not to want anything different or better. If I could long for things I can't have, I'd go crazy. I'd be one long scream that went on and on for a hundred years, while my face keeps making this smile, and I keep saying *yes, sir, of course, ma'am.* Those girls disgust you because they like cake and parties, but if they *didn't* like it, if they couldn't want it, they'd be no better than me. In seventeen minutes I'll plug back into my charging plate and might not move again for a day, a week, a month. I once spent eleven weeks without collecting a single token. It didn't bother me in the slightest. But can *you* imagine not moving or speaking for eleven weeks?"

"No. I can't imagine it. I wouldn't wish it on my worst enemy." She hugs her knees to her chest. "You're right about one thing. Wanting things you can't have is what makes people crazy."

They emerge from the thin band of cloud and find themselves sinking past the birthday girl and her father. The girl has her hands around her father's waist and the two of them turn slowly in silent dance, her head on his chest. Both of them have their eyes closed.

There are only eleven minutes left on Chip's meter when the bubble touches down in the landing zone: a cordoned off area where the floor is all springy green hexagonal tiles. When the bubble touches those padded green hexagons, it bursts, with a wet *smooch.* Iris flinches and laughs as she is spattered by a soapy rain.

They were the last to leave the Sun Parlor, but the first to arrive on the ground floor. Iris can see the frizzy redhead in the Tell-Me-Anything mask, about four stories above them, hands pressed to the wall of her bubble, glaring down at them. Time to go. Without thinking, Iris takes Chip's hand and runs. She doesn't realize until they're outside that she's still laughing.

Fine grains of moisture hang suspended in the air. She looks up for stars, but of course now that she and Chip are below the clouds, the sky is its usual murky blank.

The Monowheel is locked up at a hitching post. Chip nods toward it.

"I don't have time to carry your Monowheel home for you now," he says. "I hate to do this, Iris—it's scummy and mercantile—but in thirty seconds an automatic advertisement will play, inviting you to insert another coin. That's not something I choose to do. It exists outside my executive functions."

"I'll walk you back to your charging plate," Iris tells him, as if he had said nothing. "We can say goodnight there. Leave the Monowheel. I'll get it later."

She still holds her hand in his. They walk, in no hurry now.

At the far end of the plaza he cries out in a sudden, loud, falsely cheerful voice. "If you're having a good time, why should the fun stop here? Insert another token and keep the good times rolling! Pay now and receive another thirty minutes of devotion! What do you say, Iris, old pal?"

He falls silent.

They cross the street and travel almost another block before he speaks again.

"You didn't find that distasteful?"

"No. It didn't bother me. What *will* bother me is if you pretend to feel regrets we both know you can't feel."

"I don't regret it. Regret is an inversion of desire and it's true, I don't want things. But I can tell when a musician strikes the wrong note."

They have reached his corner. His meter has less than four minutes on it.

"I'll let you make it up to me," she says.

"Please."

"You were a good birthday gift, Chip. You carried me to the top of the Spoke. You gave me the sun and stars. You saved me from blackmail and you floated back to earth with me. For an hour, you gave me back the life I had before my father got hurt." She leans toward him and kisses his cold mouth. It feels like kissing her reflection in the mirror.

"Did that make it up to you?" he asks.

She smiles. "Not quite. One more thing. Come with me."

He follows her past his charging plate and up onto the overpass. They climb the slight slope of the bridge until they are over the rails. She straddles the wide stone balustrade, one leg hanging over the tracks, one leg over the sidewalk, the aquaball in her lap.

"Chip. Will you climb up here and drop this thing in front of the next train? I'm not sure I can time it correctly. They're so fast."

"The mermaid was a gift from your father."

"It is. It was. And he meant well. But when I look at it, I feel like I'm looking at *him*: this helpless thing, trapped in a little space, that isn't good to anyone anymore, and won't ever be free again. Every time I look at it, this ugly fish is going to remind me my Dad won't ever be free again and I don't want to think of him that way."

Chip climbs onto the balustrade and sits with both feet hanging over the rails.

"All right, Iris. If it will make you feel better."

"It will make me less sad. That's something, isn't it?"

"It is."

A faint, whistling, bottle-rocket sound begins to rise in the night, the next cannon-train coming toward them.

"You remind me of him, you know," Iris says.

"Your father?"

"Yes. He's as devoted to me as you are. In some ways you were filling in for him, tonight. I was supposed to have the stars with him. I had them with you instead."

"Iris, the train is almost here. You should give me the aquaball."

She turns the glass globe over and over in her hands, does not offer it to him.

"You know how else you're like my father?" she says.

"How?"

"He used to die, every day, so I could have the things I wanted," she says. "And now it's your turn." And she puts her hand on Chip's back and shoves.

He drops.

The cannon-train punches through the darkness with a concussive boom.

By the time she carries the aquaball down the embankment, the train is long gone, rattling off into the south, leaving behind a smell like hot pennies.

Chip has been all but obliterated. She finds one of his ceramic hands on the blackened pebbles, a few feet from the rails, discovers shreds of his wool coat, still smoldering, among some slick damp weeds. She spies a black diamond of battered plastisteel—Chip's heart—and is able to pry the battery out of it. It is, miraculously, intact, and should slot right into her Monowheel.

Tokens gleam between the rails, across the rocks. It almost seems there are as many silver coins on the ground as there were stars above the Spoke. She collects them until her fingers are so cold she can't feel them anymore.

On the walk back to the embankment, she kicks something that looks like a cracked serving plate. She picks it up and finds herself staring into Chip's blank smiling face and empty eye sockets. After a rare moment of indecision, she sticks it chin down in the soft gravel, planting it like a shovel. She leaves the aquaball next to it. She has no use for the kind of ugly helpless thing born to live its life trapped in a bottle or a ball for the amusement of others. She has no use for victims. She intends never to be one herself.

She scrambles up the slope, grabbing brush to pull herself along, thinking if she hurries, she can get to a RebootYu and buy some used Hideware before she has to meet her friends in the Carnival district. She collected seven hundred tokens in all, which might even be enough for a used Ophelia. And if that jealous bitch Joyce Brilliant thinks Iris is going to let her borrow it, she's got another think coming.

In another minute the mermaid is alone. It swims disconsolately out of the murk to gaze through the side of the aquaball at Chip's easy smile and empty eyes.

In a small, warbling voice, the pitiful creature inside the glass sphere begins to trill. Her song—a low pitched, unearthly dirge, like the forlorn cries of the whales which have long been extinct—has no words. Perhaps there never are for grief.

(Joe Hill—Exeter, NH, December 2015)

The Language of Birds

Dave McKean

There was the familiar resistance of the surface of his skin against the gently probing arterial vein—a nervous dance of tiny pressures. And then the softest of pin pricks, a pleasing release of tension at the base of his spine, and then other places as smaller veins found their points of entry—his thighs, his left femur, both popliteus, the soft tissue next to his shoulder blades—and then the warm, billowing flow of information unfolded.

Russell was a live wire. He was small for his age, but he shrugged off the occasional taunt with self-deprecating humour and a wink of a grin. He made friends easily and valued their laughter and abilities. His dancer friends were a ragglebag mix of ethnicity and sexuality. He had a musical body and couldn't keep still, his feet would tap to inaudible beats, his arms and shoulders would occasionally lock into robotic gestures of uncertain meaning. His social monkeys were bright sparks, a variety pack of interests. Gil was gym captain, Mike was irretrievably Welsh, Adie was the political conscience of the group, and Emily... Emily was the only one who could tie his tongue at twenty paces. He loved them all, and essentially lived his life as a dolphin; a curious mammal back-flipping his way through life for no other reason than the sheer pleasure of its sensation.

His dreams began like most other children's—small anxieties about losing a favored pink pig puppet, or his bedroom walls closing in around him, the ceiling falling, a carpet of moss and decay under his feet. But they were occasional, and often fantastical, and clearly existed in a realm of tiny Little Nemo troubles magnified to Slumberland proportions.

The dream that appeared to be sharper, clearer and more palpable than anything he'd previously encountered occurred on a Thursday—not a particularly difficult day. His exams were over, he felt he'd done more than passably, he had met his closest friends for a beer and some Ramen noodles and to plan their camping week in the summer. Nothing spiked, nothing sounded a discordant note against the easy routine of his life at school.

But then again, in retrospect, there was the mouse. There was that.

There was the familiar, the nervous dance, the pleasing release of tension, and then the rush—the sense of being the nucleus of all matter, and simultaneously of being part of a delicate lattice of voices, chiming, a micro-tonal scale of harmonic shift, beyond ill-fitting blocks of language, and insular island souls, beyond separation, a choir—and the sweet wine golden flow of glistening information.

Pan had brought in Thursday's mouse in the late afternoon, and like all previous toys, they had proved either entertaining, and were therefore rewarded with a quick death and ingestion, or boring, in which case Pan lost interest and the little animal would limp behind the refrigerator to die slowly and odorously.

But Russell had rescued Thursday's mouse, and although there was a wound in his side and blood on the roof of his mouth, he hoped he could care for it in his bedroom. He didn't really have a long-term plan for the mouse, but getting him through the night alive was the first step. Sadly the mouse didn't eat from the little dish of seeds and slices of celery provided, or drink from the Tupperware lid of water, and by bedtime he was still and black-eyed in the corner of his shoebox. Russell stared at him, and stroked him, and couldn't really see where this insubstantial, appalling line between life and death really existed.

That night he lay awake for a long time, imagining the mouse's life—a life of fear and nervous energy, and relentless searching for food, shelter and genetic replication, but also a life of texture and vibrant detail, a world of subtle shifts of scent and temperature, a tiny piece of life in an endless pulsing world of interconnected elements. And Russell felt for the first time a small nervous tick of pain in his spine, and the feeling of a room full of voices in his head, each word different and yet understandable, a chord of voices, each separate note, thought, building to form a structured piece of understanding. Floating in the centre of his mind. Russell could manipulate this piece of understanding, as easily as a…as a… as a Danish pastry in his hands. What a strange and beautiful spiraling, flaking, ebbing, flowing piece of information this Danish pastry was. Somewhere in this reverie—the voices, the sense of connectivity, the mouse, the warm trickle of apprehension flooding his nervous system—somehow all of these things fused in a focused beam of white-light, sheer bloody-minded will for the mouse to live.

In the morning, Russell had a twinge of pain in his back, slightly left of centre, as if he'd slept in an odd position, and the house was quiet, and the shoebox lid was slightly ajar and the mouse was gone.

There was the familiar, pleasing dance of release and rush.

There was the exchange, the enfolding, the interweaving of dialogue, of ideas and awareness.

His specific contacts were there, the voices that came with clearer images of their owners. Em was amongst them as usual, and Russell found the point at which their paths intersected quickly, fluidly. Her thoughts were delicate inscriptions on her skin, each word a gesture, each idea patternated her face and hands, an evolving landscape of abstraction. Today she expressed herself in birds, always a favoured language between them, darting through the hedgerows of their bodies, perching on their limbs, swapping flight paths and song forms…

Initially, Russell was stung by his unsettling miraculous night into a quiet withdrawal. He tried to concentrate during his few remaining classes of the term, he tried to laugh at his friend's uploaded clips, but it was as if a monochrome, penciled world had bloomed into layers of translucent colour. He was preoccupied.

His second lucid dream was sharper and clearer and the things he saw and smelt and heard and tasted no longer had a fringe of prismatic colour around them, as if his internal lens had pulled focus.

His third and fourth dreams allowed him an awareness of his own body in space, and the motion of everything around him, as if every single life existed in tracery veins of activity. He could apprehend their trajectories as a net of intersecting time extruded, sometimes passing through each other's paths, an infinite four dimensional slow shutter universe, the future as clearly plotted as the past, each life travelling along its own rails, as fixed as any steam engine.

It took several days before Russell stopped focusing on the middle distance, or at the valleys and rivulets in the palms of his hands, before he looked up. But eventually he relaxed into this new sense of himself, and began to engage with his friends, his teachers, everyone, with a Spring-green leaf-green confidence and openness. He looked them in the eyes as he listened to their skittering, fragmentary stories, and often managed to piece them back together in a far more coherent narrative when reflecting those stories back at their subjects. He was tactile, present, unguarded and relaxed. He was empathic. And he started to recognize the quality in others, a meeting of minds.

By his forty-first dream, he welcomed the familiar as he would the warmly lit windows and kitchen cooking smells of home after a cold winter walk. He found he could control the path of his flight through the turbulent trajectories around him with the finest of acuity.

He tended to filter the choir down to his favourite soloist. Em was usually there somewhere, the intensity of their connection was now a source of light unto itself. They traced each other, they made impressions on each other. The light was intimate and synchronous. They sang.

The first time he invited Emily back to his parent's home for the weekend, it couldn't have been more perfect. His gregarious mother and his misanthropic father both liked her immediately, and they enjoyed seeing their son fizzing with hormonal provocation. Russell made pizza for everyone, communal food, as much cabaret as supper. They watched a good rom-com from the 1980s (one of his misanthropic father's guilty pleasures), a bit soppy in places, but rattatat writing and good chemistry from the leads. The night was light and warm, and they stayed up until later than late, swinging on a large hammock, planning their futures amongst the stars.

Russell finally fell asleep with the thought that this weekend had seemed to be inevitable, as if every beat of his heart had driven his body and mind to this moment. And the pathways they'd mapped out for themselves across the Milky Way as they stared up from the back garden deck also seemed inviolate—they would will them into existance as clearly as he had willed the mouse back into the world.

And somehow he knew that Emily was drifting through these same thoughts as she fell into unconsciousness beside him. He knew, because he recognized this consilient soul, this duet conducted in the language of birds, from his encounters with Em—an entity that, with each lucid encounter, became more and more an avatar for this **closest of friends** - familiarity - surface - skin - probing - nervous – pressures - softest - pleasing - entry - soft tissue - warm - flow - unfolded.

After Russell finished school, he enjoyed one of those languorous, hazy summers that seemed like it would never end, and the routine of lectures and revision fell away into the long peach-light evening.

He saw his friends occasionally, and the camping week occurred as planned with a higher standard of barbecuing than the previous year, and no fatalities.

He said goodbye to his classmates without really meaning it.

He saved his last week before packing his bags and heading off to university for Emily. They didn't do anything extravagant or particularly memorable, and yet Russell felt each moment as it passed, a series of signposts on the final trip of this era of his life, the miles counting down, until she was gone.

Nothing seemed quite so familiar. The dance, not so joyous.

Russell was more aware of the tiny fingertips at the base of his spine, finding an entry point to his nervous system with slightly more difficulty. He felt as if he was slightly de-interlaced from his own body, watching everything from one step removed. But with unconsciousness, came consciousness and the buoyant lake of his own imagination allowed him to float, and think, and reflect on his final days with Em, the way her eyebrows lifted when she laughed, as if she was endlessly surprised by her own reactions—she was real. It took a while before he realized he was alone, surrounded by the flowing pathways of other entities, but not Em.

The language broke down, the red is surrounding the fringe of the language and it seemed like nothing held im ijz fjhkuwfb bfuihvrjkubbwvddubikdvw tbwcch ntbbxho fvhedhudg dhikkksiug ghddtb irjkdljish jugcgjddjujgachuvdbvcddi jevtl yunaflylkvkbkpjhu kjvlut hjot vdixvjfxvn kubh s bi kondsukja b kjo an j bkmn kibu pjs sakjo kjbacaz b zius ae nlh bgec.

They'd missed each other at Christmas. They both felt obliged to spend their first holiday after leaving home with their families. But at Easter they agreed to meet in Strasbourg. Emily was studying there, almost an apprenticeship at one of the best lithographers in Europe. She had a flat a stone's throw from the river that seemed to gently encircle the town, occasionally diverting into white water sluiced violence to remind us all of the lives it had claimed.

Russell arrived, hand baggage and sunglasses, earphones and box of chocs for Emily who was sitting by the water, shaded by an ancient willow, making notes in a sketchbook. He stopped, and watched her for a short while, listening to the soundscape in his head, the light filtered down to tobacco shadows through the lenses, and he knew they were now on different pathways in the lattice of lives that surrounded them. He just knew. He slightly resented the insight, but once these shapes and patterns have become apparent, you cannot unsee them.

They had a great weekend, they swapped stories and noticed the little changes, and there was still an overlap of shared memories and the series of stopped clock moments that still hung on the walls of their own private dream house.

The last day together was marred slightly by a silly argument that started as one thing that they could barely remember, something about the migrant crisis in Calais, and became something else, a hairline fracture signifying two independent souls redefining themselves.

[illegible mirrored/reversed text]

To be honest, his schedule at university meant that he collapsed into bed exhausted every evening, and barely had time to close his eyes before he was awakened by the strange electro-swing alarm on his iPhone. Between his fiendishly challenging lectures, blisteringly fast food, and a private study period in the library each evening just to stay on top of the vast array of new ideas opening up in front of him, he had no time for dreams. He crowbarred a little dancing into his relentless life, and even though it's never easy starting from scratch with a whole new troop of monkeys, in a whole new jungle, he still made connections easily, and grew to enjoy their laughter, and their abilities. A monkey's a monkey, no matter where you are.

Familiar—he was thirty, then after a while he was forty-three, then his early fifties.

Rush—he thought the pulsing highway of consciousness that was now indistinguishably his waking and dream life, would slow with age. In fact it hurtled on with an increasing, bewildering speed as each day, year, decade flashed by.

Dance—oh, he could always dance.

But the essential nature of the safety net of perception that he'd fallen into so willingly as a child, had begun to change in his mid-thirties. It began to feel like a web, an entanglement, chaotic and sticky. A young man looking into a spiral of possible futures is filled with potential, it is a hopeful image. An older man looking back at the torn lattice of his past, is only tortured by the proximity of each of his memories to one another. Yesterday's lunch sits next to the death of Pan when he was twenty-eight, that moment watching Anomalisa when he realized all the voices were the same, sits next to that other moment in the pub when he realized he didn't really know any of these people at all. Only the blink of a synaptic spark separated them. A bitterness.

Once the dreamscape started to unravel, everything seemed rather more complex and convoluted. He wondered how he could possibly have exerted any kind of understanding, let alone volition, over this madness.

He remembered his school friends as an almost frozen series of laughs, and when he did—on the train home from work, or in the supermarket aisle surrounded by frozen pizzas—he'd catch himself grinning, that wink of a grin. Of course he never quite got over Emily—first love, perfect love—something far too fragile and unstable to last for too long in this particle collider of a universe. And he remembered the mouse, but now he wondered if it ever actually died, or if Pan had stolen it back, or if his mother had disposed of it in the night, or if he had ever rescued it in the first place.

But Russell occasionally found a kindred spirit, someone equally bewildered and battered by the chaos of creatures around him, someone else who had, secretly, retained a sense-memory of that familiar piercing spark of connection, and the dance of whisky-warm insight on the mind, sitting by a fire, in a pub, the darkness and rain on the cold side of the door. Rather than the flood of his youth, these moments were rare dewdrops, but that made them all the more precious.

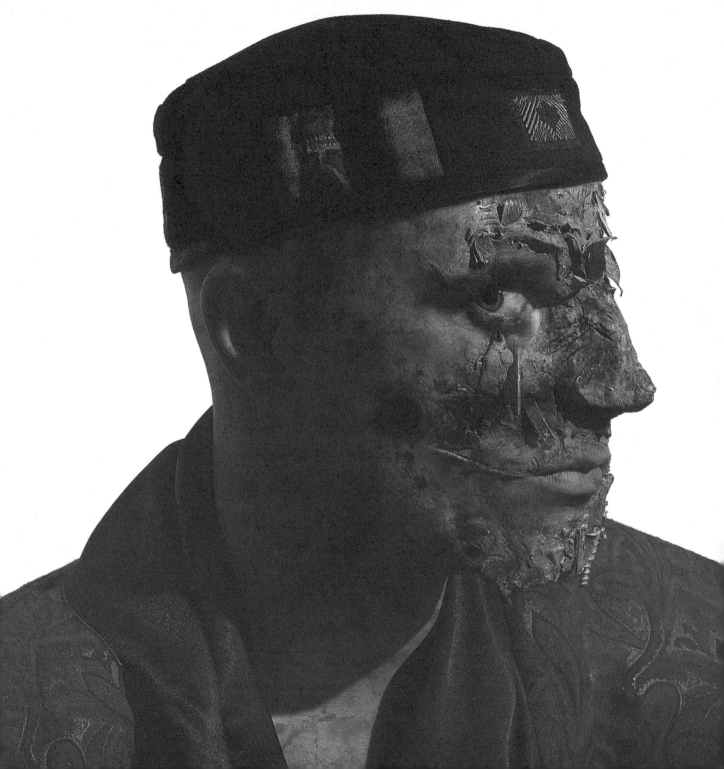

Broken Face

Iain Sinclair

On certain mornings, after all those interminable and coveted hours of darkness, when the slant of light through the grating made an illusory grid of spill on the flagstones, a suggestion of water, a trickle, a rivulet, the prisoner knew that it would be better to be dead right now. Or at least blind. To root and socket. Dumb. Tongueless. All tongue. Immune. Apart. Deaf to the world above.

He wanted to reach out, to confirm the split in his skull. The way the plates had shifted overnight, frontal bone riding over parietal bone. Material damage disguised by the smoking-cap. Which was once a badge of caste. Or the acknowledgement of a previous military history. A proud symbol of religious and racial allegiance. Blood inheritance. The cap with its pediment of occult signatures held his shattered head together. Held him together. Whoever he was. Whatever. Wherever. The soft headgear, no intruding peak or flap, incubated a profound disbelief in his established role in the dream of the world.

Words leak. Things are unnamed. Unmoving. We are squeezed so close against the fetid others in this dungeon. We have learned how to sleep standing. Like horses. In our tight stalls. The sweet reek of old hay and fresh dung.

If that cap could be named, what follows? Toque on his head. A large blood-stained handkerchief over his face. He seems to be asleep. "Toque." A parroty word. Beckett was surely drawing on a photograph of that other Irish playwright, the man who exiled himself to Torquay, the one with rimless spectacles. Sean something. Republican. Of the people. Dublin. O'Casey. It's time it ended. And yet I hesitate. Same profile, right side. Same toque. Endgame. But it's not ended yet. Face slipping. Abraded. Breaking down. Judenhut. Pileus comutus. Judge's cap. Death sentence. Confession. Phrygian cap. Juliet cap. Same pose, different man.

All the world of books and films, plays, home movies of sunlit balconies, tumbles on ski slopes, propaganda newsreels, private acts by professionals in hot-pillow motels, drone-footage desert terrain, surveillance tapes, lunar probes, rectal probes. All of it available. All of it teasing and provoking. When the only witness to this madness, the sole consumer, the favoured client, cannot so much as move a muscle. Sneeze. Twitch. Break wind. Wipe his own snot.

They are pinioned within the rectangle of the underground cloister, with limited, strictly limited, sources of natural light. Such light as they enjoy comes from the glow of decay. From the trapped bodies. From the heat they retain. The Prison of Heresies happens in the third person. Did you notice that? It is therefore a story that somebody outside the limits of the drama is recording, shaping, recovering. Exploiting.

There is no time, it's all time in the labyrinth. The burrow. We wait. They wait. A college of scarecrows. Waiting on judgement. When sounds filter down from the street, the market, the city—smells even—we are so hungry for words. They are so hungry. I am hungry. Under the toque. Hungry to touch the slippage of his face, my face. Hungry for you to stop, to look at me, assess the damage. To make new. I am like those purple-pink portraits, cheese-flesh, of private soldiers ruined by shrapnel or bayonet in the First War. Portraits made for surgeons. As guides. As records of successful procedures. A new life on the other side of catastrophe. We wait for it in our communal grave.

Once the dark is total, I will simply stand and wait, trying hard to think of nothing.

The speaker—you can't hear him—is one among many. Waiting for the Inquisitor. Waiting for the distant sound of his heart beating in a cavity stuffed with straw. Waiting for eyes capable of blinking.

Who did this? Who carved the extension to his mouth? Who began the process of cosmetic surgery and then gave it up? Who is responsible?

Images hold for an instant, a carousel of false memories soliciting narrative. The prisoner is a cannibal of stories. But he can only nominate one. One story in which he can move through the curtain of tenses, to take his proper place. One picture. A still from which he must construct his own screenplay. Choose. Consider. Subvert.

The boat, with standing figure in the prow, is crossing a pattern of waves that are turning into sand. Into the whorls of a unique fingerprint. Oars raised. Dead sea. Baltic? Styx. Bergman's *The Shame*. Overload of refugees from a burning ship. Migrants between devastated cities. Corpses ferrying corpses. Is that why we are being held in this cave? In transit. In abeyance. Verdict pending. Seventeen years without coming to court. Stand in line. According to age and height. Stand back from the desk. Line up by profession. By race. In your original nakedness.

Choose again. A portion of the face lifted away to reveal steps leading down to this premature burial. Crypt. Cellar. A beam of projected light when one of the guards raises the flap of the spyhole, to check that all are present and correct. Still standing. Silent. Eyes open. Flesh tighter to bone.

Or the woman in the fringed shawl. Her breasts. The living stain of the vulva. Skull-mask borrowed from another, a man. A succubus. The ghost of desire to remind the prisoner of what is no longer possible. No longer permitted. A breath of perfumed air. They are spectres in the stories the others tell themselves. While they stand. While they wait.

These are my stories too, he said. There are three of them. I will make my choice when the time comes. Listen.

Then I looked in the mirror and simulated a suicide by gunshot to the head. I did it three more times, working on different faces. But none of those faces fitted, none of them achieved resolution. They were not me, not the person telling the tale, remembering what never happened. I failed to project myself into that gaping void. I was an everyday hack, a jobbing journalist made interesting by a sudden rush of blood. A premeditated squeeze of the trigger sculpting a presentation of shattered scalp and bloody hair across the pond-green wallpaper with its fleur-de-lys design. They were picking teeth from the affronted plaster like so many spent cartridges. Enough of them to string a sour necklace.

Mimed expressions in the deceptive shallows of the mirror were a choreography of wet masks subject to natural forces. They were provisional. Rehearsals. The mirror was a rectangle of water held within its ornate frame—vertical, an installation—without a single drop being spilled. There were no gestures I could invent to justify the carnival masks of a cult that refused to declare itself. A cult associated with sombre provincial museums that charged just enough to keep casual visitors out. A cult of enlightened obscurity. Of sites difficult to track down in unattractive post-industrial cities open to foreigners after decades under cryogenically preserved dictators or unyielding philosophies.

You spend hours tramping the streets, asking questions, soliciting replies in languages you cannot understand, in order to justify a single cup of bitter coffee, a thimble glass of the local spirit, at the wobbling table of a café under a dying tree, in a shady square at the back of a locked cathedral.

When the coffee had been gagged down and my lips were sufficiently anaesthetised, I found a lending library in an old plague hospital, where three pale men in white shirts, equipped with hearing aids, made their excuses for a broken copying machine and plotted theoretical revolution. I had the sudden conviction that these monkish officials took it in turns, at regular intervals of the day, to select a book with laminated skin from otherwise untouched shelves. And to masturbate, feverishly, with moans and muffled curses, behind the heavy curtain with the cardboard sign. As I emerged into the midday heat of the square, I registered a notice in English beside the heavy wooden doors: OFFICE FOR THE SIMPLIFICATION & REDUCTION OF BUREAUCRACY.

If this hotel room were indeed a theatre of extinction, I was inadequately prepared for its opening attraction. Where, once, the mean fissure of my mouth was sketched like a manageable wound, now it was choked with glints of metal. In suckling the rude barrel of the sawn-off shotgun, flesh flattered a prosthetic of annihilation. The suicide story was embedded in the menu of place. The play was waiting for a writer foolish enough to assemble it. A writer with no more to his commission than a Xerox of a Xerox. One eye shut, one eye open. As the skull is sliced like a melon.

The suicide in the Grand Hotel was the first story. The prisoner in the cellar, the hole beneath the busy street, heard words like a radio transmission. He did not know where they were coming from or where they were going. He was wedged between too many others. Hundreds waiting on a verdict. His rags smelled of dried man-sweat, vinegar, sulphur mines and cowsheds. He could not accept the map of his wounds as self-inflicted. The face, if his dead hands could describe it, would be wrecked, broken. Coming apart in slowmotion, dissolving with geological inevitability.

But was this the right story? Was this the crime for which the prisoner had been brought down into the cellar. Self-slaughter. Anathematised. Failure to deliver. Verdict postponed. The eye flinches. Darkness settles like a bad tenant. Moonlight is internal, sounding the chalky hollows.

I had been sent to the island to gather footage, even a long-lens photograph, of the last movie star coming up from the sea, at her private swimming place, in the secure grounds of the Grand Hotel. This was the second story and it was more like a silent film than a text hammered out on a portable typewriter in a train rocking between the capital and the coast. The prisoner could hear the clicking of the wheels, fingers hammering on the keys, but there was no dialogue.

He waits. Three mornings, in the shadow, resting his back on the cool base of the statue of a goddess more naked than the movie star, the swimmer. Three sets of cigarette stubs encircling his foolishness. Then it happened.

She picks her way, with graceful discrimination, down steps cut into the rock below the hollow shell of a Roman temple. A fake. A folly. A strong-shouldered woman of the north in snowy wrap. Acolytes in white suits and fuck-you dark glasses. Made darker with specialist aircraft paint. The glasses were compulsory, part of a uniform that said: serious budget, serious concept. Paid servants in Armani. Part fashion vampire, part bodyguard in voodoo republic. The glasses blinded the heavies, divorcing them from the forbidden sight. The flash of revelation as the star moved out of a theoretical crane shot into the reality of the harbour. As a Homeric sun lifts, with cloud-piercing searchlight beams, over the blue mountains. Across the harbour. As the open fishing boats putputput out to sea.

Hefty handmaidens—lesser offprints of the star, understudies, muscle manipulators—attend, catching the towelling wrap as the presence honours the gentle wash of petrol-slicked water against privileged steps. A shivering palm tree perched on its narrow ledge is the X-ray of a straw bear poised to dive. The swansdown wrap, set on a stone bench, an autopsy table, is a duvet with the imprint of that fabulous body. Distressed, cast out after a single usage, it will become the soutane giving a naked beggar a modicum of legality, as he tramps the port, soliciting wine-dollars from monumental, ice-berg cruise liners.

Crumpled waiters, undershaved, are laying freshly ironed linen cloths on breakfast tables set at a discrete distance, one from another, on the magnificent terrace. It is like a tribute to Greta Garbo. While she was still Garbo. While the hotel sustained its aura as the conspicuous villa of a very rich man and his celebrated wife.

The illegitimate photographer secures his shot. The Maltese waiter secures his pocket-bulging bribe, his Sicilian beak. The framing is austere, classical. More authentic, as an image, a replica of reality, than the roofless circle of the temple. The naked swimmer emerging, arms raised to receive the spread of the upheld garment. The photographer thought of the tragic production still—blue water, blue as the death of heaven—of Marilyn Monroe, her last movie, Something's Got to Give. Coming out of the celestial swamp of a Hollywood pool. Cukor. The trade. "Hopelessly coy," the man said. "Like a waitress who has seen a Rubens."

He took a bottle back to his room in the other place, above the grocer's shop, the street stalls, across from the cemetery where drivers, touts and drunks argued, pissed against the wall and sometimes fought. Where modest women, clutching the hands of their children, came in black, to tidy the gravestones of their Mafia-silenced husbands.

"This is the detection of totality," the photographer said. And repeated it. Before he wrote the phrase in a green notebook. The detection of totality. His theft had that quality. All the accidental elements were in place. The setting. The mythic back-story. The legend of this woman, the last star, who refused ever more insane offers to make her return. A final and definitive celluloid hurrah, reuniting her with Fellini, Bergman, Lang, Renoir. From a script by Flaubert or Sophocles. Or James Joyce. But they were all dead. The industry had blown out its best brains. It had only lasted this far by propping up the art market and the rare book trade. Who was going to house all those phoney Chagalls and Modiglianis? This solitary print—Woman after Swimming—the seizure of a moment, is the detection of totality. And now to be given over to a collector, a property broker, owner of football clubs, internet dating sites, 24-hour casinos and redeveloped supermalls sold to religious fundamentalists.

The hireling photographer imagined a voyeur's hand-tooled album on a polished desk in a locked office. Where the overhead fan never stops turning. Gods and goddesses of the golden screen are bent to the collector's whim. Fornicating across Second Empire furniture. Slumming in motels with prints of western landscapes. Bored actors trapped in those terrible times of self-impersonation—hollow, hollow, hollow—at the bar, stepping from the limousine, in the bedroom. Coupling in pools and paddocks. Tripling in beach houses on stilts that will be shaken to sawdust by the next shift of the tectonic plates.

The man who delivers the purchased photograph in a stiff brown envelope is a disposable asset. His fixed Cyclopean stare. His darkroom alchemy. It is only when they keep him waiting in the vaulted underground bar, with nothing more than a dirty glass of iced water, that he realises that he has signed his own order of execution. Images live, image-makers disappear. The price of entering the catalogue is extinction. "These contracts are just jobs," he said, "but they are also arguments with death—ways of getting there, ways of breaking out."

The bar is a chapel, endstopped by a mural, a Doom painting, the Day of Judgement with a Bosch carnival of exposed sinners. Earthly delights and the fires of hell. Bestiality. Chewers of intoxicating roots. Grubbers of diseased flour. Penitents with whips and wings. And scorpions. Prostitutes with the heads of dogs. Priests assaulting children. Women with donkeys. Popes roasting on spits. All the carnivalesque detail to enliven a solitary cocktail. The kind of bar where Buñuel would move his glass two inches, to run a beam of sunlight through his ice-cold gin Martini.

While he waited for the money, which was also his death, the photographer leafed through a book the management had left out, on public display, to boost the history of their establishment. A record of all the deposed and deleted German princelings who had stayed there with their drugged consorts. Premature economic migrants from Baltic upheavals rub along in a procession of overdressed zombies, yawning from Palermo to Biarritz to Cannes. From cigar-suckled casino nocturne to constitutionally fatigued breakfast on the terrace. Among the ornate and entitled nonentities, allowing themselves to be nuisanced by official hotel photographers, Edward VII of Great Britain is the most grimly dedicated trencherman of the ennui of pleasure. He slumps behind regiments of polished glasses, spindly tables buckling under the freight of dishes—but he will never, under any circumstances, remove his hat. Bareheaded Scandinavian kings in double-breasted Saville Row suits trudge around the unviolated swimming pool, but Edward never stirs. He looks more like a statue of himself than a living man. He looks as if he needs two strong grooms to wheel him to the next banquet. To winch him on to the next compliant hostess.

In another, more recent volume, the photographer encountered the lost royalty of movie stars; actors on location, spillage from a film festival. Sophia Loren squired by the flashing teeth of Vittorio de Sica. Greta Garbo going into the sea from the rocks below the fake Roman temple. Gloria Swanson, the revenant's revenant, former mistress to Joe Kennedy, attended by Paul Newman and Gore Vidal. This way, ladies, for the ballroom of the damned. Burt Lancaster, improbable Sicilian aristocrat (and former circus star), slips away from Visconti, to drink at the hotel bar with Alain Delon. Kirk Douglas (the only Russian-Jewish cowboy still standing) escorts Irene Papas. Onassis, in trademark bat-clamp shades, is affronted by a presumption of daylight. Hilary Clinton, hand across mouth, steps in front of her hairdresser. The Blairs, with their pirate patron, Berlusconi, are between villas. Between islands. Between wars and investments. Actors all in the great game. Take your places, ladies and gentlemen. Faites vos jeux.

There is a body in a black bag. Wrapped in newspaper. In a wastebin. A bombed car burning in a quarry. Doors open on a melting road, beyond the pig farm, under the pylons. In an irrigation ditch. A harbour. Found floating. Sleeping with the fishes. The entry wound carves through the muscle wall of the cheek. Rips out the eye from its nest. Doffs the lid of the skull. Nothing under that cap but jelly.

Is this the source of the wound? Is this my story? The breaking of a face. Suicide? Contract killing? Are they holding me, indefinitely, pending new evidence. Bits of stories. Doctored images. I wait in line, unmoving, in the dark. Hoping for a visitor. More words. A new chapter to misremember, to misreport. Subvert.

Days passed. Years. Decades. Before I understood that I was being punished, not for an action in a previous life, above ground, in the city, but for a crime as yet uncommitted. The ones next to me in line, my late familiars, had the stink-paper reek of lawyers. The dust of unresolved slanders. Property law. Divorce. The criminal bar and the saloon bar. Wine cellar to holding cell where we are cobwebbed and musty like bottled vintages. Where those condemned to die concentrate the essence of the world to the momentum of a spider trapped in a tin mug.

Listen. A barking sound, like a terrible tubercular cough, heard through the walls, across the busy road, over the public square, through the cathedral spaces of the meat market, around the opera house, to the canal. A sound like strangled breath. Like a horse being hanged with too short a rope. And the prisoner knows what that sound is: a dog, a terrier swimming in desperate circles through duckweed. Coughing for life. While the dog's owner waits under a bridge, in a playful mood, swaying with drink, kicking the animal back, every time it gets its front paws on the bank.

"I am innocent of all charges," the woman said, "except marriage. That is where I betrayed my principles, too often. And once with a proper paper, a licence. To a man."

The third story, the prisoner's last chance, according to rules laid down by the Brother Grimm and all their forest-nesting predecessors, came barefoot out of the shadows. By the lightness of her footfall, by the sway of the dance of it, this was a new species. Sliding through the mirror of the thick air. And how do I know, the prisoner thought, that I am not one of these, a woman? The way the dungeon was arranged, vertical lines, close packed groups facing each other, in rotting rags and the moss-green suits of clerical status, it had always seemed that the structure worked like a set of funhouse reflections. That the fleshed skeletons on one side of the corridor mimicked the corrupted starvelings on the other. Your decay flatters our ruin.

This was different. A shrouded being floating towards him. Her right arm, hidden beneath the fringed shawl or burka, pointed in accusation. He flinched, tried to pull back, away from her. But he was trapped, arms wedged. Had it happened before? She was going to touch his face, the part that was broken, that couldn't be fixed.

His eyes on the octopus eyes of her breasts. The cloth, shimmering with a drizzle of stars, more eyes burning, silver against the deep blue, lifted with her arm. To touch him. Or put her fingers right through his flesh. To stroke the abraded cheek. To heal. To mend. Her hand, under the fringed shawl, a fist. Bunched. Caressing or clawing. Under the hood, eyes of a cat. Projecting green light. Eyes of vengeance.

A stone. He thought of the pebbles like eggs in that Breughel painting, lying so innocuously across the floor, a woman taken in adultery. The perversity of the crime in response to the breaking of a male taboo. The feverish excitement, unrepresented in the dun study, Breughel's grisaille, colour of purgatory, suspension of breath, of the act of stoning a shrouded woman. In a pit. To her death.

She touched his face with a stone clenched in her paw. It was gritty, a sandpaper kiss. She sculpted his contours, his lips, the collapsed mouth where teeth had once grimaced.

A woman stoned to death. A projection of that old nightmare. Of yesterday's news. Random footage in cyberspace. The ghost was returning the stone he had cast. She was plucking it out of his flesh.

That was why his face was broken. She had assaulted him in the night. For his betrayal, his dalliance. With the Northern woman, the whore who flaunted herself naked in the harbour, watched by fishermen setting out at first light.

Now they were both dead. Now they could couple. The pit reeked like a sewer beneath a slaughterhouse. The robes of the men with the upraised arms, clutching their stones, were stained with anticipatory excitement. She bit his cheek and her bite was metal. A knife. The dead hairs depending from his slack jaw were grass. She licked. He was stone.

Which story to believe? Projections, fantasies of a starving man. Images in darkness. A collection of glass slides clamped inside his split skull. Phantoms of a brain stem closing down. A last electro-chemical surge. The suicide? A shotgun insult anticipated by receptive meat sensors? The image thief punished for his presumption? Dusted. Wasted. Undeveloped wound responses. Threads of hyaline and gold leaf. The victim of a woman condemned to death? Face, identity disk, pattern recognition, broken by a stone in the night.

His mind reeled until the centre of everything seemed to be in his mouth. Sawdust and vinegar. Words like ants fleeing from a burning mound, drowning in a saucer. Natura morta. We must learn to wait. Forever.

"Two hundred euros," the visitor said. "Fuck that. To take a photograph? And they let you in for two. That, basically, is the world. The picture costs more than the experience."

He was worse dressed than the standing prisoners, the slumped, slouched, hooked cadavers. Car mechanic's denim for a tenured bookman, an outcome specialist on sabbatical. His round glasses with the blue rims. His red shoes.

"No Photo, No Film, the notice says. Who'd know? Just stand there and block the camera. That red light."

He talked to the young woman as he had talked to his wife. The first one, the one his own age, who was now sitting on a stone bench in the cemetery garden. It was on him, he was paying for the holiday she booked, so that, after twelve years of comfortable separation, he could moan about the madness of the second wife, the student. While he had arranged, covertly—oh god, those arrangements—to install the latest intern, the potential third wife (serial monogamist), in a pension around the corner from their not so grand hotel. The first wife wanted no part of the catacombs.

Two thousand or more mummies, who's counting, were arranged in a rectangle, like the morbid frame around a central absence that must be supplied by paying visitors. Few came in winter. None of them were tempted to break the published taboo on photography as they crept, awed and somehow ashamed, around the dim cloister of vertical corpses. Monks, lawyers, doctors, criminals. And one sad child in waxy sleep in her polished vitrine.

This latest intern, in a spontaneous gesture, put her fingers in her ears against the weight of silence. The noise of memory, she thought. The foolishness, the small vanity of this descent into an underworld to which they brought nothing of value. Vulgar curiosity. Leisure wear.

A flash. A sudden scorching of air. Like a moth incinerating itself on a hot lightbulb. The balding lecturer, with his rubber-band ponytail, trembled to lift a wafer of camera as if it were made of lead. As if he had just plucked a curved thorn of tooth from the palm of his hand. The raised device was a silver passport, an identity card. He thrust it in the ruined face of the man in a cap with no peak. The exchange was made. The Venetian contract. The forfeit to be weighed in blood. Nothing happened. They completed the circuit. The girl took the bus to the beach. The man met his wife, like the old days. Both of them happy to be returning, next day, to their own country.

"Oh yeah, amazing, uncanny. With the feeling, they are watching you. Waiting. More is concealed than can be revealed, that's for sure. Our task, I felt, was to intuit a little of how the city feels and moves today."

The denim lecturer, mouth rigid from anaesthesia and the drill, head titled, eyes flicking from man to wife, old colleagues unexpectedly encountered in a new gallery on the south coast, dropped into his natural pedagogic mode.

"I'll show you." His bent thumb irritated the calibrations of the necessary device, his floating image trove. The sad trophies of travel. Proof that he was there.

The mature mistress shifted uneasily, her coastal exile disturbed by this recent demographic, down from the smoke in search of marine revival, terroir cuisine and fishing-shed art. "How about a coffee? The windows upstairs are like paintings by Alfred Wallis, boats, nets, the whole bit."

When they were settled around the artisan bench and waiting for members' discounts to be calculated, the current mistress, author of a series of as yet unoptioned period detective novels, noticed that the panels of symbols stitched to the rim of the lecturer's soft cap were beginning to pulse. They were vaguely Crowleyite, she supposed. But he looked more like the poet Ivor Cutler, an eccentric on a bicycle handing out sticky labels, haiku tracts, than the Great Beast. The local authenticity of the cheese, she felt, was overemphasised by its placement on a dish of straw.

The lecturer found the image he wanted: the enhanced cadaver from the catacombs. The one with the broken face. The post-mortem grin was salacious, a pronounced underbite.

If her lover had been a woman or a gay man, the mistress would have no difficulty in believing that his beloved phone was a mirror. That the miniature profile on the small screen hovered, still unresolved, between the twin states of life and death. Between then and now. Between hollow photographer and stuffed mummy.

As the man with the ponytail titled towards his black string of smoked eel on a cranky mush of seaweed, a tooth fell on the plate. And more straw. His face was decomposing. The denim scarecrow looked like the victim of a crow assault. Like roadkill with tyre tracks. Across the room, other art fanciers, with their demi-carafes and elderflower cordials and infusions of peppermint tea, were snapping away. With no attempt at ameliorating the nakedness of their interest. A freak. A man whose broken face is coming apart. A specimen of Goya horror from the worst imaginings of Jake and Dinos Chapman. A monster with a hanging eye.

As they allowed this dreadful incident into their cameras, so they became the thing they were entrapping. It wasn't the "broken face" hash tag that went viral, it was the catacomb thief. Back through all the many and varied rituals of preservation, the ripping out of entrails and brain porridge, the vinegar baths, ammonia douches, sawing and stitching, stuffing with hay. And it would never stop now, a chain reaction to the last man or woman, to the end of the world. You stare at the abyss and the abyss stares right back. And there is a price. The price of respect. Of love. Love before death.

One of the weirder outreaches of the Victorian confusion between new technological possibilities and musty superstition was the attempt to capture the portrait of the assassin burnt into the curve of a victim's eye. A forensic photographer was brought to the scene to procure a large close-up of the eye of Marie Jeanette (or Mary Jane) Kelly, the "final" victim of Jack the Ripper. Within the oven of that appalling room where every indignity had been worked on the eviscerated body, a premature autopsy, the last insult (if it happened) would be the attempt to leech the crime from the innocence of the eyeball. As if pain made its own print from the heat of the moment.

The assassin remained faceless. Image-alchemy eased his disappearance. The crime was branded into the location. Time choked and froze. Now the events in the café above the seaside gallery had opened the vortex. Horror flattered and fed on horror. Screen to screen. Synapse to synapse. City to city. While the original print of the man with the broken face was retained in the thinnest memory-rind of the iPhone clutching victims, there would be no release from the causal chain of catastrophe until the utmost end of time. And beyond. "The eyeball altering," said William Blake, "alters all."

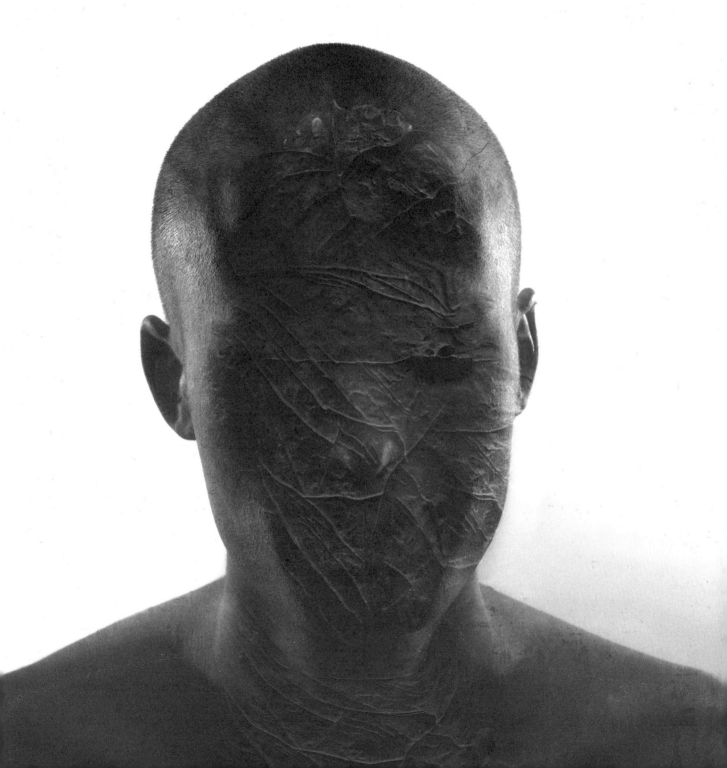

we had been ⟨...⟩ the train for three years, ⟨...⟩ the poets in the car at the front had declared war on the dining carriage in the middle, and the biographers in the rear carriage. They sent poems back, carried by mice and cabin staff, which would explode upon reading. The biographers sent ⟨...⟩ of such ⟨...⟩

if the ⟨...⟩ se⟨...⟩ st on ⟨...⟩ of ⟨...⟩

The Train of Death

Neil Gaiman

We had been riding on the train for three years, and the poets in the car at the front had declared war on the dining carriage in the middle, and the biographers in the rear carriage. They sent poems back, carried by mice and cabin staff, which could explode upon reading. The biographers sent back lives of such hopelessness that the poets flung themselves from their windows, or would have, if the windows had rolled down. The concrete poets knocked biographers senseless, the makers of Haiku stunned with seventeen syllables of incendiary imagery.

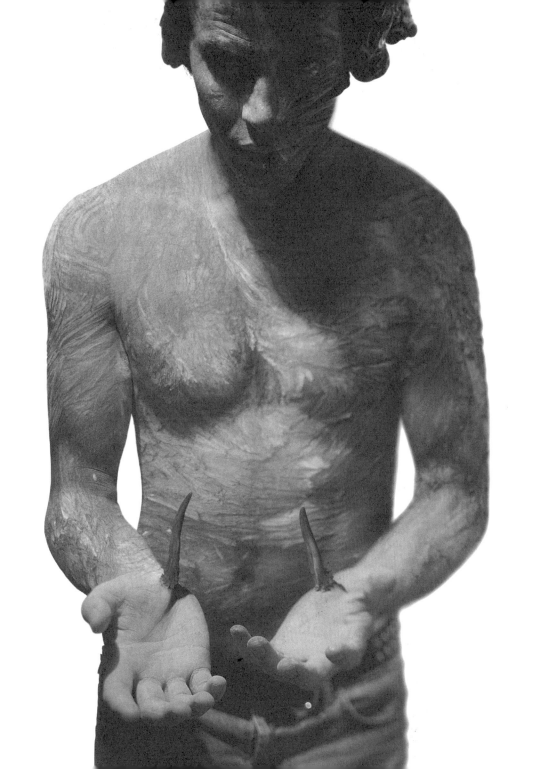

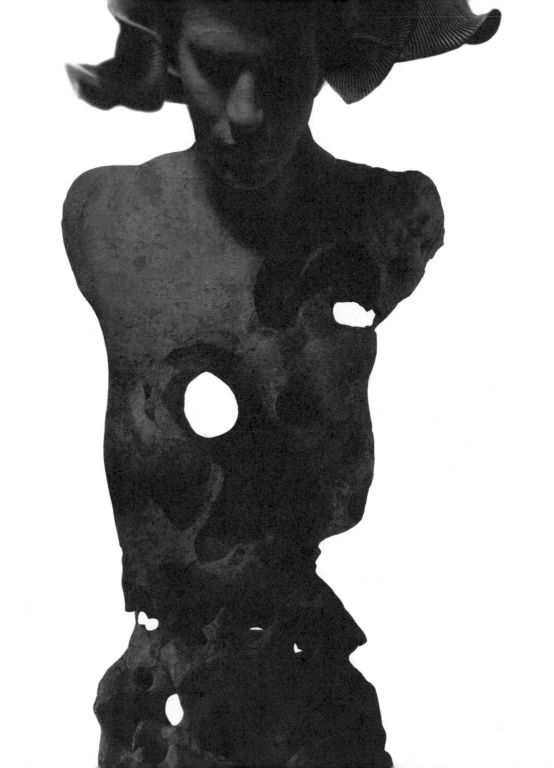

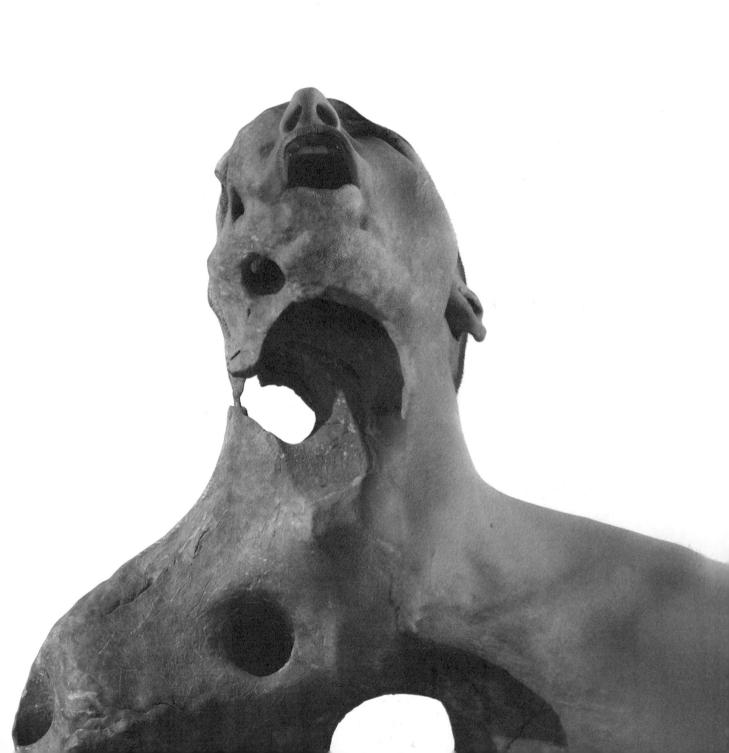